The Confessions of Frances Godwin

BY THE SAME AUTHOR

The Sixteen Pleasures
The Fall of a Sparrow
Blues Lessons
Philosophy Made Simple
The Italian Lover
Snakewoman of Little Egypt

The Confessions of Frances Godwin

A Novel

ROBERT HELLENGA

B L O O M S B U R Y

NEW YORK • LONDON • NEW DELHI • SYDNEY

Published by Bloomsbury USA, New York
Bloomsbury is a trademark of Bloomsbury Publishing Plc

All papers used by Bloomsbury USA are natural, recyclable products made from wood grown in well-managed forests. The manufacturing processes conform to the environmental regulations of the country of origin.

LIBRARY OF CONGRESS CATALOGING-IN-PUBLICATION DATA

Hellenga, Robert, 1941-
The confessions of Frances Godwin : a novel /
Robert Hellenga.—First U.S. Edition.
pages cm
ISBN 978-1-62040-549-9 (hardback)
1. Latin teachers—Fiction. 2. Mothers and daugthers—Fiction. I. Title.
PS3558.E4753C66 2014
813'.54—dc23
2013044568

First U.S. Edition 2014

1 3 5 7 9 10 8 6 4 2

Typeset by Hewer Text UK Ltd, Edinburgh
Printed and bound in the U.S.A. by Thomson-Shore Inc., Dexter, Michigan

Bloomsbury books may be purchased for business or promotional use. For information on bulk purchases please contact Macmillan Corporate and Premium Sales Department at specialmarkets@macmillan.com.

To the Memory of my mother,
Marjorie Johnson Hellenga,
high school Latin teacher.

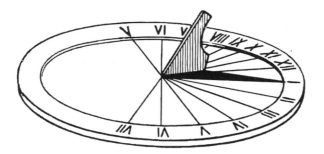

Transit umbra, lux permanet.

The layout is important. And the feast.
Rock bottom basis: please remember these
procedures by which feasting's managed. Here
I mean the rule of strict conversion: dirt
turned into green beans, green beans set
upon a fine white dish, the dish itself
scorched earth, stone crushed to powder.

Layout of spread platters. Who will eat and
What and in what sequence: dirt to grass,
grass to calf, calf to the sharpened edge
of slaughter. Taking turns is important.
We share the room, its white-flecked space,
blue vaulted ceiling, wainscot of woods' frilled
branching, founded in stone and sea.

The layout is important. Proportion,
consonance of form and formal interchange.
Good manners. Dinner plates rise out of
ground. Our table's rooted in the lives
of trees, the cloth upon it meadow
weave. We take our seat. A place is set
for each in turn. Earth is our banquet,
our hall; the feast, richly concocted of desire,
limitation, murder, serves us all.

—Lisa Ress, "Setting the Table, Eating What Is Served"

A Note to the Reader

B efore I begin let me say that I seriously considered writing these confessions—which are really a kind of spiritual autobiography—in third person so I could get a little ironic distance on myself, could see around myself, know more than I know myself. But that would have been to create an illusion. All narrators are first-person narrators. You can't get ironic distance on yourself, can't see around yourself, can't know more than you know. So what's the point of pretending? Besides, I'm an old—well, older— woman now. Is it likely that the police will come knocking at my door again with their warrants and handcuffs and Miranda rights, or that the Vatican will come down on me like a ton of bricks, the way Pope Gregory VII came down on the Henry IV at Canossa? In the unlikely event that either of these things happens, I'll just say I forgot. I'll just say that I made it all up.

PART I: 2006

1

∞

Do Not Resuscitate (2006)

At the end of May 2006—my last Commencement—my students marched across the stage at Galesburg High School. I watched them throw their hats into the air even though Mr. Walters, the principal, had made it perfectly clear that they were not to do so. And afterward we said good-byes. I would miss the students, most of them, I would even miss the obligatory school functions—the faculty meetings, the parent-teacher conferences, the endless round of games and band concerts, and the union meetings (I'd been the steward for five years)—that had been my life after my husband's death. The students were looking ahead, I was looking back; they were letting go, I was hanging on. But now I had to let go too. The Latin program was being "phased out." I'd protested, organized demonstrations, clipped articles about the Latin Renaissance in the United States and articles about the successes of our own program, which had strong enrollments and which was regarded as one of the best in Illinois. But to no avail. The state was more than a million dollars behind in its payments to the school district and cuts would have to be made.

I had several weeks to clear out my classroom, but I wanted to get it over with, so I started in on Monday. This classroom had been my home, my second home, for forty-one years. Everything in it had a story to tell. Every object whispered to me. The window ledges and the long tables in the back of the room were crowded with models of Roman buildings—enough to recreate the whole city of Rome, at different eras, and half of Pompeii before Vesuvius. We'd started, years ago, with a jigsaw puzzle of the Roman Forum and Capitoline Hill and moved on to three-dimensional puzzles of the Colosseum, and the Baths of Caracalla, still standing (glued, varnished, repaired with packing tape), and then, with the help of George Hawkinson, who taught physics, and Dan Phillips, the ingenious shop teacher, we'd moved on to more substantial models: bridges, arches, a Roman villa, even a model of the Pont du Gard aqueduct that could actually carry water for about half an hour before it started to leak.

The walls were crowded with pictures of Rome and famous Romans from Scipio Africanus to Marcus Aurelius; pseudo-Latin quotations from *Harry Potter* were flanked by a *Spartacus* poster and pictures of neoclassical architecture, including the old Galesburg city hall, and by Doonesbury cartoons of the president, invisible but wearing a Roman military helmet as he jousts with reporters about weapons of mass destruction, about Abu Ghraib, torture, the war, Colin Powell, Hurricane Katrina.

The students got extra credit for translating the dialogue into Latin. Some were quite difficult, maybe too difficult, but they did a good job and we took *Id adfer* as our motto. *Bring it on.* How could the administration object to that?

I had to laugh at the cartoons, which had caused a certain amount of trouble. I left them tacked up on the bulletin board. The

6

principal and some members of the school board had wanted them down, but the students had kicked up a fuss, invoking the first amendment.

Bits and pieces from our last *Roman Republic* tournament were still scattered on three game boards in three different corners of the room. I sorted out the faction cards and the statesman cards, the forum cards, the event cards, the scenario cards, the province cards, the war cards, the Talents (marked in Roman numerals), the chits and markers and personal treasury boxes. I could see that the late-republic game had ended in defeat for all the players because four active war cards had come into play at the end of the combat phase. *Game over.* At the end of the wars the advanced Latin students had given me a used copy of the Warwick *Vergil Concordance* that had once belonged to a Miss Allison Connolly of London, Ontario. Paul and I had driven past London more than once on our way to the Stratford Shakespeare Festival and I pictured Miss Connolly in her classroom, a classroom much like mine, the big red concordance open on her desk as she looked up a word. I felt sad for Miss Connolly and sad for myself, too, as I ran my finger over the names of my students, who had signed their names on the half-title page. But the inscription made me laugh:

> hanc ego de caelo ducentem sidera vidi;
> fluminis haec rapidi carmine vertit iter.

I recognized the lines from Tibullus's "To Delia": "I have seen her draw down the stars from the sky; she diverts rapidly flowing rivers with her spells." And I recognized Jason Steckley's bold handwriting. And his sense of humor: the woman in the poem is a witch who can not only draw down the stars from the sky and divert rapidly flowing rivers with her spells, she can make the earth open up and lure spirits from their tombs; she can chase the clouds from the sky and make it snow in summer! She can make old men who used to mock young lovers put their aged necks in the halter of Venus! Well, it was all fine with me.

It was almost four o'clock, time to shift some boxes. I had left a lot of books that would have to be discarded, and had already packed the ones I wanted to keep in banker's boxes: my dark blue Oxford Classical Texts, my red and green Loebs—green for Greek, red for Latin. I thought I might take up Greek again, read *The Odyssey*. I'd probably have to learn the language all over again, but that was all right. Maybe this time I'd master the optative mood, which was worse than the subjunctive in Latin. It was one of these banker's boxes that did me in. It was too full to handle easily and too heavy with the weight of the big concordance, which I'd put on top. Or maybe it was just too heavy with the weight of memory. Whatever it was, I felt something tear inside me as I tried to lift it. I thought it was my heart ripping in two, but it was part of my abdominal wall. My internal organs were trying to get out. I tried to push them back into place, exerting gentle pressure. But it was like trying to force the lid down on the books in the banker's box.

I got to the pay phone in the lobby and called my neighbor, Lois— my oldest friend (and enemy)—who brought me home. She wanted to go out and buy a truss at Burgland Drugs. But I said no, even thought my insides were protruding. I kept caressing the protrusion, as if it were a baby.

My doctor saw me that afternoon, late. Lois took me. He poked and prodded and palpitated. It was not an emergency, but even so, two days later I was on the operating table.

Just before the anesthesiologist came to administer the anesthetic, the nurse handed me a sheet with a long list of boxes to check. Liability precautions, I suppose. They don't give you much time to think it over, but I looked over the list and checked a box that said "Do not resuscitate." I wasn't looking forward to having loads of unstructured time on my hands, but I wasn't depressed or suicidal. On the contrary. It's just that at that particular moment I thought my story had come to an end, and that it would be appropriate to exit the scene quietly and unobtrusively. I didn't really care one way or another. There was nothing coming up on the horizon that I wanted to deal with: a library board meeting on Thursday; a fund-raiser for the animal shelter on Saturday afternoon; a hair appointment sometime the next week.

The only thing worth mentioning was the forthcoming translation of Catullus that I'd done for a small press in Brooklyn. But what had been a source of joy had become a source of anxiety. The jacket designer had put the wrong Catullus on the cover, not Gaius Valerius Catullus, the poet, but Quintus Lutatius Catulus (with one "l"), and I hadn't managed to garner a single blurb. I used to think that blurbs sprouted like mushrooms, but now I know that you have to impose yourself—beg, grovel, plead, call in favors, cold call. I'd written to all the Latinists I knew and to some I didn't know, though blurbs from high school Latin teachers were not what was needed, so I'd written to all the poets who had given readings at Knox. But so far, no responses, and the deadline for jacket copy was rapidly approaching. To tell you the truth, I didn't want to face the issue. I'd already begged, groveled, and pleaded enough. And I didn't really have any favors I could call in.

Do not resuscitate. Well, that certainly got their attention. The nurses. The surgeon (Dr. Parker, my neighbor in Loft #5), the anesthesiologist. They were all right there, crowded around. "You can't do that," they said, sequentially, and then in one voice. "We always resuscitate."

"Then why do you have the little box?" I asked.

When it became clear that they weren't going to repair the hernia unless I unchecked the box, I unchecked it, drew a heavy line through the box, and wrote "Okay to resuscitate." It wasn't a big deal. I didn't really care one way or another.

"Don't worry about your clothes," the nurse told me after the doctors had disappeared behind the curtain that had been drawn around my gurney. "They're right here in this plastic bag. There's a little lock on it, see?" I saw. I wasn't at all worried about my clothes. "And I'm going to pin the key to your gurney."

"Okay," I said.

"So they'll be right here when you come out of surgery."

"Okay," I said again.

"Don't worry," she said.

"I won't," I said.

The surgery was what they call microscopic, performed with a laparoscope, which comes from the Greek for "flank" (*laparo*) and "to see" (as in "to scope out something"). The laparoscope has a camera on the end of it. It was all beyond me, and I couldn't tell you, even if my life depended on it, how they inserted some mesh to replace the damaged tissue. But it was minimally invasive. Band-Aid surgery. In and out the same day, though someone had to be there to drive me home. That was Lois.

I was a little woozy when I came to in the recovery room, but not bad. I could have driven myself home, but Lois was there, and I didn't make an issue out of it. Besides, they couldn't find my clothes. Lois had to go back to Seminary Street to get some clothes for me; she had a key to my apartment (Loft #1) and I had a key to hers (Loft #2). My wallet was in the locked plastic bag with my clothes. My driver's license, Illinois state ID, insurance cards, and so on. My keys, too. But I wasn't worried. Lois drove me home, let me into my apartment. She wanted to fix some supper for me, later on, maybe have a glass of wine, or two, but I told her I just wanted to rest. Actually, I wasn't tired, but I wanted to be alone. Besides, the *Complete Seinfeld* DVDs had arrived from Amazon. Lois had to make a second trip down to the mailbox, in the little elevator room on the first floor, to bring it up. She was curious, but I didn't open it till later.

As a grief counselor at the Banks-Connolly Funeral Home on Carl Sandburg Drive, Lois had been full of advice at the time of my husband's death, and she was full of advice now about preparing for the end of life. She couldn't emphasize enough, she said, the importance of getting my papers in order, and she gave me another copy of the little pamphlet she'd put together on the subject.

But, as I pointed out, not for the first time, I already had my papers in order: long-term care insurance; a living will; hospice information, from when my husband, Paul, had been in hospice (though hospice, I knew now, wasn't a place you went to in order to die in peace; it was an organization that sent someone to your house—a Mrs. Adama in Paul's case—to help you through the process).

"What about your funeral?" Lois asked.

"Stella can take care of it," I said.

"Humph," Lois said. Lois had put together a number of pamphlets—in addition to the one on getting your papers in order— on preplanning your funeral, on dealing with grief and loss, on what to say and what not to say to the bereaved. (Don't say, "He's in a better place," or "At least she lived a long life"), and one on the importance of "sharing your stories."

"Write it all down, Franny," she said, "you've got time now." She pulled a copy of "Share Your Stories" out of her large handbag. "Your life with Paul, all those years in the classroom, the troubles with Stella, and Jimmy." As if Lois had any idea about what had happened to Jimmy.

She was still there when someone from the hospital arrived with my clothes. The dog, Camilla, barked up a storm and rucked up the runner in the long hallway, but she did that every time someone came to the door. I made her sit before I opened the door. I thanked the person for bringing my clothes, told Camilla "okay," and went back to my desk, Paul's railroad desk that we bought at auction when they tore down the old Burlington depot. I thought that if I sat down on Paul's stool at the desk, Lois would realize that it was time to go.

"That's a story right there, isn't it?" she said. "They tell you not to worry about your clothes, and then they lose your clothes and your wallet and your keys."

I had to laugh. "You're right," I said. "I'm going to get started right now."

"You're sure you don't need me to stay?"

"I'll be fine, Lois. But thanks."

Lois's pamphlet went on and on, like the list I'd been given in the hospital, and I was thinking, once again, that it wouldn't have been so bad to check out during the surgery. I was almost sorry I'd unchecked the do-not-resuscitate box. Of course, if I hadn't unchecked it, then Dr. Parker wouldn't have repaired the hernia and I'd be walking around with a truss.

I wrote down the story about the clothes in one of Paul's beautiful dark red Clairefontaine notebooks, put a number "1" at the top of the right-hand corner of the page, and then capped my fountain pen. Enough for one day. I was too tired to share any more stories. I opened up the *Seinfeld* box. A large box that looked like a little refrigerator. It was a complete set of DVDs. It was used and hadn't come directly from Amazon, so I hadn't gotten free super-saver shipping. The seller had wrapped it up in an old Kansas City *Star*. I glanced through the paper. A military convoy had been attacked by a suicide bomber in Afghanistan, Michael Jackson had been cleared of all counts of child molestation, the Detroit Pistons had defeated the San Antonio Spurs in game three of the NBA playoffs and were looking forward to game four. I folded up the paper and put it in the blue plastic recycling sack in the laundry room.

Kramer's coffee table book was part of the package. I was a little disappointed. It wasn't about coffee tables, and it didn't have little legs on it.

I couldn't decide between my two favorites episodes, "Wedding in India" and George's conversion to Latvian orthodoxy, so I watched them both. I took Camilla out for a short walk and when we came back I shrugged off my clothes and climbed into bed and she lay down on a pile of old quilts that had accumulated on the floor on my side of the bed.

In the morning I poured myself a cup of coffee and leafed through Lois's pamphlet again till I came to "Share Your Stories."

Why not? I thought, mentally emending "stories" to "confessions."

I could think of a lot of reasons, in fact, and if you keep on reading you'll probably come up with a few more.

Nonetheless I sat down at the long, narrow harvest table in the living room, uncapped my Pelikan Souverän 600, and started to write, and I kept on writing for two weeks, filling more than seventy pages and going through a full bottle of Aurora black ink. I'm computer literate, of course—I have all my lesson plans, and all my translations, on my MacBook Pro— but I wanted to share my story in ink, wanted the ink to flow from my pen onto the creamy Clairefontaine paper as if it were my own dark blood.

I'll begin at the beginning—the Shakespeare party in Paul's attic—more than forty years ago.

PART II: 1963–1964

2

Santa Maria in Trastevere (1963)

P aul and I joined our bodies—if not our souls—together for the
first time after the annual Shakespeare's birthday party in the
attic of Paul's big Victorian house on Chambers Street. Saturday,
April 27, 1963. I'd been around the block a few times, but never
with a man who knew what he was doing, and it made quite an
impression on me, opened my eyes. Did Paul seduce me, or did I
seduce him? Let's just say that I made myself available. Lois was
upset and threatened to report us to the dean, but that was only
because she was jealous.

Lois and I had sat next to each other in the front row of Paul's
Shakespeare classes during our sophomore year. And as seniors
we'd both taken his seminar on Shakespeare's Roman plays. We
were attracted by his energy, which was calm and flowing rather
than nervous and jumpy—a river, not a waterfall. You could see it in
his eyes as he leaned back against the chalk board at the beginning
of every class, making eye contact with first one student and then
another. "Friends," he'd say in a deep rich voice.

So this was our third Shakespeare party. At the first party Lois, an English major, played Hamlet's mother in the closet scene and I got stuck as one of the fairies in the play within a play in *A Midsummer Night's Dream*. At the second party—our junior year—I did a knockout Portia—"the quality of mercy is not strained"—with Lois as Nerissa, and Rita Johnson, who taught French, padded out as a fat Shylock, though she couldn't have weighed more than a hundred pounds. At the third I got to do the balcony scene in *Romeo and Juliet*, but according to an ancient Shakespeare party tradition—one that predated Paul—the gender roles were always reversed in this scene, so I played Romeo to Paul's bearded Juliet.

After the party, Lois's boyfriend dragged her off. I stayed behind in the attic and was pretending to be asleep on one of the old couches when Paul came up to put the makeshift costumes and hats away. Paul's wife—a lovely woman, elegant—was in New York, visiting her parents, who lived in a large rent-controlled apartment on Central Park West. She was a native New Yorker and loved to talk about New York, the greatest city in the world. She felt trapped in Galesburg: no Zabar's, no MoMA, no Metropolitan Museum, no Central Park, no Lincoln Center . . . Lois and I knew nothing of these magical places, but we resolved to live in New York after we'd been graduated, preferably on Central Park West.

Paul and I began a torrid affair—at least that's how I thought of it at the time, though "torrid," from Latin *torridus*, meaning parched or scorched, is perhaps not the right word. "Scorched" maybe, but not "parched." Paul's wife was going to stay in New York till the middle of June, so we had no logistical problems. I would walk down Kellogg Street, where no one was likely to see me, then over to Chambers. I'd circle around and come up the alley and cut through a gap between the end of the privet hedge and the neighbor's garage. I'd wait on the back porch for a minute, sometimes two, holding my breath and (standing on tiptoe) looking through the little window into the kitchen and admiring the picture of a big artichoke on the far wall before knocking on the door. If Paul was reading at the kitchen table he'd look up and smile. If he wasn't in the kitchen, I'd have to pound on the door and wait.

I felt very grown up. Safe, too, because we had a clear *terminus ad quem*: as soon as the term was over Paul would be leaving for New York, to join his wife for a few days, and I would be leaving for Rome, to take an eight-week course in spoken Latin. *"Quo fata trahunt,"* I said to myself, *"retrahuntque sequamur."* Wherever fate leads us, let us follow.

I was graduated from Knox College in June and left for Rome a week later. Leaving Paul. Leaving my family. My mother had hoped I'd get to see the Pope—John XXIII—before he died, though she wasn't a big fan of the changes that were coming out of Vatican II. "The Pope can go to hell if he wants to," she liked to say. "That's his business, but I'm not serving meat on Fridays."

One of the announcers at the Radio Vaticana had come from Galesburg. His father still lived here. You could see him—the father—mowing the lawn in front of a small brick house on Cherry Street. My mother called him, but he said he couldn't arrange an introduction to the pope and didn't think his son could either. In any case, Pope John was already dead by the time I got to Rome.

My mother, who'd gotten wind of my affair with a faculty member and who was very upset about it, wanted me to go to confession before I left for Rome. It had been a long time.

"You know," she said, "Father Gordon at Saint Clement's is very understanding."

"He's not supposed to know who I am."

My mother waved her hand. "When was the last time you made a full confession?"

My father used to drive us in to Saint Clement's on Saturday afternoons, but that was before I went off to college. "At least talk to him," my mother said. "I don't want you flying over the ocean in a state of mortal sin. What if the plane crashes?"

"It's not going to crash, Ma."

I wasn't sure how my mother found out about the affair. Lois? Probably not. She—my mother—wanted my father to complain to the dean, but I wouldn't tell her who the faculty member was—my *współpozwany* as she kept calling him. My co-respondent.

I was a classics major and my mother suspected Professor Davenport, who had directed my honors thesis on Catullus.

"Let it go, Anka," my father said.

"She's in a state of mortal sin, Kazik. I don't want her flying over the ocean in a state of mortal sin."

This scene was repeated for the last time on the day before I left. I refused to give up Paul's name; my father, whose name means "keep the peace" in Polish, refused to complain to the dean; my mother was weeping in her room and wouldn't come downstairs. My aunt came over and fixed sausages and cabbage for our supper, and a cucumber salad, and half a cheesecake from the bakery on Seminary Street.

The next morning my father took me to the airport in Peoria. My mother managed to come down to say good-bye before we left.

"Was it that Professor Davenport?" she asked as I was getting into the truck.

"Ma, he's fifty years old."

"So," she said. "Your father's fifty-two."

"How about Professor Hanson?" I asked. "Or Professor Goddard?"

"Franciszka," she said, turning red. "What are you talking about? They're women. Don't tell me . . ."

"Ma," I said, "don't worry, okay? Besides—"

"At least go to confession when you get to Rome," she said. "Or maybe you could go before, in the airport in New York. They have churches in airports. Do this for me, will you? Maybe they'll have a new pope while you're still there."

"If they do," I said, "I'll tell him you said hello. I hope it's not that sour-faced Cardinal Montini."

Ma came over to the truck and reached through the open window and held my head in her hands and kissed me.

"Ma," I said. "I love you."

I cried halfway to Rome, a traveler sensing the gravitational pull of home. The stewardess kept asking if she could help me, but my tears were tears of sorrow mixed with joy, and I was enjoying every one of them. I thought about Paul's kisses, and Ma's last kiss as we were pulling out of the drive, and I thought about Lois, who was going to spend a big chunk of the summer detasseling corn before going to the University of Illinois in Urbana. I was going to Loyola University in Chicago, a good Catholic school. Even so, I was leaving my old life behind, and I wouldn't be going back home in the fall. But I'd already said good-bye to my old life, the night of the Shakespeare party. I'd crossed a line that night, crossed the Rubicon. The die had been cast. *Alec iacta erat.* And so I was sad. But I was happy, too. I'd negotiated a grand passion, my first adult love affair. Just what I'd needed at that time in my life. I'd handled it well. There were no loose ends.

I'd been encouraged by Professor Davenport and by Miss Buckholdt, my high school Latin teacher, to take the course in spoken Latin taught by Father Adrian, an American Carmelite friar from Philadelphia who taught Latin at the Pontifical Gregorian University in Rome. In the fall I'd be going to Loyola on a generous scholarship, living in Rogers Park. No turning back now.

They turned off the cabin lights about ten P.M. Chicago time. I turned on my reading light and took out the Loeb Ovid from my backpack, but none of Ovid's heroines spoke to me. They offered warnings rather than invitations. Why did things always go wrong for the women who were loved by the gods? I didn't know, but I knew that I was undergoing a kind of metamorphosis. But what was I turning into? A tree? a cow? a bear? a stag? a flower? a rippling mountain stream? a bubbling fountain? a woman?

I went to sleep on that thought, and when I woke up we were over the North Atlantic, and I was feeling a little shaky. Maybe I *should* have gone to confession? What if the plane *did* crash and I *was* in a state of mortal sin? Which I was. What about Paul's wife, a woman who had always been very kind to me? In my dreams Paul and his wife had been laughing about me as they tried to explain these things to my mother. "I found her up in the attic," Paul was saying, "after the party." And my mother said, "I just hope they elect a new pope soon so she can go to confession in Rome."

By the time the charter flight landed at Ciampino, the military airport, I had regressed to my pre-first-adult-love-affair self. I needed help, physical as well as spiritual. There was no subway into the city; there were no shuttle busses. I had to heave my suitcase and my L. L. Bean backpack onto a regular city bus. I didn't understand at the time that I was supposed to buy a ticket before I got on the bus and punch it on the bus itself, and I almost got arrested, but I pretended not to understand the policeman who checked our tickets. And in fact, I didn't understand him. The policeman wrote out a ticket and handed it to me. I put it in my backpack. I still have it. (There was a policeman at each end of the bus, to keep people without tickets from jumping off.)

Rome was a *casino*, a madhouse. Pope John had been in the ground—in the cave under Saint Peter's—for over a week, but no one had gone home after the funeral. They were all sticking around the center of Rome waiting for the election of a new pope. Not just cardinals and their retinues, but priests, monks, friars, journalists, pilgrims, students, tourists, from all over the world.

The students in Father Adrian Young's spoken Latin course were going to stay in the Carmelite convent on the Janiculum, a big hill on the left of my map, just south of the Vatican. But I couldn't get into my room till Sunday, and I was sorry I'd come a day early. My Italian was based on three years of Italian at Knox superimposed on a solid foundation of Latin, augmented by a book written by one of my professors called *Italian Is Easy If You Know Latin*. So I could get around all right; I could read the street signs, ask directions. But I couldn't get close to the American Express office in Piazza di Spagna to cash a traveler's check. The piazza was too crowded to negotiate with a large suitcase and a heavy backpack. It was like Disneyland. I couldn't find a *pensione*; even the cheap places near the station were full. My backpack—containing Lewis and Short's *Latin Dictionary* and the Gildersleeve and Lodge *Latin Grammar*, which we were to have with us in class at all times, as well as my own Catullus, Ovid, Vergil, and Helen Gurley Brown's *Sex and the Single Girl*—was so heavy I was afraid I was going to fall over on my back. I managed to take a rogue cab from the station to the convent and used up almost all my cash. I knew I was being cheated. My Italian was okay, but not good enough to deal with the cab driver.

I left my suitcase and backpack at the convent. I had only ten thousand lire left but I didn't feel like making another attempt to get to the American Express office. So I spent the afternoon on the

Janiculum, the eighth hill of Rome. On a bench, reading Ovid. Nothing to eat. The sun started to set behind me, and I started to feel a little uneasy, so I walked down to Santa Maria in Trastevere, not an easy trek in the fading light. My feet twisted and turned on the uneven cobblestones. I passed a strange lighthouse and then the Roman Finnish Institute and the Embassy of Finland to the Holy See, and kept bearing to the right and downhill—toward the city center—till I came to a poorly lighted street that ran along the Tiber. I was able to consult my map and find my way to Piazza Santa Maria in Trastevere. I was thinking that the proximity of the church would protect me, but by nine o'clock the church was closed. At least there were a lot of young people in the piazza, and two different men asked me if I was lost and needed help. I hadn't gotten very far in Helen Gurley Brown's *Sex and the Single Girl*, but I was far enough in to know that I didn't want any adventures, at least not that kind of adventure, at least not now. I sat at the fountain, telling myself that this *was* an adventure. I tried to imagine myself telling Paul about it. I realized that I still needed to get Paul out of my system, but I wasn't quite sure how to do it. Lots of young people were necking on the stone steps that circled the fountain in the center of the piazza, and I wondered if their butts were starting to hurt like mine.

What was I doing? What did Rome mean to me? As a classics major? As a lapsed Roman Catholic? Maybe the new pope—when he got elected—would give me some good advice. I hoped it wasn't Montini. I couldn't imagine any words of sympathy or kindness coming out of that pinched mouth. Actually, I *could* imagine them. And did. "Father," I'd say, and he'd say, "Child, you've lost your way." Maybe I'd even discover a vocation. My mother's cousin was a big-deal nun in the Clementine order in Chicago, and I used to stay in the convent once in a while. The nuns were happy. Why was I surprised?

"All I know about love," I thought, "is . . ." What? I couldn't think of a single thing that I knew about love, and I was homesick. For the farm, for the old Sunday evenings at home, my mother playing Polish folksongs and Chopin drinking songs on the upright piano at which I'd been forced to practice a half hour a day, seven days a week. (Yes, Chopin did write some drinking songs.)

I'd been terribly homesick when I first went off to college, even though "home" was only five miles away. I went home every weekend for a while, and then every other weekend, then once a month, then hardly at all. I told myself it would be this way with Paul. At first . . . then . . . and finally . . . but it didn't happen that way.

What did I want to happen right at that moment, sitting on the steps of the stone fountain outside Santa Maria in Trastevere? I couldn't think of anything. A good restaurant? I didn't have any money, and besides, I wasn't even hungry. I hadn't planned well. What I wanted was to go to sleep and wake up calm and refreshed, but that's hard to do when you're having some kind of psychosexual crisis.

What I really wanted, I see now, was to go to confession. Ma had been right. I needed to clean out my attic.

I slept, sort of, on the steps of the fountain, using my backpack as a pillow. In the morning I spent my remaining ten thousand lire on some postcards and dragged myself back up the hill to the convent. I sat on a bench on the edge of the hill, overlooking the city, and wrote to my folks, to Lois, in Latin to the classics professors at Knox, and to Miss Buckholdt, my Latin teacher at the high school, and in Italian to Professor Marino, who'd written *Italian Is Easy If You Know Latin*. I told them that Rome was wonderful, even as my tears were falling on the postcards and smearing the ink. But I didn't write to Paul.

A nun sat down next to me on the bench. She had a small suitcase and a heavy backpack, like mine.

"Are you all right?" she asked in Italian, and I was able to understand her.

"A little bit lost," I said in Italian. "*Perduta.*"

"A 'lost' woman?" she said in Italian, laughing. "Or do you mean you don't know where you are?"

"That too," I said.

I was glad to discover that she was a student in the program. We were both waiting for the convent to come to life. It was still early. We couldn't get into our rooms till afternoon.

We continued to talk in Italian and I had to concentrate. Her sister was coming from Ireland, she said. She had tickets for a papal audience on Wednesday, but now that the pope was dead, her sister wasn't coming.

"If your sister's from Ireland," I said, "then you must be from Ireland, too."

She laughed. "Yes," she said, "but I've lived in Italy for over twenty-five years. I teach at a convent school in Florence, a *liceo*. They're sending me to this program because they need someone who *speaks* Latin."

I recognized a critical moment: we could switch to English or stay in Italian. It was my option, but I waited.

"*Hai fame?*" she asked. *Are you hungry?*

"*Si*," I said, feeling more confident.

She dropped her suitcase off at the convent and we walked up and down the path at the top of the Janiculum. She treated me to a cappuccino and a dolce, which we ate sitting on a bench overlooking Regina Coeli prison.

"It used to be a convent," she said. "Two convents, actually."

"And now it's a prison?"

"Some people would say it's always been a prison."

"But not you?"

She tossed off another nice laugh. There was nothing mean or sarcastic about it. It rang in the air like a wind chime.

We walked down to Santa Maria in Trastevere—a half-hour stroll in daylight—and went to mass together.

At the beginning of the mass itself the priest said a few words about the change from Latin to the vernacular that was just around the corner.

"*Error magnus,*" I whispered to Sister Teresa. *Big mistake.*

Sister Teresa took communion, but I stayed in my seat, trying to lose myself in a mosaic of the annunciation that was hard to see clearly because of the baldacchino over the high altar. An angel with a third feathery wing attached to his head appeared to be shaking his fist at the Virgin Mary. The Virgin didn't look very happy.

After mass we tried to speak in Latin as we were walking back up the hill.

"Did King Evander point out the Janiculum to Aeneas?" I asked.

"*Nescio,*" she said, *I don't know,* and that was as far as we got.

I hadn't been able to cash a traveler's check, so she treated me to lunch, a sandwich from the same cart where she'd bought the cappuccino and the dolce. Lots of people were taking the air.

At three o'clock we were able to move into our rooms. I lay down on a firm, narrow bed and tugged my shoes off with my toes and slept till the next morning.

Father Adrian was not a gentle man. He was a "tough-love" kind of priest—I was familiar with the type—who didn't spare the rod of ridicule. It's one thing to rattle off the list of deponent verbs that take the ablative. It's another thing to stand in front of nineteen other people, twenty if you counted Father Adrian, and use one of these verbs in sentences illustrating the passive periphrastic in the perfect, imperfect, future, pluperfect, and future perfect tenses.

There were nineteen of us. I was the youngest. My pal, Sister Teresa, was in the middle, about forty-five. The group included several priests and two German school teachers, with their big German-Latin dictionaries. The rest of us had our Lewis and Shorts.

At first I didn't see how I could hold out for eight weeks, but by the end of the third week we had watched the eruption of Mount Vesuvius with Pliny the Younger, taking turns summarizing passages from the letters he wrote to Tacitus; we had entered the cave of the Sibyl with Aeneas, and fought the second Punic War with Polybius—seventy thousand Roman soldiers slaughtered by Hannibal's mercenaries at Cannae. All these exercises were challenging, but they were easier than sticking to Latin during the informal sessions after supper, where the main topic of conversation was the papal conclave, which began two days after our first class. Between classes Sister Teresa and I would walk to the north end of the park, where we could get a view of the dome of Saint Peter's. We couldn't see the Sistine Chapel, on the far side of the basilica, nor could we see the chimney. But we thought we might be able to catch sight of the smoke signal if we were there at the right time. The priests in our group were the biggest gossips. They listened to Radio Vaticana and pored over the accounts of the proceedings in *L'Osservatore*, the Vatican newspaper; and they entertained us with the conspiracy theories dating back to John's election in 1958, when Radio Vaticana had announced the election of a new pope and then said that black smoke had mistakenly been identified as white smoke. And then with the conspiracy theories surrounding his death, barely two weeks earlier. Had he been murdered to prevent him from doing further damage to the

Church? Had he secretly been a Freemason? Had the 1958 conclave been contaminated by outside influence—threats of a nuclear attack on the Vatican by the Soviet Union if a conservative anticommunist pope were elected? If such a threat had in fact reached the cardinals, then John's election would have been invalid, and John would have been an antipope. Probably not, I thought. Sister Teresa and I were both glad that Father Adrian did what he could to put a stop to this kind of gossip, but the Church really knew how to put on a show, and it was impossible not to get caught up in the excitement.

The class usually met in a room in the convent, but on occasion we went outdoors and declaimed poetry in the park, sometimes attracting a small audience. It was embarrassing. Like doing tai chi exercises in public. Father Adrian had an iron will. No one thought of resisting. And he enjoyed embarrassing everyone. Teaching us humility, I suppose. He always called on Sister Teresa to declaim dirty poetry. But she didn't seem to mind, wasn't bothered by Catullus or Propertius. I envied her her high spirits, and her inner peace. I'd never really admired inner peace in others. Inner peace always seemed like a negative quality rather than a positive one. A damping down. But not in the case of Sister Teresa, who had the energy of a young horse. Like our old black Lab, she was thick and solid, all spiritual muscle.

I went with her to seven-o'clock mass every morning that week at Santa Maria in Trastevere. The mass was celebrated in the small chapel, cordoned off to keep out the tourists. I kept glancing up at the mosaic of the annunciation, over the high altar, that I'd admired on my first Sunday. A little pamphlet told me that it was by Pietro Cavallini. The extra wing, I could see now, was really the wing growing out of the angel's left shoulder, and the angel wasn't really shaking his fist at the Virgin, he was offering her a two-finger blessing. The Virgin was holding a book in her left hand, her fingers curled under the cover to keep her place. God observes from a little window at the top as a dove—the divine sperm, the divine *Word*—wings its way on a shaft of light toward the ear of the unsuspecting Virgin.

I was no longer hung up on belief. Is it true or not true? Did God really impregnate the Virgin Mary? Did Jesus really rise from the dead, physically? Or are these stories just metaphors? These questions had been very important when I was in high school, but they no longer troubled me. I stopped worrying about all the misdeeds of the Catholic Church, which I'd thrown in my mother's face—the Spanish Inquisition, the Great Schism (three popes at one time!), the dysfunctional attitude toward sexuality, the persecution of the Jews, Father Gordon's predecessor (who'd disappeared after a scandal involving an altar boy), and so on—and just let myself experience what I was experiencing as I knelt next to Sister Teresa in what was probably the earliest Christian church in Rome—certainly the first to be dedicated to the Mother of God—built on the site of a club for Roman soldiers, a site where oil had gushed forth on the day of Christ's conception, heralding the coming of the Messiah; a site where popes and antipopes had engaged in internecine warfare long before the scandal of the Avignon papacy. What I was experiencing was a feeling that I was a part of a larger whole. I couldn't really follow the sermons in Italian, but I'd get the general drift, and that was usually enough, though one sermon in particular, during the third week of the program, stands out in my memory. At least the end of it does. "You need only one little word to be saved," the priest said, several times. I listened as hard as I could, even cupping my hands behind my ears, but the priest lowered his voice to a whisper when he pronounced that one little word, and I couldn't hear it. I could have asked Sister Teresa, but I didn't want to raise the issue of salvation with Sister Teresa, a Dominican, very well educated. She taught Greek as well as Latin in the *liceo* in Florence, which was run by an order of Irish nuns, though the lessons were all in Italian.

The next Saturday, after the one-little-word sermon, I went to confession. It was a week and a day after Giovanni Battista Enrico Antonio Maria Montini had been elected and chosen the name "Paul." By this time the evening gossip had turned from conspiracy theories to speculation about the new pope's intentions. I was not an eager disputant in these slow-moving Latin bull sessions, but I was hoping that he'd do what he said he was going to do: follow the path laid out by his predecessor. Sister Teresa and I had our doubts, which we shared on the way down from the Janiculum.

"You could make your confession in Latin," Sister Teresa said. We were speaking in Italian as we walked along via della Lungara.

"Right," I said, as we passed the guards standing outside the big front door of Regina Coeli.

"You could go to Saint Pat's if you want to do it in English."

"Saint Pat's?"

"In via Boncompagni. There are four Irish churches in town."

"Italian is fine," I said, and we stopped talking for a while.

I thought Italian would be less traumatic than English. But kneeling in the deep shadows of the confessional I started to speak in Latin. "*Pater, pecavi . . .*"

"*Piano, piano,*" the priest said. *Slow down.* "Did Father Adrian send you to test my Latin?"

"Non," I said.

"Start over," he said. "This time in Italian."

Was this what I'd been wanting all along? I thought so. Clean out my attic, as my mother liked to say.

"I've committed adultery," I said. No, not adultery, fornication. Not sure of the word, I tried *fornicazione* and hit the jackpot. "I've been disrespectful to my parents, especially my mother. I've told lies." I stopped there. The priest waited for me to go on, but I thought it was enough, especially *fornicazione.* And then everything happened that was supposed to happen. The priest asked me to consider the seriousness of my sin and its effects on others, and to promise not to repeat it. I agreed to everything, and then he absolved me, in Latin, *"in nomine Patris, et Filii, et Spiritus Sancti."* I was in a state of grace. It was like standing in a cold shower, or plunging into Lake Storey, after jogging on a hot day.

Sister Teresa, who had already made her confession, was waiting for me at the fountain in the piazza, her fingers working a rosary. Penance? You always had to wonder about other people's sins. She looked up at me, her face a question mark. My own face answered her. No need for words. We walked along the west bank of the Tiber, not talking at first, and then talking slowly and carefully in Latin all the way to Ponte Sublicio and then back up the east bank all the way to the Corso, and then backtracking through some smaller streets, not knowing exactly where we were and not caring, till we found ourselves in Campo de' Fiori, where Giordano Bruno had been burned at the stake for proposing that the sun was just another star and that the universe contained an infinite number of inhabited worlds.

We wandered around till almost eight o'clock and then ate in a restaurant on one of the little side streets that branch off the campo. Lots of diners had great big brown flowers on their plates. I didn't know what they were. Neither did Sister Teresa. They weren't flowers; they were deep-fried artichokes. Not little baby artichokes, but medium-size ones. Like everyone else, I'd been having a hard time in class. Father Adrian kept pushing and pushing us. But sitting with Sister Teresa, pulling the leaves off my artichoke, sprinkling them with fresh lemon juice, my mind had become calm. I could see things clearly, but I wasn't sure if it was because of the artichokes or because I'd received absolution.

If I close my eyes I can still see Paul sitting on a bench on the Janiculum overlooking Regina Coeli. Not the new pope, Paul VI, but Paul Godwin, my Shakespeare professor. It was the fifth week of the course. We'd been declaiming Catullus 2 and discussing the possibility that some lines were missing between 2(a) and 2(b)—a famous crux in the famous poem about Lesbia's sparrow. I was able to shine, since I'd done my honors thesis on Catullus, and when Father Adrian realized that I was familiar with the crux, he asked me to lead the discussion. I had to step up in front of the class and ask questions in Latin. And respond to questions too.

"Quid omisum est?" What's been left out?

And so on. Pretty basic, but pretty exciting, too. And soon it was time for lunch.

With my eyes still closed I see myself walking with Sister Teresa along the edge of the Janiculum. I see us buying two gelati, in little cups—my treat this time. And then I notice Paul and I realize that this is not the first day he's been sitting on this bench.

At first I think I must be mistaken. But there's no mistaking Paul, though he's looking very Italian. He's peeling an orange with a knife and putting the peels down on a napkin spread out on his lap. Sister Teresa and I walk on by, and my sense of being free from sin is soothing. Especially in Sister Teresa's presence. We're on an elevated plane, above the world, looking down on Paul. Paul, I think to myself, will be a welcome challenge, a test of strength.

Sister Teresa and I had both done well in class, discussing the pros and cons of the missing-lines hypothesis, and I was feeling strong, even as I thought about Paul. His touch. His fingers on the inside of my leg. His smell. Not cologne, but some kind of shaving gel. I'd seen it in his bathroom. But I was experiencing these sensations as if they were happening to someone else. Someone I'd been long ago. Well, not that long ago. About six weeks ago.

It was good to be with Sister Teresa, good to walk in the circle of her happiness, her gusto, her goodness, which was not the kind of goodness that makes you uncomfortable, that makes you want to spoil something.

I liked the way she stood up to Father Adrian. She was the only one who was not afraid of him. I thought *he* was a good person too, but his was a different kind of goodness. You did things his way. You pronounced Latin with a soft "g", as in Italian, and "c" as "ch." Ecclesiastical pronunciation. But Sister Teresa pronounced it her own way, the classical pronunciation, and after a while Father Adrian pretended not to notice. I liked the way she sang *Gaudeamus Igitur* in the convent basement. Her soprano voice was sweet, high, and loud at the same time.

I wanted to touch Paul, to comfort him. He had not wanted to accept the end of the affair, but now it was over. We inhabited two different worlds. We were not Romeo and Juliet but Dido and Aeneas. I was Aeneas—destined to move on—and he was Dido, destined to remain behind.

I took Sister Teresa by the hand, which made it difficult to finish my little cup of gelato, but it didn't matter. I'd been putting a lot of effort into my new life. I no longer wanted all the beautiful outfits I saw in the shop windows. I was imagining a future devoted to good works. But I was very vague about this. I was letting one thing happen at a time. I was letting myself be led.

My own intention, which I kept secret, even from Sister Teresa, was to fast regularly, and to help some of the other students who were having difficulty in the class, and not to speak to Paul unless he spoke first. He was there the next day, and the next, feeding sparrows, eating more oranges.

But it annoyed me to think of him sitting there every day, so smug. What was he trying to prove? I finally asked Sister Teresa to wait by the ice cream truck while I spoke to someone who, I said, might be an old teacher. "If you see me raise my hand," I said, "please join us right away. *Statim*? Okay?"

And so I sat down next to Paul. "How long are you going to keep this up?"

"As long as it takes."

"I thought we decided . . ." I said, not sure exactly what we had decided, if anything, and then I asked: "How did you get here?"

"With love's light wings," he said, "did I o'er-perch these walls; For stony limits cannot hold love out."

"Paul," I said, "stop right now. We're not going to play Romeo and Juliet again. Once was enough. Besides, everything has changed."

"I had to see you, that's all. I'll go if you want me to."

"You know that's not what I *want*. Not like that."

"What *do* you want?"

Paul was wearing his Italian suit. I never was impressed by men's suits, but this one was beautiful, light brown, linen, striped, and I knew that he wore it only on special occasions.

"I'm not going to apologize," he said, "if that's what you want. For being here, I mean." He paused. I didn't say anything. "You loved me once."

I didn't recognize the quotation, but I pretended I did. "Paul, I'm not going to talk to you if you talk in quotations."

"It's not a quotation. It's just something I said."

"You're the one," I reminded him, "who warned *me* not to fall in love."

"Ah, Frances," he said. "that love, so gentle in his view, Should be so tyrannous and rough in proof."

I answered him with a quotation of my own: "God's will is our peace," I said, and I was immediately sorry I'd said it. What was I talking about?

"*La sua voluntade è nostra pace*," Paul said. *His will is our peace.*

I raised my arm, and Sister Teresa joined us immediately.

"*Piacere*," she said to Paul, *a pleasure*. And without even being introduced they began to speak in Italian. I knew that Paul knew Italian, but I hadn't realized he was fluent. At least he sounded fluent. He said something that I didn't understand, and Sister Teresa laughed. Maybe she needed a break from speaking Latin.

"*Nonne Latine loquamur?*" I said stiffly. *Shouldn't we be speaking Latin?*

Sister Teresa laughed again. "But you were speaking in English," she said in Italian.

The sun was high in the eastern sky, over the prison. It was a beautiful day, but all the people looked sad to me—the man in a wheelchair whom we saw every day, the couples strolling hand in hand. You could hear the noise of the ice cream vendors over the bawling of portable radios. I felt almost ashamed of my own inner strength, my own vision. I was like a person in robust health in a group of invalids, though I was a little annoyed that Paul and Sister Teresa spoke too fast for me to keep up. Sister Teresa was saying something about riding on a donkey when she was a child in County Cork, and Paul was explaining that his suit actually came from Ireland. He showed her the label on the inside of the jacket. I looked too: BRIAN & BRADY.

Sister Teresa told Paul about Father Adrian and the spoken Latin course, and then they were talking about me. Sister Teresa reached over and touched me. She said that I was a shining example for all the students, a real angel.

Paul said that I'd been a shining example to the students in his Shakespeare classes, too. He was in Rome, he said, because he was sure that Shakespeare had spent some time in Italy. Too many descriptions in the plays matched up with actual sites in Italy.

"Shouldn't you be in Verona?" she asked.

"Absolutely," he said. "In the very first scene of *Romeo and Juliet* Shakespeare mentions a grove of sycamore trees 'that westward rooteth from this city side' that's not mentioned in any of his sources. If I could find that grove . . . but there are other things, too, and I wanted to start in Rome."

In the late afternoon, after the lessons, the three of us went to a puppet show in the park, ostensibly a show for children but with intrusive erotic overtones for the adults—Pulcinella's huge nose, for example, and the wooden spoon that he uses to beat everyone, or Columbina's cleavage and perky stance, and all the erotic byplay, which I had trouble following, though Paul and Sister Teresa laughed and laughed. The puppet theater was a little square shack about the size of an outhouse with a sign in front admonishing children not to throw stones at the puppets.

That night we walked to Campo de' Fiori for more deep-fried artichokes at Al Pompiere. Paul said the dish was called *carciofi alla Giudia, artichokes alla Judaea.* We were all native English speakers, but we conversed in Italian. I was ready to brain Paul for paying so much attention to Sister Teresa, but I drank too much wine and invited him to come to seven-o'clock mass with us in the morning at Santa Maria in Trastevere. I didn't know if I wanted to stop him in his tracks or if I wanted him to taste what I had tasted.

That night I lay on my back, opening myself up, praying for strength, listening for instructions, trying to imagine my way back to a time before we had complicated everything. If there'd ever been such a time.

I did not expect the spiritual life to be smooth sailing. Not at all. I welcomed Paul's presence as a challenge. Paul was just the sort of problem you'd expect to crop up.

At mass he knelt between us, and I told him to get his butt off the pew and kneel up straight. Which he did.

After mass Sister Teresa pleaded a cold, brought on by a dreaded *colpa d'aria*, a *blow of air*, a draft. Paul and I spent the day saying good-bye. He did not make a fuss, did not attempt to talk me into, or out of, anything. I could not detect any irony in his questions, nor sarcasm in his comments about the church. No comments about Jesus being a great moral teacher, or being the son of God in the sense that we're all children of God. In short, he didn't make fun of me. He took me seriously. He wished me well. He applauded my decision to work on weekends in the soup kitchen at the old Maxwell Street market in Chicago.

We sat on a bench looking down at the prison, Regina Coeli, and I told him about my conversation with Sister Teresa. Most of the prisons in Italy, he said, had originally been convents.

We walked down the hill to via della Lungara and had coffee in a bar across from the waiting room of the prison. I told him I'd been going to confession.

Later we sat by the fountain in Piazza Santa Maria in Trastevere. Waiting. For what? For Paul to leave.

I told him that my mother hadn't wanted me to fly across the ocean in a state of mortal sin, told him about my mother's simple faith, as if she were one of Tolstoy's peasants with immediate knowledge of God. (I'd read *Anna Karenina* twice.) This was going to be easier than I'd thought.

"You're happy," he said.

"And you?"

"I'm happy too."

And that was it. Or, it might have been.

We said good-bye at the foot of Ponte Sisto. It was three o'clock in the afternoon.

I watched him walk across the bridge, waited for him to turn back for a last look. If he'd turned back I might have waved good-bye, but he didn't look back. It's a long bridge with three piers. I could hardly make him out as he turned up the Lungotevere dei Tebaldi. And then I ran after him. Over the bridge, then left along the river. I took the first turn to the right and found him in Piazza Farnese. Turning into a bar.

"Don't go!" I shouted as I saw him going into a bar.

He didn't hear me. He was talking to the barista when I went in. I watched as he ordered a beer and sat down at a table and picked up a copy of *Corriere della sera*.

I sat down next to him. Out of breath.

"You're sure you want to do this?" he asked.

"I'm sure," I said.

"I like it when you tease me," he said.

"I'm not teasing," I said. And I wasn't. I *was* sure. My body was burning, in fact. I couldn't think of anything except holding him in my arms, feeling his warm skin next to mine, his warm breath in my ear. I longed for him, as if he were far, far away instead of sitting right next to me.

That night, while the new pope was addressing a crowd—a throng—of 250,000 in nine different languages (Latin, Italian, French, English, German, Spanish, Portuguese, Polish, and

Russian), Paul and I walked along the Janiculum, looking down at the city and up at the stars.

"It's hard to believe," Paul said, "that Rome is at about the same latitude as Galesburg, so if we were in Galesburg we'd be looking up at the same night sky. Well, in another six hours."

"I took Professor's Lynch's astronomy course," I said.

"Right," he said, and we both looked up at Boötes the Herdsman, my first constellation except for Orion and the Big Dipper. And beneath Boötes, Virgo, and the Coma Berenices, all of them sinking down into the Tyrrhenian Sea in the west.

I did not go to confession again in Santa Maria in Trastevere. In fact, I was pregnant when I flew back to Chicago. It was too early to be sure, but in my heart I *knew* that Paul had planted his seed.

I didn't go to confession again, at least not a proper confession, for many, many years. But I've never forgotten what it was like to be free from sin. If only for a couple of weeks. It's a great feeling, but it doesn't convulse the entire being.

3

The Blessing (October 1964)

As far as Ma was concerned, the world was coming to an end. At least *her* world was coming to an end, winding down. Our first Catholic president had been assassinated exactly one year earlier; Vatican II had thrown the church into turmoil; my mother's fears about the importance of fasting on Fridays were coming true; and "Dominique," a song by the Singing Nun, had been replaced in the number one spot on the charts by "I Want to Hold Your Hand." Elvis Presley had been bad enough, and now the Beatles, who had appeared on *The Ed Sullivan Show*, were coming up behind him. By April they dominated the charts. In another three weeks—on Monday, November 23, to be exact—Latin would cease to be the official language of the Roman Catholic Church. And finally: her only daughter had disgraced the family by having a baby out of wedlock.

Baby Stella had been born in March. Paul and I weren't married at the time, not till his divorce was final. And then we were married before a justice of the peace, not by Father Gordon in Saint

Clement's. So as far as my mother was concerned, we weren't married at all. (Of course, in my mother's eyes Paul hadn't been married in the first place, since he wasn't a Catholic.)

I'd spoken to Ma a couple of times on the telephone, but we hadn't been out to the farm, and they hadn't seen baby Stella, who was now seven months old. So when my father called to see if Paul would like to help slaughter a hog, I thought "truce," or at least an invitation to negotiate a truce. But it was also a test. Was Paul up to slaughtering a hog? I wasn't sure. I let him talk to Pa on the phone, so Pa could issue the invitation in person.

We were still living in the house on Chambers Street, which was up for sale. Paul's wife, his ex-wife, Elaine, was rich but not vindictive. Illinois was not a no-fault state, so she had to sue on grounds of adultery. Paul did not contest, of course, so there was no problem, but the court wanted some names and dates—proof—and I was named as co-respondent, the *współpozwany*.

I was taking classes at the college to fulfill the state education requirements. I was hoping to take over the Latin program at the high school when Miss Buckholdt, my old teacher, retired. I'd been one of her star pupils and she'd been happy that I was going to Loyola. Then disappointed, of course. She was the one who'd interested me in the spoken Latin program in Rome. She'd always wanted to try it herself, and maybe she would once she retired.

The weather was cold, but not too cold. The hog weighed almost two hundred fifty pounds, a little heavier than usual because we were slaughtering late. It was a Canadian Lacombe gilt that my father favored. Next year we'd slaughter a Berkshire. My uncle's preference. One hog a year for the two families.

Ma and my aunt Klaudia were cooking pierogis in the kitchen and canning cherries at the same time. I said a few words in Polish to Izabella, the exchange student who was helping her. I didn't know much Polish, and she answered me in perfect English. She was on the swim team at the high school, so she had to be driven into the YMCA, where the swim team practiced, every morning at five, which was when the team practiced. Ma didn't drive and didn't want to learn, which was very inconvenient out on the farm. She didn't care. She went shopping with my aunt once a week. My cousin Jerzy loved to drive and my father had bought him a car so he could drive Ma around, but now he lived in Boston. Another cousin, Michal, who lived on the next farm, drove Izabella in to swim practice every morning in the car, a Studebaker. The top looked like the tower of a submarine. He was in love with her. He was big and strong, good looking, too, but too shy to put himself forward.

The cherries were in jars in a pressure cooker on the stove. More jars were being sterilized in a steam bath on the woodstove on the porch. When you opened the kitchen door you could feel the heat.

Paul sat at the table, drinking a glass of warm buttermilk that my mother had forced on him, listening to Aunt Klaudia, who was holding the baby and explaining the difference between hot pack and raw pack. Ma preferred hot pack; Aunt Klaudia preferred raw pack. So they took turns, hot pack one year, raw pack the next, just the way Pa and my uncle took turns with the hogs, Canadian Lacombe gilt one year, Berkshire the next. I sat next to Paul. He offered me some of his buttermilk, but I shook my head.

"If you'd gone to mass yesterday," Ma said to me, "you'd have heard Father Gordon say it in Latin. Three more weeks and it's gone." She cut her throat with her finger.

"The old Tridentine mass," Paul said. "It goes back a long way."

"You see," Ma said, looking at me, "he knows more about it than you do."

"Father Gordon doesn't really know Latin anyway," I said. "He's just memorized it. Like a parrot."

"Aren't you Miss Smarty Pants," Ma said. "Who hasn't been to mass for how many years?"

Paul said, "They've been preparing for this for a long time now, but I'm afraid they haven't done a very good job. A lot of misinformation, confusion."

Ma poured some more warm buttermilk into Paul's glass. "I know," she said. "We been getting all these instructions about the responses. We have to say one thing instead of another, 'The Lord be with you' instead of '*Dominus vobiscum.*' 'And also with you' instead of '*et cum spiritu tuo.*'" Aunt Klaudia welcomed the switch to English, but Ma had no stomach for changes in the liturgy.

The buttermilk was a kind of test, though I don't think Ma realized it. She made all my boyfriends drink warm buttermilk. She couldn't understand how anyone could drink it cold, right out of the refrigerator. I had to laugh. Paul didn't like milk in any form. He even put orange juice on his cereal. But he drank the buttermilk.

"I think it's nice," my aunt said, "for everybody to know what's going on. We have to go with the times. Nobody understands Latin anyway. Except Frances. And maybe you, Paul."

This was the first time one of the women had uttered his name.

"You don't just throw out the old ways," Ma said. "Everybody in the world hears the same words. Gets the same blessings. Now they want to change all that." She paused. "The Pope can go to hell if he wants to, that's his business—"

"But you're not serving meat on Friday," I finished the sentence for her.

"It's good to suffer a little bit once a week," Ma said. "To remind you of somebody else's suffering. Next they'll be saying it's okay for the priests to get married." She crossed herself.

"Eating fish is not suffering," I said.

"You had to love the pope," Aunt Klaudia said. "The old pope. Pope John."

"He was a nice man," Ma said, "but he made a lot of problems for everybody."

"He started Vatican Two," I said.

"Vatican Two," she said. "What about Vatican One? Tell me what was Vatican One? Does anybody remember Vatican One?"

"That was more than a hundred years ago," Paul said.

"You see, Franny," Ma said (again), "your husband knows more than you do, and he's not even a Catholic."

"Ma, he just looked up all this stuff in the *Columbia Encyclopedia* to impress you."

"Well, it's nice that he went to all that trouble."

Baby Stella started to cry. "See, Ma," I said, "you're upsetting the baby."

Pa got out a bottle of potato schnapps. "Here," he said, "rub a little of this on her gums."

"Put that away," Ma said. "Give her to me, I'll change her diapers."

"Ma, sit, sit. I'll change her. Where's the diaper bag?"

"It's on the couch," Ma said, picking up the baby and going off into the living room, which was right off the kitchen. I could hear her singing in Polish, a song that she used to sing to me. I could remember the words, but not what they meant:

A la la Kotki dwa
Szary bury oby dwa
la la Tatusiu
Tru la lu la lu

When my uncle, who'd gone into town to get a new rope for the block and tackle, returned, Pa got out the bottle of schnapps again. It was part of the drill.

The pierogis were cooling on a tray on top of the stove, where the dog, an old Norwegian elkhound, couldn't get at them.

Either my uncle was growing a beard or he just hadn't shaved for several days. "So you're the new husband," he said, looking at Paul. His voice was raspy. "The new helper." He looked at me. "And this is the baby." Ma was standing in the doorway to the living room, baby Stella over her shoulder.

The conversation, which had been awkward, turned to food—always safe. My uncle ate a pierogi. "You buy these at the A and P?"

"Get away with you."

"Klaudia buys them frozen, don't you?"

"One time I try, that's all. You going to kill that hog or we should go home."

Pa filled three shot glasses and handed one to my uncle and one to Paul. This was another test, not as difficult as the warm buttermilk.

"*Na zdrowie!*" my uncle said. *To health!*

"*Na zdrowie!*" Pa said.

"*Na zdrowie!*" Paul said.

And then they tossed back the shots.

We'd managed to avoid the question that was on everyone's mind. At least on Ma's mind. *Is this a valid marriage? And, what attitude should we take toward it? And, is there any point in talking about it to Father Gordon at Saint Clement's?*

But I knew that the question was already moot.

Paul and Pa and my uncle went out to slaughter the hog. It was an important occasion. Time for man talk. It was a mystery. Pa would have something to say to Paul. Threaten him? Probably not. That was my mother's department. Probably tell him that he'd better take good care of me. I see them stop. Facing each other. I can almost hear their voices. But not quite. But I can see that they're laughing.

"So. This new husband of yours," my aunt said. "He looking after you?"

"I don't need anyone to look after me."

My mother put her fingers under her eyes and pulled. It made her look like my grandmother, who used to wear a red ribbon as protection against the evil eye. I thought *I* might need a red ribbon before the day was over.

"I heard he does all the cooking."

"Where'd you hear that?"

"At Pete's market."

"Why'd you go to Pete's?"

"They had lingonberries on sale."

"You didn't call me?" Ma said.

I watched through the window as my uncle threaded the new rope through the block and tackle and attached it to the pulleys. Paul and Pa and my cousin Michal—who was in love with Izabella—had gone to get the hog, which they would hang from a tree limb. A fifty-five-gallon oil drum full of boiling water sat on a piece of cattle panel laid over a charcoal fire. I could see the men talking. Paul was doing fine so far. He knew how to talk to my parents, not saying too much, but not bashful either. He was wearing a flannel shirt. Old. Just right for the occasion. I'd never seen it before. He'd been talking to our neighbor on Chambers Street, Willie, who ran the M&W Meat Market downtown, getting some tips on slaughtering. This was the sort of thing he loved, the sort of thing he thought of as "real life."

I went outside with my camera to take a picture as Paul and Pa led the hog up from the sty, the pen, like the heifer in the Keats poem. The sty, which was next to the barn where the driveway forks, was always kept clean. Pigs are clean. The hog had his own toilet area in one corner and a wallow in another. My uncle tested the water three times. Flicked the water off.

The three men and Michal stood around the drum, talking, my uncle holding onto the rope around the hog. Pa handed his pistol to Paul. A long-barrel Colt .38 that I'd learned to shoot with, over Ma's loud objections.

After some more discussion Paul placed the pistol at the hog's ear. The hog knew something was going on and wouldn't stand still. You have to be careful.

I took a picture and the hog looked up at me. Paul pulled the trigger. I took another picture. The hog went down slowly. Good for Paul. I'd seen it take as many as three shots. The body convulsed on the way down. I looked away as my uncle slit its throat. Then I took another picture as they tied the back legs together. It took all four of them to drag the hog up to the tree by the back porch and hoist it up with the block and tackle over a sturdy limb. Pa put a clean pail under the hog to catch the blood. For blood sausage. My uncle cut it open, and Michal was elected to pull the guts out and bury them so the dog wouldn't get at them.

And then we all went into the kitchen. The men washed up and drank more schnapps. Paul had blood on his flannel shirt. It took half an hour for the hog to bleed out. The men drank more schnapps.

The hardest part was getting the hog from the tree into the drum of hot water. My uncle cut the head off. I did not take a picture of this, but I took one of the men carrying the hog, on a pole, and maneuvering it into the drum. It was hard to raise it up high enough. Paul put his arms around the hog and lifted. They got it over the edge and down into the hot water. Tail first. Headless. The open neck on top. They left it in for about half a minute. Just enough to scald it, not cook it, and then they flipped it over, almost knocking the drum over, for another twenty seconds, and then they hung it in the barn, legs spread.

I went back inside and made myself comfortable in the kitchen while the men skinned the hog. It took a long time. I washed up some dishes while Ma held baby Stella, and Izabella and Aunt Klaudia put the cherry jars on the porch to cool. Ma had run the soapy dish water so hot I had to grab each dish or glass and set it on the counter to cool before I could dry it.

The men came back in, ate a plate of pierogis, drank more schnapps. I could see that the day had been a success, and the women could see it, too. Paul had passed the buttermilk test (though Ma never realized that it was a test), and the schnapps test, and the slaughtering test.

But what about me? I was being tested too, though I wasn't sure exactly what the questions were. There was baby Stella, who had incipient diaper rash. Hmmm. Not good. Ma wasn't happy with my plan to teach Latin at the high school the following fall instead of staying home with Stella. But she liked the fact that Stella would have to come out here during the day.

"Ma," I said, "why don't you learn how to drive? That would make everything so much simpler."

"Are you sure you want your mother driving out on the highway?" This from Aunt Klaudia.

"It's just Blackburn Road over to Kruger Road and into town. One right turn and one left turn at the stop light on Old Thirty-four."

Ma threw up her hands. She said something in Polish to my aunt. Keeping an eye on Izabella and on Cousin Michal.

"They're in love," Aunt Klaudia said aloud, nodding at the young people. "Your ma's worried."

I nodded.

"What do you know now that they don't know?" my aunt went on.

"The woman cries before the wedding," my uncle said, interrupting, "the man after."

My aunt turned to Paul: "What about you?"

"No tears yet," he said, and I could see he was enjoying himself.

I started to make noises about getting Stella home. It was late afternoon. The hog would have to cool for a couple hours before sectioning. But Ma told me to sit still. She put an uncut loaf of bread on the table cloth and a strip of white cloth. And a bottle of wine.

"Ma," I said, "enough."

"Do this for your mother," Pa said. He was standing behind my mother rubbing her shoulders.

Aunt Klaudia acted as the *starosta*, the governor, the one who runs the show.

"Stand up," Ma said. "You too, Paul." It was the first time Ma had used his name. "Give the baby to your uncle," she said to me.

Paul and I stood next to each other at the table and Aunt Klaudia joined our hands together over the bread and tied them together with the strip of white cloth. She made the sign of the cross over the bread. "May they always have bread beneath their hands," she said.

Aunt Klaudia sprinkled the bread with salt, to remind us that life will be difficult at times and that we'd have to learn to deal with troubles.

Pa poured the wine so that we'd never be thirsty, so that we'd enjoy good health and good friends.

"Anka," he said to Ma, "you want to do the blessing."

We stood in a circle around the table and Ma blessed us with holy water. "I got it from Father Gordon after mass," she said. "I hope it works okay."

"I know it will, Ma," I said. "Thank you." And I knew then that we were going to be happy. And we were happy, right up to that last year.

Paul and I had our differences. He loved Homer, I loved Vergil; he turned to Plato for his metaphysics, I turned to Lucretius; he loved Faulkner, I loved Hemingway; he reread *War and Peace* every three or four years, I reread *Anna Karenina*; he was a lapsed Methodist, I was a lapsed Catholic; Paul played the blues. His heroes were Dr. John, whom he'd met once in Cincinnati, and Otis Spann. My musical heroes were Bach and Chopin. Paul could read music, but he could also play by ear and could play in any key. He'd just grab a handful of notes and off he'd go, left hand rock solid, right hand dancing. I needed to learn things one measure at a time. Paul liked his eggs poached; I liked mine soft-boiled. He was careless with money and had expensive taste in clothes and wine; I was careful. Paul couldn't find things; I could find anything. "Just by thinking," as Paul used to say. He liked his Shakespeare on the stage ("in the body") and always served as dramaturge for college Shakespeare productions. I liked my Shakespeare in the study. He preferred Florence; I preferred Rome. Paul wasn't afraid of anything, especially authority; I was more cautious. I obeyed the rules—most of the time—at least till late in life. He wanted to sail out into the deep water; I wanted to hug the shore (though in the end I let myself get blown out to sea). He wanted to buy an eight-inch Cassegrain telescope so we could see out to the edge of the universe, but I said they were too expensive and so we made do with the smaller telescope that we'd given to Stella one Christmas. Paul liked driving fast, which was bad for our insurance. He even had his license suspended for a year. I hadn't gotten a ticket in more than forty years. Paul was a superb cook and did all the cooking. I didn't start to cook seriously, with some imagination, that is, till after his death. I took it up partly to pass the time and partly to taste life twice, taste the past. He read the *New York Times* and had an opinion about everything; I read the *Galesburg Register-Mail* and worried about the school board elections and the price of hogs and the new aluminum castings plant on Kellogg Street. He loved cars but didn't know anything about them; I had no interest in cars, but I knew how to change the oil in our old Oldsmobile and put in new plugs and points. Paul had wanted to buy a Mazda Miata when they first came out in 1994 and were all the craze, but I always stood in his way and we bought an Oldsmobile station wagon instead. Later, at the end of his life, he bought the old sports car that had been left, so to speak, in our garage when Dr. Potter's widow moved into assisted living at the Kensington. Paul offered her the price of a Mazda Miata, and she took it. By this time he had to lug around an oxygen tank.

Paul wrote with ball point pens, which he lost as soon as he used them. We had to keep a huge supply. I wrote with a Pelikan Souverän 600. Not the most expensive pen in the line, but the most beautiful. Paul fancied spaghetti strap dresses. I had a closet full of them. I wore them around the house and even in bed, fooling around with Paul, but I wasn't comfortable wearing them in public. I controlled the money—the checkbook—and gave Paul an allowance. He never had anything left.

Paul was sexually adventurous. I was not exactly innocent, but I let Paul show me the way, and it was like riding in a sports car with the top down. Like the little sports car in the garage that he never got to drive. Except a few times around the parking lot. There was barely room for the two of us and his portable oxygen tank, but we used to sit in it with the garage door open and keep an eye on the cars pulling in and out of the parking lot, and the people who walked by. Plato's cave? Or the catbird seat?

But these were the sort of differences that hold two people together, like the gravitational field that keeps two binary stars orbiting around each other, or around their common center of mass. Like Sirius A and Sirius B.

The *real* problem, the real heartache, was more complicated. Paul did not go gentle into that good night. And that wasn't the worst thing. The worst thing was that we squandered most of that last year. And there was nothing I could do about it now. It was too late. The show was over. The gavel had come down. The verdict had been delivered. The final score had been registered at the scorer's table. The manuscript had gone to press and it was too late for revisions. The deadline had passed.

I blamed Paul; I blamed our son-in-law, Jimmy; I blamed our daughter. I blamed everyone but myself.

PART III: 1995–1997

4

Circles of Doors
(October–December 1995)

We were married for thirty-three years. Where did the time go? I suppose everyone who lives long enough wonders the same thing. And they do what I've been doing. They look at old photos and wonder why the same pictures appear over and over again: Paul shooting the hog behind the ear; Paul and Pa and Michal with their arms around the pig carcass while my uncle pulls on a rope, like three men embracing the same woman; the enormous pile of leaves that the choir kids raked up in the fall; the garden after we'd planted it at the end of May and then after we'd put it to bed in October. But I was glad I still had the photos. The rakes had long spindly fingers.

After Paul's divorce was final we sold the house on Chambers and bought a big shingle-style house on Prairie Street. When I think of "home," that's what I think of—Prairie Street, not the farm—though Paul kept on with the hog slaughtering till Pa had his first heart attack in 1978 at age sixty-six. Paul taught Ma how to drive so she could drive the Studebaker into town to the Hy-Vee or the library. He talked cooking with the women, learned to cook pierogis and borsht and even cheese babkas. He talked local politics with the men. My uncle was a brakeman on the railroad; Pa was a mechanical engineer and union steward at Maytag. Ma came to live with us for a couple of years after Pa's death. Paul spoke at their funerals and served as a pallbearer.

Ma got to see a copy of Paul's book, *Shakespeare and the Invention of the Inner Life*, before she died. She didn't read it, but she kept it by her bed. The book received some national attention and Paul was invited to spend a semester at the University of Verona.

By the time we went to Verona in the fall of 1985 both my parents were dead, my aunt and uncle too. Miss Buckholdt had come out of retirement and was teaching a couple sections of Beginning Latin, and in 1995 Father Viglietti—who'd replaced Father Gordon—had been hired to teach two sections of Latin 3. The Latin program had been recognized by the Illinois Classical Association as one of the best in the state; I had received the Farrand Baker Illinois Teacher of the Year Citation and had published several translations, including a translation of Catullus XXXI, celebrating his return to his old home in Sirmio, in the *New Yorker*.

Paul was diagnosed with lung cancer in August 1995, just before the start of the fall term. Against the doctor's advice he decided to teach that term. Two sections of Shakespeare I. Histories and Comedies. He was sixty-three years old; I was fifty-five; Stella was thirty-two.

By his birthday in early November he was having trouble breathing. His big classroom voice had been reduced to a loud breathy whisper, which he tried to correct, unsuccessfully, by pinching his vocal cords together.

Shortly before Thanksgiving the choir kids came, as they always did, to rake the leaves in the big lot north of the house where we had our garden—tomatoes, lettuce, arugula, and herbs. Paul and I always put the garden to bed while the kids were raking, but this year he was too weak. He tried to stack the logs that Mr. Friend, who looked after the yard, had dumped in the drive, cut short so they'd fit in the old coal fireplace, but he couldn't manage it and I got the choir kids to do it. He sat in a chair at the edge of the garden and took pictures of me pulling up the tomato plants, and of the kids hauling leaves to the back of the lot on a big tarp that was starting to fall apart—documenting the occasion, as he did every year. Kodak moments that he wouldn't be around to remember.

There were still lots of green tomatoes on the plants. I thought I'd picked them all at the end of September. "We're still in the tomato business," I said to Paul. "For a while, anyway." We always let the green tomatoes ripen in the basement. In the dark. We'd usually eat the last tomato in January. They tasted great, as if they'd gained strength there on the shelves, in the darkness. On shelves. On an old trunk. On the seats of old wooden chairs.

I pulled up the stalks and stuffed them in garbage cans and yard waste bags. On Wednesday I'd drag them out to the curb.

Autumn is my favorite time of year. Well, it's probably everybody's favorite time of year. People often announce this preference the way they announce the fact that they don't like hospitals or funerals. As if it set them apart from others. But this year was so sad that I thought it did set me apart, apart from everything old and familiar. Or maybe it put me at the center.

The wind had torn all the leaves off the maple trees that Paul had planted in the parkway and most of the leaves off the big oak tree at the back of the lot. The students piled the leaves against a shed in the back and helped me pull up the cattle panels we used to stake the tomatoes and put them on top of the leaves to keep the leaves from blowing away. I didn't bother to cut off the bits of rope we used to tie the plants to the cattle panels.

"You should be singing," I said to one of the choir kids. "How about 'Autumn Leaves'?"

"The jazz ensemble does that," he said, and suddenly it took my breath away. Remembering the song. How I'd loved that sentimental old song in high school. And then I'd grown out of it. But now I was growing back into it.

"Are you all right?"

No, I wasn't all right. I was thinking that we'd just paid almost seven thousand dollars for a new furnace and central air and that now we were going to have to sell the house. Paul was dragging his feet, but it would have to be done.

Paul made his way to the back to take a picture of the huge pile of leaves sloping down from the shed at the back of the lot. So many leaves. Thick as autumnal leaves that strow the brooks in Valombrosa. Paul and I took a bus once from Florence to Vallombrosa to see the leaves for ourselves. We walked a long way into the woods, and when we got back, the last bus for Florence had already left and we had to spend the night in a lovely old hotel.

It was time to write a check for the choir kids. Paul had gone back into the house to get the checkbook. The wind had suddenly stopped, as if it had nothing more to say.

The writing was on the wall. Paul would be starting chemo right after the holidays and had finally agreed to sell, so it would be our last Christmas in the old house and everything glowed in the candlelight of nostalgia as we waited for Stella to arrive from Iowa City. Winter is not a good time to sell, but I'd already talked to a realtor and I'd already put our names on a waiting list for one of the apartments, or "lofts," on Seminary Street, where there was an elevator. It would be our last redoubt. So we had a plan. At least *I* had a plan. The plan included reading Shakespeare aloud. And maybe Lucretius, too, and Catullus, of course. It included listening to Bach and Chopin, and to Otis Spann, Pinetop Perkins, Dr. John, Roosevelt Sykes, and others. It included getting Paul's old 78s out of the attic and maybe having them transferred to CDs. It included getting Stella's telescope out of the attic and setting it up on the balcony outside our bedroom so we could keep an eye on the stars. It included playing some Brahms waltzes for four hands, and listening to the Metropolitan Opera on Sunday afternoons. It included getting all our old photos in order, to pass on to Stella, so she'd have a record of a happy marriage, a happy family. With a little judicious editing, of course.

Paul's plan was to finish a long article, maybe a short book, on Shakespeare and Lincoln—*Lincoln's Shakespeare*—that had been simmering on the back burner for several years. He'd already done a lot of the leg work, combed through the Lincoln papers and Herndon's biography, and had decided to work it up into a proposal for the National Endowment for the Humanities. I was going to type it up for him on the computer. The project was a natural for Paul. He'd taught Shakespeare for thirty-eight years in a classroom overlooking the east lawn of Old Main, where Lincoln, in the fifth debate with Stephen Douglas, had first denounced slavery as a moral evil.

"Listen to this," he said, lying on his back on the couch and looking down through his half glasses at his handwritten draft.

"Paul," I said. "It's Christmas. Why don't you take it easy. I'll light a fire." I'd laid a fire in the fireplace but we hadn't lit it. "Besides, I've got to get the capon in the oven." I didn't say what I was thinking—that this would be our last Christmas in the old house.

"'Lincoln's fellow citizens,'" he went on, "'took their Shakespeare seriously. In the spring of 1849 three different theaters in New York were mounting performances of *Macbeth*, Lincoln's favorite play. The new *res publica* had apparently triumphed over the tyranny and discord distilled in that play, but the victory was not secure, and in Macbeth himself Lincoln saw the dangerous tendencies of the post-Revolutionary generation.

"'John Wilkes Booth, of course, modeled himself after Brutus, slaying the tyrant—'" He interrupted himself: "You think she'll get here this morning?" he asked.

"At least she's coming," I said.

She, Stella—our hostage to fortune—had dropped out of the Iowa Writers' Workshop to go to New York and now was back in Iowa City working as a dispatcher for a trucking company. We'd been expecting her the night before, Christmas Eve, but she'd decided to drive to see her boyfriend, Jimmy, who was in prison in Ames, Iowa, for a parole violation. Stella had given us the impression that Jimmy was a student in the Iowa Writers' Workshop, when in fact she was going to encourage him to *apply* to the workshop. He had so many stories and had been lionized by the fiction writers, hungry for material, even before he'd been sent back to prison.

Paul had been thrilled when Stella had been admitted to the workshop while she was a senior at Knox, where she'd done well in a very active undergraduate writing program. She'd published a dozen poems in *Catch*, the campus literary magazine, and won several prizes for poetry, including the Davenport Prize. She'd put together an impressive portfolio. Paul read all her poems and was her biggest fan and toughest critic. He was not so thrilled when, at the end of her second year at Iowa, after she'd completed her course work, she dropped out of the workshop to go off to New York with one of the visiting fiction writers, though she herself was a poet. But he put a good face on this turn of events—the best face possible: "Nothing bad can happen to a poet," he said. "Everything is material."

I was less sanguine. I couldn't understand how anyone could be so careless about her future well-being. "How much experience do you need to be a poet?" I asked. But I kept one of her early poems on the refrigerator, replacing it with a fresh copy when necessary:

> This morning I saw the sun rise from the Fourth Street
>   bridge;
> I saw a freight train curving west on the Graham cutoff
> and a switch engine backing into the classification yards.
> I was at the Outpost when the custodians came for coffee.
> I took my coffee to the Gizmo patio
> And started to write a poem about the man I'd seen from
>   the bridge,
> hopping the freight train. I didn't know where he was heading,
> I still don't, but I'm going to find out.

There was a light covering of snow, enough to make it beautiful and enough so we had to worry about Stella driving her banged-up Honda SUV on I-80. I went out to the kitchen to peel potatoes. Paul sat at the piano for a while and riffed on an old song in the style of Dr. John, with lots of flourishes and curlicues:

> Good and bad times,
> Honey, well that's okay.
> Good and bad times,
> Honey, well that's okay.
> It's you and me babe,
> Till the end of my days.

"Keep on playing," I shouted, but Paul was tired. He lay down on the couch again and looked at the cartoons in old *New Yorkers* that had been stacked on top of the stereo speakers, some of them dating back ten years.

I'd managed to bang the artificial tree down from the attic. One huge box and two smaller ones. The tree stood in the front window, unadorned; we were waiting for Stella so we could decorate it together.

I read the poem aloud to Paul. He grunted.

"Do you think she ever found out?" I asked.

He didn't look up, but I knew he was listening. "Yeah," he said. "Straight to jail."

"I meant the man in the poem," I said, "not Jimmy."

"The man in the poem *was* Jimmy," he said. "At least he's behind bars. Again."

I added another small log to the fire.

"She drives a hundred miles from Iowa City every week to see him, that's admirable. She says he's doing really well in prison . . . He's going to be in a Shakespeare play."

"*Titus Andronicus?*"

"No," I said. "*The Tempest.* Caliban. I think she does better this way than when they're together. It appeals to the nurse in her."

"When did she ever want to be a nurse?"

"I mean she likes to nurture. She's got a big heart. Too big. I've always thought," I said, getting back to the poem, "that the man hopping a train was Stella herself."

Paul grunted. "Yeah. And I used to think that nothing bad can happen to a poet. But that was before Jimmy."

I went to the kitchen and put the capon in the oven.

Lois stopped by in the early afternoon. She was having dinner with Jack Banks out at the funeral home, but she poked her head in to say hello and to drop off a bowl of her famous cranberry relish with horseradish. And a bottle of Châteauneuf-du-Pape. And a small wrapped present for Paul. Paul wasn't supposed to drink, but we opened the bottle anyway and each had a glass in front of the fire.

Stella didn't arrive till late afternoon. The capon was keeping in a warm oven. The water was ready for the potatoes. I was afraid to ask how Jimmy was doing in prison, but Stella told us anyway as we plowed through the capon and the mashed potatoes and Lois's cranberry-horseradish relish. She listed the facilities—forty-six buildings on one hundred acres, three housing-unit clusters with fourteen housing units, a fifteen-bed health care unit; the courses he'd been taking in carpentry and cabinet building; the average number of daily inmates (1,515), et cetera, as if he were enrolled in a fancy liberal arts college. And she told us about their plans to invest in a used Kenworth T2000, or maybe a Pete 379 with a double box sleeper. She was going to go to truck-driving school, and when Jimmy got out, they were going to go on the road together, hauling produce from the west coast.

In stories, the freewheeling bad boy is always the one who has the most interesting adventures, the one whose transgressions make him whole, but I didn't think it was going to work out this way with Jimmy. Neither did Paul. "Stella," he said, "just because you're a poet doesn't mean you don't have to think about money. It's part of growing up. Look at Shakespeare. He wrote for money, don't kid yourself. He did it all: writing, acting, part owner of the theater. And when he got enough he retired and went back to Stratford and bought the biggest house in town."

"Whatever I know about money I learned from you."

"Touché," Paul said. "I'll admit it; I don't know a lot about money, but at least I've got some common sense. How much does one of those big trucks cost? My guess is over a hundred thousand dollars. Where are you going to come up with a hundred thousand dollars?"

"We've got a plan, Pa, believe it or not. We're going to work for Jimmy's uncle in Milwaukee when Jimmy gets out. His uncle's a produce broker."

"You want to go to truck driving school?" I said. My heart was sinking rapidly. "No chance you could get back into the workshop to finish up your degree? Then you could teach . . ."

"I don't want to teach, Ma. There's more 'material' out on the road than in the workshop, that I can promise you. I've had it up to here"—she tipped her head back and raised her hand, palm flat, up to the level of her nose—"with workshop poems."

"Like white onions," Paul said.

"Right," she said. "No bite." They both laughed. "We wouldn't try to buy a truck right away, but Jimmy's uncle knows the people at Lincoln Trucking. They always need owner-operator teams, and the Lincoln terminal in Springfield—close to home—has got a full basketball court, a weight room, a movie theater, a spa, two good restaurants . . . We'll need help with the financing, of course, when the time comes, but Jimmy's uncle's going to take him into the business."

"Jimmy's uncle must be one hell of a guy," Paul said.

"He's very supportive," she said.

"How does he feel about his nephew serving time for aggravated assault?"

"Battery," she said, "not aggravated assault."

"How's the play going?" I asked, before Paul could make matters any worse.

"Jimmy's going to be a star," she said.

The man who has everything—in this case Paul—is usually the one who gets the best Christmas presents. Especially when he's dying.

That was fine with me, but I was annoyed that Lois had given Paul, in addition to the wine, a Mont Blanc roller ball that I'd seen in my Fahrney's catalog for almost four hundred dollars. What did she think she was doing? Still trying to get his attention? Paul had had a brief affair with Lois while I was in Rome one summer with a group of Latin students from the high school. I'd never held it against him, had no right to, because I'd had an affair of my own, and we didn't have the stomach for recriminations. What was the use? These affairs were like bone fractures that are stronger after they've healed than they were before. But over four hundred dollars? Not even a proper fountain pen. It would disappear the first time Paul used it, like all his other pens.

Stella gave him an autographed copy of Saul Bellow's *Henderson the Rain King*, a first edition, from the Book Shop in Iowa City. It would be just the thing for us to read aloud together.

My present was a photo album I'd been working on with Paul's old single-lens-reflex Leica. Black-and-white, thirty-five doors in all. I copied out a little-known Sandburg poem, "Circles of Doors," that was so different from his usual stuff that you'd hardly recognize his hand. Doors with knobs and doors with no knobs, doors that opened slow to a heavy push, like the big front door, so big we couldn't find a replacement for the old wooden storm door, and doors that jumped open at a touch and a hello, like the door to the little balcony off our bedroom. French doors framing the piano, a shot of the little door in the basement wall that opened into a crawlspace beneath the side porch, painted white, the paint long chipped away. A shot of the open bathroom door, taken from the second landing, halfway up the stairs. Somehow the angle made the toilet and the sink look classy, romantic, glossy. And I hoped that Paul could hear me, whispering, like the speaker in the poem, I love him, I love him, I love him and sometimes only a high chaser of laughter, four or five doors ahead, or four or five doors behind.

Paul and I were looking back. Stella was looking ahead. "All I want for Christmas," she said, "is tuition money for the truck driving school in Iowa City."

Maybe I should have kept my mouth shut, but I was too upset. "You know," I said, "I always read Ann Landers in the *Register-Mail*. It's somebody else now—'Annie's Mailbox'—but it's the same thing. Doctor Wallace, too. He went to Knox, you know."

"I know, Ma."

"I keep reading the same thing over and over, the same letters. 'My boyfriend is a great guy, but if I get out of line he hits me sometimes. I know I deserve it, because I really know how to push his buttons. He doesn't want me to go out with my girlfriends . . .' The letters aren't signed, but half the time I can hear your voice, Stella. What's the answer? Counseling? Get professional help? What I'm thinking is, get the hell away from this guy. What I'm thinking is, It's as plain as the nose on your face. And what I'm wondering is, What are these buttons anyway, and where are they? What I'm wondering is, Where do these dopey girls come from? And why do they make me think of you and Jimmy and the guy from the workshop who knocked you up and left you in Brooklyn? It all goes back to Howard Banks. We practically had to lock you in your room that night."

Howard Banks, Jack Banks's son, had asked Stella to the senior prom but Howard's reputation was such that Paul had absolutely refused to let her go. That night—the night of the prom—Howard drove his father's hearse into the path of a BNSF freight train in nearby Cameron, where the Burlington Northern tracks cross the Santa Fe tracks, killing himself and three of his classmates.

"Howie? You're still mad at Howie?"

"If your father had let you go to the prom with Howard Banks you'd be dead now."

But Stella didn't see it that way. "If I'd been with him he'd be alive now. He would have been wearing his seat belt."

"A lot of good a seat belt would have done when the train hit the hearse."

"Well, if I'd been with him he wouldn't have tried to beat that train."

"Why do you pick these losers? Howard Banks, the visiting writer—I can't even remember his name—who took you to New York. Brooklyn. I can't remember them all."

"Howie was not a loser. He was smart and he was fun and he was sexy and exciting, and he didn't take any shit from anyone."

"He got kicked out of school for cheating," Paul said, "more than once, and he got arrested for breaking into the school one night and fucking with the bell system."

"It was great," Stella said. "In the morning the bells kept ringing every five minutes. Nobody knew what to do. Mr. Collins and the dorky assistant principal kept running up and down the halls shouting at everybody, trying to get us to stay in our classrooms. You should have seen Mr. Collins. His big moon face was as purple as a grape."

Stella stopped talking and looked around. "I can't believe we're still fighting about Howie Banks," she said. And then she said, "Merry Christmas," and Paul told me to write a check and to get the money out of the credit union on Monday.

"Thanks, Pa," she said. "It's four thousand dollars."

I wrote out a check and let the ink dry and handed it to Stella. She folded the check in half and put it in a wallet that she fished out of a black canvas tote bag, and then she was gone, and Paul and I were sitting next to each other on the couch. We didn't say anything for a long time, and then Paul started to snooze and I cleared the dining room table and cleaned up the kitchen.

Can you imagine anything more sad? Even sadder than Vergil's *lacrimae rerum*—the tears of things. I can't. And yet I was able to step back from my own sadness, as I was wiping the counters, and observe it, as if I were watching a film, or reading a novel. And as I did so, I was aware of an undercurrent of joy. The kind of undercurrent you can sometimes hear in a Chopin étude or a Bach fugue. Our little drama was playing itself out against a background of joy. Our life together had been good. Sadness wasn't the worst thing. What would have been really sad would have been if we hadn't been sad at all.

5

⌘

Do Not Go Gentle
(January–October 1996)

In the middle of January—Paul just back from his first round of chemo—the retired doctor who had lived in Loft #1 of the Seminary Street apartments from the time it was built died and his widow moved into the Kensington. We were on the waiting list and the Seminary Street office called. It was a beautiful apartment, with large windows looking out onto the street; *"proprio in centro"* we might have said if it had been in Italy. *Right in the center of town.* A large living room, two bedrooms, two baths, walk-in closets in both bedrooms. Paul wasn't impressed, till he saw the sports car in the garage. Under a tarp. The real estate agent and I struggled with the tarp. Paul wanted the car. The doctor's widow didn't want it. It had been sitting in the garage for thirty years. Paul hadn't gotten his Mazda Miata, hadn't gotten a Thunderbird or a Corvette. It was his bargaining chip. I gave in. He offered the widow the price of a new Mazda Miata, and she took it. It wasn't a midlife crisis. It was a pre-death crisis. We put our house on the market.

> Enjoy the elegance of this Victorian shingle style: Baccarat
> crystal chandelier, coffered ceiling and patterned parquet floor
> in dining room, four bedrooms, unreconstructed kitchen, side
> porch, balcony. Built in 1895. One of Galesburg's premier
> homes.

We moved in February, before the house had been sold. I was teaching Roman Civ., and *Aeneid* ii, iv, and vi in Latin 4, plus an extra
section of Beginning Latin, and Paul, still recovering from his first
round of chemo, was on the phone every day with the young woman
from the University of Illinois who'd been brought in to teach his
classes and who had her own ideas about how to teach Shakespeare.
So: it was a difficult time. Our first night in the new apartment was
like a lot of first nights. Unsettling. Another milestone. Like your
first night in your college dorm, like your wedding night, like lying
in bed at night after the birth of your first child, like your first night
at home after that child has gone off to college.

The piano, an old Blüthner grand with eighty-five keys, had been
sold to a music store in the Quad Cities, traded, actually, for a good-
quality Yamaha electronic piano. Paul and I had watched the men
from the music store wrap up the piano and take it down the front
steps, and then we had stood in the front window and watched them
load it onto a smallish van.

"This is a mistake," Paul had said, and I had thought maybe he
was right, had thought maybe I should run out and stop them before
they drove away. But I hadn't. "It's a done deal," I said, and Paul
started to cry. Just a little bit. Just a few tears. I had pretended not to
notice.

More than two thousand books—eighty some banker's boxes—
had been sold to a dealer in Springfield. Another two thousand

were in boxes in the garage. Paul's old railroad desk, too big for the little "study," was on the long interior wall that we shared with Lois. The movers had set up our bed in the bedroom, at the east end. Two windows opened onto the deck, but we were at the north end of the deck, so no one would be walking by our apartment. A sofa bed had been installed in the study, the rugs had been spread out on the floor, the furniture had been set in place. Everything else was in disarray. Lois was coming in the morning to help, and Sophia, my regular cleaning lady.

Lois called in the morning, before I left for school, and offered to do a shopping for us, and Paul asked her to get some scallops. He wanted to cook some scallops for supper that night, or if not scallops, then wild-caught shrimp. Cooking, for Paul, was a way of relieving stress, though he'd insisted on walking up the outside stairs instead of taking the elevator, and he was too tired. The cancer was announcing itself, making its presence felt. He was going to need oxygen pretty soon. His face was aging, the skin tightening over his cheek bones. His green eyes were looking larger and larger. He was losing weight. He sat in a rocking chair at the edge of the kitchen, wearing his favorite sports jackets—Brooks Brothers— and his Sulka tie, kibitzing while I tried to organize the kitchen.

There were no bread crumbs, no panko, but Lois brought butter and lemon. And we had a glass of wine while Paul told me what to do with the scallops.

Lois had bought enough scallops for all three of us. I sautéed them in butter, closely supervised by Paul, two minutes on a side, and we squeezed lemon over them and ate them on buttered toast. Delicious.

I got Paul set up at his desk with his Lincoln books and his Riverside Shakespeare, and for a while the new book and the NEH application seemed like real possibilities. Paul sent me to the college library for books and more books. The literature on Lincoln is enormous. Every item opened new doors, new corridors to be explored: Sandburg's biography, the *Herndon Papers*, Charnwood's *Abraham Lincoln*, journal articles that had to be photocopied.

Arthur Jamieson, a colleague from Knox's Lincoln Center, stopped by once a week to chat. Paul wrote notes with Lois's Mont Blanc roller ball, which he'd managed to hang on to, using one of his Clairefontaine notebooks with a deep red cover.

I transcribed them onto the computer. I don't think of myself as a tech person, but I had mastered Microsoft Word, which had replaced Word Perfect. I set up function keys, and I created headings for the document map so Paul could move around the document freely.

The oxygen tank slowed him down. Once you start the oxygen, you have to keep on. The oxygen machine sat next to the door of the half bath. It had a very long plastic tube that could reach through the whole apartment, though it sometimes got tangled, like his shoelaces. If I wasn't home, and Lois was out at the funeral home, Paul would have to call Cornucopia, the deli down below us, and one of the student workers would come up and untangle him. I arranged to have my lunch period free at the high school so I could check on him at noon. And Lois, of course, was always ready to help.

In the evenings we read Lucretius, in Rolfe Humphries's fine translation; we read my translations of Catullus—and Paul knew enough Latin to ask intelligent questions about some of my choices. We read Shakespeare, too—Lincoln's Shakespeare: *Richard III*, *Hamlet*, *Macbeth*. Lincoln liked to recite the opening soliloquy of *Richard III*. He preferred Claudius's "O, my offence is rank" in *Hamlet* to the famous soliloquies. And he kept coming back to

Macbeth's speech to his wife after the murder of Duncan: "Better be with the dead."

What was Lincoln reaching for? What about Paul?

When Paul was especially agitated we read the copy of *Henderson the Rain King* that Stella had given him for Christmas, or, if the weather was clear and not too cold, we'd do some star hopping out on the deck with Stella's telescope. I'd taken Astronomy for my science requirement at Knox, and we had the copies of Mike Lynch's *Illinois StarWatch* and Terence Dickinson's *Nightwatch: A Practical Guide to Viewing the Universe* that we'd given to Stella along with the telescope.

Paul wasn't afraid of dying. It wasn't fear that poisoned his last months; it was anger, and irritability. "Sixty-five years old," he'd shout—though actually he was only sixty-four when he died—"and I can't even untie my own shoes."

"Why don't you let me put in some new laces," I would say. "Those laces are too long. That's why they get tangled up when you pull on them, and they're full of little knots." But he didn't want new laces; he wanted the old laces to work properly, and the new, shorter laces remained in a box on top of his dresser. They're still there. His laces continued to tie themselves into knots till he couldn't put his shoes on any longer and had to wear slippers or sandals with Velcro straps.

I came home at noon one cold, clear day in March and was surprised to find the garage door open. Paul, who was using a wheelchair now, had managed to wheel himself down to the garage and wrestle off the tarp that covered the sports car. He was sitting in the car, which was facing out, with his portable oxygen tank on his lap. I pulled the Cutlass Cruiser in beside him.

"How's it going?" I asked.

He shook his head. "I want to drive around the parking lot," he said. He was wearing a pair of leather driving gloves. "They were in the glove compartment," he said.

The garage opened onto a city parking lot with entrances on Mulberry Street and Seminary Street and an exit onto Main Street. You could circle around.

"I'll go with you," I said.

"You'll have to get a new battery first," he said. "And change the oil, if there's any oil in it."

"Why don't you call Jones and Archer. They'll send someone over this afternoon, then we can drive around when I get home."

"I want to do it now," he said. "And I don't want anyone else touching the car."

"I grew up on a farm," I said. "I know how to put in a new battery, but I can't do it right now. George Hawkinson is coming to Roman Civ. to demonstrate the principles of the Roman arch. We're going to start a model of the Pons Fabricius. Why don't you take it easy this afternoon and I'll put in a battery as soon as I get home."

He wasn't happy with this plan—there was no patience left in his system—but there wasn't much he could do about it except call Jones and Archer (the garage on Kellogg Street where we had our Oldsmobile serviced), which he didn't want to do.

"We'll have to get more air in the tires, too," I said. "We can use the pump we got for emergencies. If I can find it. The one you plug into the lighter. If there's a lighter."

A brown UPS truck drove past the garage. And then a semi backed into the loading dock of the furniture store to the north. The cab blocked the opening. We couldn't have driven out even if the car had been ready to go. Paul started leaning on the horn, but no battery, no sound.

*　　*　　*

George Hawkinson, who taught physics, had a way of explaining arches and demonstrating bridge construction that never failed to engage my Latin students at all levels. It never failed to engage me.

How do you span a space? The Greeks depended on beams, which limited the space you could cover to the length and strength of your beams. Look at Agamemnon's tomb at Mycenae! One long beam. The Etruscans had arches, of course, but no one else really explored the possibilities of arches till the Romans.

We rearranged the desks so everyone could see.

George already had his wooden centering, attached to a wooden base, on my desk at the front of the room. The centering would support the "stones" till the keystone of the arch was in place.

He constructed the arch by placing *voussoirs*, or wedge-shaped stones, made out of some kind of casting compound, around the wooden centering, dropped the keystone into place, and removed the centering.

The arch was very stable as long as you kept the wooden supports at the outer edges in place to contain the outward thrust. This is the key. An arch, unlike a beam, carries weight under compression, not tension. But you have to contain the outward thrust.

He invited one of the larger boys to press down on the top of the arch. The boy put a lot of weight on the arch without demolishing it. Impressive.

Then George removed one of the wooden supports. The arch gave way under minimal pressure.

He replaced the support, laid down the centering, and rebuilt the arch. "What can go wrong," he asked, "if the arch is supporting a roadway? You've got your constant load. That's easy to calculate: snow cover, the weight of the bridge itself. But you've also got nonconstant loads. Pedestrians. Vehicles.

"As long as the stress line is contained in the arch itself, the arch will hold. But if you put too much weight and the sides of the arch start to bulge out of shape . . . In other words, when the compression is greater than the stress line, the arch will collapse.

"You can keep this from happening by adding spandrels and by filling in the space between the spandrels with concrete, and you've got your roadway."

George pointed out the relevant features on the model of the Pont Saint-Martin, in northern Italy, that we had constructed the previous year. The Pont Saint-Martin is a single semicircular arch spanning about thirty-five meters and supporting a one-lane road. The Pons Fabricius, the oldest bridge in Rome, is more complicated than the simple and beautiful Pont Saint-Martin. It consists of two arches instead of one, spanning half the Tiber from the Campus Martius on the east to the Isola Tiberina, the two arches supported by a pier in the river itself. A third, small arch in the center allows water to pass through unobstructed in case of a flood. The bridge has been in continuous use since 62 B.C. George set up three teams: one to make scale drawings, another to make the *voussoirs,* a third to construct the wooden centerings.

In retrospect I see that Paul and I were the two large arches, and Stella the smaller arch in the center, and that Jimmy put so much weight on the bridge that the arches bulged out till they no longer contained the stress lines, and the bridge collapsed.

I didn't take out the old battery till Saturday. It was larger than a normal car battery. I took it to an auto parts store and paid a hundred twenty-five dollars for a replacement, and for six quarts of oil and some lithium grease. I installed the new battery, sprayed the terminals with lithium grease, drained the oil, cleaned the oil pan, added new oil. I decided not to bother with plugs and points unless I had to.

Paul sat in an old canvas deck chair and kibitzed, his oxygen tank on his lap, impatient, like a man who hasn't lived up to his own expectations and doesn't know what to do about it.

"Paul," I said. "You don't know the first thing about cars."

"You're right," he said, "but I know this is a beauty."

We got Paul into the driver's seat, with his portable oxygen tank. We couldn't figure out the complicated seat belts, which were really harnesses, but we weren't planning to go out on the highway, weren't planning to leave the parking lot, in fact. We sat for a while, the oxygen tank between us, and then Paul turned the key and the engine roared, literally roared, the way a lion roars, deep in the throat.

Paul engaged the clutch, killed the engine. The silence was startling.

He turned the key and the engine roared again, a huge sound, like a jet plane, and he pulled out into the parking lot in a series of small jerks before he got the clutch under control. The car slammed to a halt when he hit the brake. He started up again and turned to the right, past the other six garages. Then he turned left and circled around the two rows of cars parked in the center of the lot.

He shifted to second gear, briefly, then back to first. We went around twice, and then Paul managed to back the car into the garage.

We sat for a while till the engine stopped ticking. We'd gone only what? Not even a hundred yards on the ground. We'd started out side by side, but Paul had driven a lot farther than a hundred yards in his imagination, had left Shakespeare and Lincoln far, far behind, and me along with them.

In April we sold the house, contingent upon some repairs. Stella persuaded us to hire Jimmy, out of prison now. He was a good carpenter, she said. He could do anything.

Let me tell you something about Jimmy Gagliano—Jimmy Gagg. What a piece of work he was. Worse than Howard Banks, worse than the writer who took her to New York, worse than all of them put together.

Paul and I didn't encounter Jimmy till Friday afternoon, though he'd already worked a week. He and Stella were staying in the house on Prairie Street, sleeping on the floor. He'd come over to pick up a check, and I got off on the wrong foot by addressing him in Italian. He looked at Stella: "You tell your mom to talk to me in Italian?"

"Sorry," I said. "I thought . . ." But it didn't matter what I thought.

He was strikingly handsome, tall, with muscles like little mice running up and down his arms, under his tattoos, some profes-sional—bat wings, two snakes intertwined—and some prison, the ink bleeding so you couldn't make out what they were. He gave off a kind of hum, like a sports car idling, waiting for the light to change. I could see why Stella, or any woman, would be attracted to him.

Stella herself was nervous, the color had drained out of her. She stood in the bay window and the light from the afternoon seemed to shine right through her.

I asked Jimmy to carry up some boxes of books from the garage. We had a little cart in the garage he could use. You could convert it from a two-wheeler to a four-wheeler.

"On the clock," he said, looking at his watch. "I'm keeping track of my time."

"Of course," I said.

He projected an air of menace, cocksureness. Beating you back with his eyes and his tattoos, and his way of speaking his piece in short outbursts that didn't leave any doubt about what was on his mind, but that interfered with normal conversation. He kept his head down when he spoke, as if he were in attack mode.

"I'm a truth teller," he said. "So let's cut right through all the bullshit right at the get-go." He was speaking to Paul, who was hooked up to the oxygen tank. "You've been sitting here with your books and your fancy electric piano and your fancy food and I've been behind bars, locked up in a cage. Like an animal. You don't have to remind me, but you don't have to avoid the subject, either. You probably have a lot of questions. Go ahead. Ask me anything you want."

"Fuck you," Paul said, and I guess it was the right thing to say. At least it slowed things down. Jimmy laughed.

Jimmy stacked the boxes next to Paul's desk. "You read all these books?"

"Every one of them," Paul said, though it wasn't true. At least not one-hundred-percent true.

Jimmy shook his head.

"I hear you're a Shakespearean actor," Paul said. *The Tempest.*

"We did a short version," Jimmy said. "But I was a natural. But you know what? If I was Shakespeare I'd have put Caliban in charge of the whole island."

"Then I guess it's a good thing you're not Shakespeare."

"Good thing for Prospero. Good thing for you. Not for me. I'm Caliban, and Stell here is your precious little Miranda. And I know what you're thinking."

"Jimmy," Stella started to protest.

"Shut up, Stell, I can handle your old man without your help."

"You don't have to 'handle' me," Paul said. "How about just talking to me. Like one human being to another."

"This island's mine," Jimmy said, striking a pose. "By Sycorax my mother, Which thou tak'st from me."

"No wonder they sent you back to prison," Paul said. "I could never get the story straight from Stella."

81

"A friend of mine," Jimmy said. "Somebody stole his dog. Up in Milwaukee. He asked me to get it back for him. That guy that stole it put up some resistance. That's all. It was all bullshit."

"Why were you carrying a knife while you were on parole?"

He shook his head at the stupidity of the question. "You know what I learned from doing that play?"

"What?"

"Everybody's on stage. All the time. That's what I came away with. You're on stage. I'm on stage. Your wife's on stage. Stell here is on stage."

"On stage?" I said.

"The world's a stage," Paul said. "You're not the first one to notice. But why did you need a knife?"

"To cut through all the bullshit." He looked around. "You're on stage right now. You're nervous, aren't you, but you're trying to act like you're having a good time shooting the shit with me. Like Prospero shooting the shit with Caliban." After a pause he asked if we had anything to drink.

I looked at Stella, who was wearing tight jeans and a man's blue shirt. She was thirty-three years old. Her life had not worked out the way we'd hoped, and our hopes had been pretty flexible. But here she was, and my heart ached with love.

"There's beer in the refrigerator," Paul said, "and a bottle of wine on the counter, already open."

"He's not like this when we're alone," Stella said to me. "He's just nervous around Pa."

"Not like what?" Jimmy said, swinging his head around like a wrecking ball.

"You know how you get," she said, "around other people."

"How do I *get*?"

"Like you are now. You wear this mask long enough you won't be able to take it off."

"Get him a beer, would you," Paul said to me.

"I tell you what," Jimmy said to Stella. "You tell your daddy to give you the keys to that car in the garage and we'll get the hell out of here, take it down to Iowa City tonight. Burn out some of the carbon."

"No insurance," Paul said.

"I'm not going to wreck it. I'm just going to drive it."

Paul shook his head. "It needs new tires before you take it out on the highway."

"Next week," Jimmy said. "Put it on your auto insurance policy. I'll look out for some tires."

"You won't be able to afford them," Paul said.

"I will when I leave here," he said.

Jimmy did good work, I'll say that for him. By the end of the first week he'd patched the room over the porte cochere and replaced and primed the curved trim on the bay window. But he couldn't let go of the car. He wanted to know how much Paul had paid for it, but Paul wouldn't tell him. He offered to buy the car—said he could get the money from his uncle—but Paul wasn't interested in selling.

The struggle over the car escalated. Paul was in bed at the end of the second week when Jimmy came to get his check. Jimmy stood in the doorway. "Prospero"—he had started calling Paul "Prospero"—"Let me ask you something, Prospero. Can you still get it up? I mean, a man in your condition—"

"Jimmy!" Stella tried to intervene.

"Jimmy," I said. "How much do I owe you? I'll write a check right now. At twenty dollars an hour a forty-hour week would come to eight hundred dollars. And I'd appreciate it if you wouldn't look at me that way."

"What way?"

"Like you're sizing me up."

"You're still a good-looking woman, Mrs. G," he said. "You deserve better than that old man in there. And that car in the garage. It's just sitting there. What a waste. Like you."

"It's Mrs. Godwin," I said. "And that old man in there is my husband. Stella's father. We've been married thirty-two years. And you can go to hell." I got the checkbook.

"Just around the block, Mrs. G. What, you think I'm going to wreck it? That car needs to be driven, burn the carbon out."

"I'm making out a check for eight hundred dollars," I said, "even though you didn't really put in forty hours."

"You can't stand it," he said, "can you, to see someone who's alive? You sit up here in your nice little apartment and look out the window at the nice little restaurant across the street and worry about where you're going to put all your nice things and where you're going to hang your nice pictures. While you're waiting around for that old man to die. I never saw such an ornery sons-a-bitch."

"It's 'son of a bitch,'" I said, "not *sons*-a-bitch."

"Ma, he doesn't mean anything. It's just the way he talks."

"Shut up, Stell."

"Her name is Stella."

"Her name is what I say it is."

Paul appeared in the doorway with his oxygen tank, his half glasses on a cord around his neck.

"Look who's here," Jimmy said. "Dead man walking."

"Get the fuck out of here."

"Dead man talking. Listen to that, would you. Prospero speaks."

Jimmy started to leave. Stella got up to go with him.

"Where are you going?" I said to Stella.

"I'm going with."

"You stay here, Stella," Paul said.

"Pa," she said, "you're both crazy."

That night, Friday night, Jimmy simply took the car. I hadn't thought to hide the keys, which were on a key holder in the laundry room. But the car was gone, and the keys were gone. We wouldn't have known it if Lois hadn't called to say that our garage door was open.

Paul was in slippers and a robe. He was in a hurry. He struggled out of the armchair in the window alcove—a chair that now seemed to swallow him whole—and took the stairs instead of the elevator. A train was going by, making a huge noise. There was an empty space next to the Cutlass Cruiser.

Back in the apartment I heated a little leftover coffee in the microwave.

Paul called the police and told them that the car had been stolen—I begged him not to, but I didn't beg very hard—and was probably on the way to Iowa City. And that the thief, Jimmy Gagliano, was a convicted felon out on parole.

Jimmy was pulled over at mile 284 on I-80, about ten miles west of the junction with 280, and taken to the Scott County Jail in Davenport, Iowa. I drove to Davenport and brought Stella back to Galesburg. We barely spoke, and she wouldn't come in the house. She got into Jimmy's truck, which was in the parking lot, and drove back to Davenport.

"Sorry, Ma," she said out the open window as she was leaving. "He didn't mean it. But Pa was such an asshole about the car. Why couldn't he just let Jimmy drive it around the block? He didn't have to be such an asshole."

She called in the morning, but I refused to bail Jimmy out.

We got the local Amoco Station to bring the car back from Davenport on the back of a truck.

A week later Stella told the prosecutor that Paul had given her the keys and asked her to drive the car to Iowa City to burn out the carbon. There was no case. Jimmy was released.

Paul started to worry, and by the end of the week he was convinced that Jimmy had been coming into the house during the day while I was at school. That he was rearranging things, moving things around, helping himself to a few things, like the pen from Lois.

We had the locks changed. The locksmith told me that it happens all the time—old people wanting their locks changed, convinced that someone's coming in and moving stuff around. Their children call and tell him (the locksmith) not to change the locks.

We had an alarm system installed. Paul had to sign a three-year contract with ADT. There were sensors on the windows and the door. When I came into the house I had forty-five seconds to deactivate the alarm by punching in a code. Paul was afraid that someone could look in the window and see me punch in the code. He wanted me to hold my hand over the alarm keypad when I punched in the code. I had to register with the city. Another fifty dollars. I had to give the code to the cleaning lady, who'd worked for us for years, and to the hospice care nurse, and to Lois. Paul didn't like this and wanted me to change the code every week, which I refused to do. We were allowed two free false alarms. Then a fifty-dollar charge for every false alarm.

Paul wanted a German shepherd. I pretended to object, but we'd always had dogs when I was a kid, and we'd had a black Lab when Stella was growing up, Sparky. I could remember looking out through the little window, just big enough for a fifty-pound block of ice, that had been knocked in the back wall of the kitchen on Prairie Street, watching Paul as he dug a hole for Sparky while Stella knelt beside him, rubbing the dead dog's neck. The hole wasn't quite big enough, and Paul had to lift the body out and dig some more while Stella pushed her face down into the soft neck. So I didn't have much enthusiasm for the idea, but I didn't push back too hard. I picked out a mid-size German shepherd mix at the animal shelter. I had to tell them we had a fenced-in yard, which was true in the old house, or they wouldn't have let me take the dog. Which I named Camilla, after the warrior virgin in the *Aeneid*, who could run so fast that when she ran through a cornfield the blades of grass turned to ashes, so fast that when she ran across the sea she didn't get her feet wet.

And, finally, a gun. This time I really did dig in my heels. But Paul insisted. I got my application for a FOID card out at Farm King, where they took my picture but then used the picture on my driver's license for the card. A week later I bought a long-barrel .38 at the gun shop across the street—Collectors.

"Odd choice for self-defense," the owner said. "For a woman. The long barrel, I mean. Not a .38."

"It's what my husband wants," I said.

I still had my father's old .38, the one Paul had used to shoot a hog every fall. But something prompted me to get a new one, and in retrospect I have to wonder if I already had a contingency plan in mind.

I took a firearms safety training class, offered one afternoon a week at the police shooting range out at Lake Storey. I hadn't fired a pistol since I'd left home. My parents' home, that is, so I was glad for the lesson. The instructor explained the Isosceles stance, which is what you see in cop shows, and the Weaver stance, which is the way I'd learned to shoot in the first place, and the modified Isosceles and the modified Weaver, with your gun arm locked instead of slightly bent.

We put on ear plugs and I fired a hundred rounds with a .22 caliber and another hundred with the .38.

He said the same thing as the gun dealer. "Odd choice for a woman for self-defense. You don't need the long barrel, for one thing."

I told him the same thing I'd told the gun dealer. "It's what my husband wants."

"Then he should be the one getting the lesson."

"He's got lung cancer," I said. "He can't get out anymore. It's a long story."

He waited, but I didn't tell him about Jimmy. I fired another hundred rounds with the .38, using a modified Weaver stance, pretending to aim carefully, but spraying the shots around. My arm was sore.

Paul kept the gun in a drawer of the bedside table, loaded.

Camilla didn't poop for three days after I brought her home, but after that she did everything that dogs are supposed to do: barked when someone came to the door, slept on a rug by Paul's side of the bed, investigated the wastebaskets, licked Paul's hand, waited to see what was going to happen next. But it wasn't enough.

Paul was never the same. He complained that I'd gotten rid of too many books. Where was the catalog of the Impressionist exhibition at the Art Institute? Where was Robert Fitzgerald's translation of *The Odyssey*? What had I been thinking when I sold everything to the dealer from Springfield? And why hadn't I organized the books that we did manage to keep, which I had shelved at random just to get them out of the boxes. There were more boxes in the garage. But his number-one grudge was that I'd sold the piano. The piano had been in reasonably good shape when we sold it, though it was going to need some work, more than the man who tuned it could manage.

I played through my limited repertoire—Bach, Brahms, Chopin, Gershwin—on the new Yamaha, but Paul complained that the sound was too thin, and we abandoned the plan to work up some Brahms waltzes for four hands.

Paul's colleagues from the English Department came to visit—the old guard, most of them older than Paul. They'd bonded at the beginning of Paul's tenure and had traveled together over the years. No doubt they could see in Paul signs of their own demise, which didn't stop them from confronting the mystery head on. "Life, like a dome of many-colored glass," Ed Wilson, who taught the Romantics, liked to say, "stains the white radiance of eternity," and you couldn't tell if he was being serious or ironic, or something in between.

Paul continued to work on *Shakespeare's Lincoln*, but he couldn't sit up on the tall stool at his desk and had to work at the harvest table. He didn't have much stamina, and I could see that he was treading water, still reaching for a thesis, a big idea. Something beyond the facts, something beyond one-damn-thing-after-another. What was the problem he was trying to solve? The question he was trying to answer? The mystery he was trying to clarify? Not what or how or where or when, but why? Why did it matter? Why did anything matter? Who cared?

As far as I know, Jimmy never came into the apartment, but he did come back into the house on Prairie Street, a week before the closing. I went over to the house to walk though it one last time and make sure everything was in order. He had ripped the chandelier out of the ceiling—the chandelier that I had rewired myself—and smashed all the crystal dangles, which sparkled on the dining room floor. I called the insurance company. I was so angry I could hardly speak. Connie said she'd send someone over. It was only four blocks away.

I collected some of the broken dangles in a grocery bag for the insurance company, and swept up the smaller particles. Then I walked through the house. I realized what Paul was feeling because I was feeling it too, something deeper than anger. This old house had been our life. Once upon a time it had been our new house, after Paul and Elaine (Paul's first wife) sold the house on Chambers, and I remembered how it had been when we walked into it the first time with the real estate agent, almost two years after we were married. Empty, but full of promise, full of the future, full of love making and Christmases and Shakespeare parties. Now it was empty again, waiting for someone else's future to arrive. Upstairs in our bedroom I looked out at the street through the leaded glass windows, looked down at the lot next door and thought, for just a minute, that it was time to call Mr. Friend to till the garden. From my little sewing room in the back of the house I could see the leaves the choir kids had raked to the back of the lot and wondered if the Simpsons, the new owners, would cart them up to the garden and compost them around the tomato plants and the zucchini to keep the weeds down.

I climbed the stairs to the attic, opened the windows at both ends and turned on the attic fan. I walked through every room in the house, counting the doors, but I lost count before I got to thirty and for a moment I was Paul's high chaser of laughter, five or ten doors ahead, or five or ten doors behind. And then the bell rang. Connie from the insurance office was at the door.

I filed a police report, but I didn't give them Jimmy's name, and I never told Paul what had happened.

It was harder and harder to get Paul in and out of the car, even with his new light-weight oxygen tank, but we managed three or four times a week. We'd sit together, Paul in the driver's seat—the cockpit—with the garage door open. The car never moved, but Paul didn't need to leave the garage to drive farther and farther away. He was leaving me behind. And Stella, too. We heard nothing from Stella. Not a word. Not a phone call. Not Prospero and Miranda, I said to myself, but Lear and Cordelia.

We did what we could to hold on to scraps of ordinary life. I did the cooking now, with Paul in his wheelchair at the edge of the kitchen, kibitzing. Paul had always done his own laundry. He liked his underwear folded in a certain way, with a kind of military precision. I had trouble getting it just right. But I managed.

School started at the end of August. I'd get Paul settled in the morning. Lois would check in on him at ten o'clock, before going out to the funeral home. I arranged to come home at noon to fix some lunch and take the dog out. The hospice nurse came at two o'clock. I could usually be home by four.

I'd take the dog for a long walk along the tracks, down to the college, then through Standish Park, then down Simmons Street and then home. The same route every day, but everything seemed fresh and new to the dog—every bush, every tree, every trash container, every strip of grass on the parkways, the old cross-ties that had been stacked by the bridge over South Street.

I was teaching Catullus 2 on the day Paul died—*Passer, deliciae*, on the death of Lesbia's pet sparrow. When we got to lines 4 and 5, one of my best students, Jason Steckley—the "son" in "Steckley and Son, Funeral Directors"—raised his hand: "Does this mean she lets the bird touch her, you know, her clit, with his beak?"

The room became very quiet. Except for the sound of the lawn mower outside. I did a double take, looked at the lines again:

et acris solet incitare morsus
cum desiderio meo nitenti

"Jason," I asked, "What are . . . are you using for a crib?" I was pretending to disapprove and at the same time trying not to laugh. I couldn't imagine myself asking such a question at that age, and in fact I didn't think the lines supported this reading. I'd have to think about it. *She offers you her fingertip to nibble and urges you to bite it sharply.* Hmm.

And when I did think about it, I did start laughing. It was the sort of thing that if it got back to somebody's mother and somebody's mother complained to the principal . . . But we had a sort of tacit agreement that things like this didn't get back to anyone's mother. So I kept on laughing.

I was laughing on the way home, thinking how I would frame the story for Paul, how much he would enjoy it, but when I got home, Paul was dead, and Lois was sitting on the edge of the bed. Camilla, on the floor, had not come to the door to greet me.

"I'm here to help," she said. "Just give me a job." Then she added: "I already cleaned him up."

"Thank you, Lois," I said, "but I'll be all right."

"I want you to go deep into yourself," Lois said, "and focus on your breathing. It's hard, but I don't want you to worry if your mind wanders. Don't ask where it went. It doesn't matter. Just bring it back to your breathing. In and out, in and out. You can't go deeply into yourself if you allow yourself to be distracted. I want you to slow everything down. You don't have to do anything else. I'll be right here. I've already called Banks's. They'll do the removal after Dr. Franklin signs the death certificate, but you don't have to worry about that."

"Call them back," I said. "I'll call Steckley's."

"Steckley's? But I already told Jack . . ." Jack was Jack Banks.

"I don't care what you told Jack, you can tell him to cancel."

"But Frances . . . Why?"

"Because Jack Banks is a Republican and Frank Steckley's a Democrat. Paul wouldn't want to be buried by a Republican. Besides, Frank's son is one of my best students."

"But I already told—"

"Do I have to call him myself?"

"Of course not. It's just that . . ."

"Call him now. I don't want their van showing up here. Call him from your place. I'd like to be alone for a few minutes."

"I know this is a difficult time—"

"Out, Lois. Please. I have some things to say to Paul, and I'd just as soon you weren't fluttering around here."

"I was just trying to help."

"You've been very helpful, Lois. Now just go."

Alone with Paul (and Camilla) it wasn't fear I felt. It was anger. I couldn't shut it off, and I said some hard things.

"Oh, Paul Paul Paul," I said, running my hand over the stubble on his cheek. "We made a mess of things, didn't we. We squandered our last months together, and now it's too late to make things right. It didn't have to end like this. The doctors gave you a year. Gave us a year. We had that year together. One year. Our last year. Twelve months. Three hundred sixty-five days, more or less. Time to slow down, time to sit quietly and not trouble the universe, time to let go. Ah, Paul, maybe I don't know what I'm talking about now, but I know this: we squandered it, half of it. We wasted it. We flushed it down the toilet. You didn't go gentle into that good night. You went cursing and bitching and blaming me for everything. It didn't have to be that way. I did the best I could. But you were angry the whole time. I sold the house because I had to. What else could I have done? You couldn't manage the stairs any longer. At the loft we've got an elevator. I had to sell most of the books, too, half of them. What did you want me to do? There was no room. I got five thousand dollars from that dealer in Springfield. It's a lovely apartment with great high ceilings, but all you've done is bitch about your books and about the piano, and about the noise the trains make. Galesburg is a railroad town, for Christ's sake. Maybe it was hardening of the arteries. That's what Dr. Franklin said. He thought you might be bi-polar, wanted to put you on lithium, but you wouldn't do it. You never played the piano anymore anyway, and Stella didn't have a place for it. The Yamaha piano is perfectly nice. You didn't have to cover your ears every time I played. And you couldn't let up about Stella, could you, just because she wanted you to let Jimmy drive the stupid car.

"And Lois was here. 'I didn't want to call you at school,' she says, and she reaches over and touches your shoulder. You were wearing your new Egyptian cotton pajamas from Hammacher Schlemmer. 'I cleaned him up,' she says. 'There wasn't much. He's hardly eaten anything in the last few days. I'll take care of everything.'

"Think of that, Paul. Lois was the last person to wipe your ass. Lois the grief counselor. Now she's dating Jack Banks. *Dating!* Think of it. And all of a sudden she's an expert on death: 'I'll take care of everything.'

"'Then I want you to call Steckley and Son,' I told her."

"'Steckley and Son?' she said. 'I've already called Jack. As soon as they get the death certificate they'll do the removal.' 'The 'removal,' I said. 'That's what they call it,' she said. 'Call them back,' I said. 'Tell them Steckley and Son are going to handle the arrangements.'

"I wish you could have seen the expression on her face: 'But why?' she kept asking. 'I already told Jack—Mr. Banks—' You'd think she was working on commission."

I could almost feel Paul's presence, palpable in the bedroom. I lay down beside him and started to run my hands over him, over what was left of him. He was like a spring that has lost its resilience.

The real grief came later. That night. After the removal. Camilla had barked furiously at Frank Steckley and his assistant, and I'd had to put her leash on and keep her in the living room while they wrapped up the body and carried it down to the van. I told them they could use the elevator, but they wrapped Paul up in some kind of contraption and slid him down the stairs. I followed the van to the funeral home. After making the arrangements for cremation; after buying a burial plot in Hope Cemetery, one that was big enough to hold two urns; after gathering some material for the obituary—all in one afternoon—I walked through the apartment touching things: Paul's toothbrush, his books, a copy of the National Endowment for the Humanities application that was still on his desk.

In the evening Father Viglietti from Saint Clement's came over and sat with me for a while. He didn't come at me with promises and assurances about God's plan. He wasn't that kind of priest. He just let me cry. He brought a bottle of good wine, which we drank as we ate the cold chicken and salad that Lois had brought over earlier.

My friendship with Father Viglietti was based on Latin, and on our work together, and on the shared conviction that, appearances to the contrary, life was not meaningless, though his conviction took a more highly articulated shape than mine, one shaped by the church year and by something more mysterious. He was a religious priest and answered to the provincial of the Clementine order, not to the arch-conservative Bishop of Peoria, and while this created a certain amount of friction, it also gave him a certain amount of freedom.

We usually spoke Latin to each other, but that night we spoke English.

"Tell me about Paul's death," he said. I told him about Lois, and he laughed.

"I think you could call it a good death."

"Not good for me," I said.

"It's Faulkner's birthday today," he said.

"So?" I said. "Faulkner? It was Paul who loved Faulkner. I loved Hemingway."

"How's the Catullus coming?"

I'd been working, off and on for years, on a translation of Catullus. I shrugged. "Slowly."

'You should get back to it," he said.

"Something to do now that I'm a widow? I gave them *'Passer, deliciae'* this morning," I said. "Now it seems like it was weeks ago. And Jason Steckley asked if she was letting the bird nibble on her clitoris."

"That must have livened things up."

"It stopped everybody cold."

"Frances, I'm going to take your classes for the rest of the week."

"You can do that?"

"It's a done deal."

"I mean take time off."

"I can do whatever I want."

'You don't have to ask the bishop?"

"I answer to the provincial, not the bishop."

"Of course," I said. "Are you up for the Battle of Cannae in Roman Civ.? Second Punic War. Not the *decisive* battle, but the most interesting, the one where Hannibal ties brush to the horns of the oxen, sets the brush on fire, and stampedes the oxen through the Roman camp?"

"We'll get through it," he said.

I opened my Oxford Catullus. Well worn. Number five. "*Vivamus, mea Lesbia, atque amemus.*' Let us live, Lesbia, and love. The students are supposed to translate the whole thing for tomorrow. Make them conjugate *vivamus* and *amemus* out loud," I said. "And they probably won't recognize *assis* as the genitive."

"The 'genitive of price or value,'" he said.

"Very good, Father," I said. "It's too sad, isn't it. *Soles occidere.* The sun sets every evening and comes up again in the morning, but once our sun sets, it'll never rise again. Paul's sun won't be coming up in the morning."

"I want you to remember something, Frances. If your life isn't meaningful right now, it's not going to become meaningful by being prolonged forever."

"Then what's the point of heaven?" I said.

"I said 'if your life isn't meaningful *right now*,'" he said.

"Nothing means anything right now," I said.

"If nothing means anything," he said, "you wouldn't be grieving. Do you remember the would-be disciple who wants to follow Christ, but he wants to bury his father first?"

"Let the dead bury the dead," I said.

"Right. But why such a harsh rejoinder?"

"I'm sure it's a metaphor for getting your affairs in order."

"Of course it is," he said, "but getting your affairs in order and burying your father are two different orders of magnitude."

"Maybe Our Lord just wanted to make himself disagreeable. That's not surprising."

Father Viglietti laughed. "'Our Lord,'" he agreed, "could be very disagreeable. But in this case I think he recognized that the man was at a crucial point and wanted to shock him. The man was at the threshold of a new and abundant life. We all reach this point. We have to go forward or go back."

"Do you think I've reached that point, Father?"

"Frances, I do."

"It doesn't feel like it. I mean it doesn't feel like I'm at the threshold of a new and abundant life."

"Of course not," he said. "It never does."

That night I took Camilla out, but instead of walking her along the tracks down to Berrien Street and then over to Prairie, I stopped in the little park by the depot and let her off the leash—for the first time. I didn't know if she'd run away or not, but I was going to find out. If she wanted to run off, I thought, I'd let her go. If she wanted to stay, she'd come back. She ran off toward the depot, stuck her nose in a garbage can, headed for the tracks, then turned around and ran like the wind, ran as if she hadn't run in ages, and she hadn't. She ran to the edge of the park, Seminary Street, then back to the depot, then in a circle along the parking lot, down to the Girl Scout garden on the edge of Mulberry, past the car rental place, then completed the circle and repeated it three or four times—I lost count—before coming back to me and flopping herself down. I was crying without knowing it. I buried my face in her neck, dried my tears, and we walked home off leash. "Cammy," I said, "you're a good dog. You know that? You're a very good dog, *canis optima.*"

And she *was* a good dog. She sat with me while I sorted Paul's clothes out and put them in banker's boxes for the Salvation Army. I wasn't going to be one of those widows who kept sniffing their husbands' clothes for a year or two. The only thing I couldn't part with was Paul's "Italian" suit, which as far as I know is still hanging in the very back of our closet, though it's become invisible. Paul, I believe, was cremated in his pajamas. That doesn't seem quite right, but I can't really remember. It all happened off stage. And she sat with me while I sorted through Paul's papers, which also went into banker's boxes. And she stood next to me at the semiprivate commitment ceremony in Hope Cemetery, while two of Paul's colleagues read, as per Paul's request, Browning's "The Bishop Orders His Tomb at Saint Praxed's Church," and Yeats's "Long-Legged Fly." And at the apartment afterward, where everyone came for drinks, she was a good hostess. Greeting everyone. Mingling with the guests. Making everyone comfortable.

Stella was not at the service. How much can you forgive? How many times? And the worst thing was: No one asked about her. Men and women who'd known her since she was a baby. Not a word. And I understood this. There's enough grief, they were thinking, without mentioning Stella's absence. But it was embarrassing.

6

Milwaukee (February–March 1997)

S tella called at the beginning of February. I hadn't had any
contact with her since she'd driven off in Jimmy's truck in
June. I hadn't been able to reach her to tell her that her father
had died, had been reduced to ashes, which had been buried in
Hope Cemetery. And I could hardly contain my anger. It was the
only feeling I could grab onto to steady myself. "Your father
died and you couldn't give me a call? You couldn't pick up the
phone?"

"Ma," she said, "I'm sorry. It's just . . ."

"I called Jimmy's uncle and asked him to give you the message.
Did he tell you? Did he tell you that Pa was dead? He told me to leave
a message at TruckStopUSA in Ottawa. I called and talked to the
manager. She said she'd give you the message."

"Ma," she said, "I'm sorry."

"I found out your schedule, sort of. I drove up to TruckStopUSA
on Christmas Day because I thought I could catch you. I ate
Christmas dinner with the manager, Ruthy, the one with the long

red hair. I didn't realize she's your pal. Turkey breast and mashed potatoes and gravy. You know what she told me? She told me Jimmy wants you to get a boob job, she told me he wants you to get stitched up tighter. Down there, you know."

"Ma, Jimmy's none of your business."

Stella and Jimmy were hauling produce for Jimmy's uncle and Stella wanted me to invest in a truck, a White Freightliner Century, she explained, with a small box sleeper, 470 horsepower, dual 150-gallon tanks, all aluminum wheels, engine brake, and more than a million miles on the odometer. Most of this was lost on me, except the million miles on the odometer. A million miles. That was like a light year, beyond comprehension.

Two weeks later I drove up to Milwaukee, east into bright sunlight, the weather cold, twenty degrees, but clear. Steep hills of dirty snow marked the entrances and exits. I had no intention of "investing" in a truck with a million miles on the odometer, but I wanted to see Stella.

On the way I listened to a cassette, Paul reading Shakespeare, then switched to Wisconsin Public Radio.

I hadn't been to Milwaukee in years. Paul and I had gone up a couple of times, the first time just to have a look-see, the second time when Paul gave a talk at UW Milwaukee. We stayed in the Knickerbocker Hotel, near the lake, and ate at Karl Ratzsch's. And Mader's.

I was wondering if I needed therapy. I was walking into the wind. I had nothing to hang on to. I got off the expressway too early and drove past a big cemetery. The thought that nothing will last was comforting. I looked forward to a time when I'd be past all this. All this what? Stella, and Jimmy too. It was the thought that Stella was unhappy that bent my mind backward. Maybe Paul should have let Jimmy drive the stupid car. It was still sitting in the garage. Lois had helped me get the canvas tarp back in place so I wouldn't have to look at it every time I came home.

I found 409 North Broadway—Gagliano Bros. Produce—in the middle of the market. Broad sloping sidewalks were covered by enormous black awnings. The sidewalks were crowded. The market was loud; I recognized some of the languages—Italian, Sicilian maybe, Spanish, Yiddish, Polish—but not all of them. It was hard to hear over the noise of the two-wheelers and the metal wheels of the hand trucks. The market was smelly—garbage lined the high gutters—and vulgar: men in heavy coats shouted curses as they unloaded the trucks backed up to the sidewalk. It was the sort of "real life" that Paul loved. The men were dark, and handsome. Their hair was blue-black, but I was looking for a red-headed Italian. Tommy Gagliano, aka Tommy Gagg. I found him in his office in what looked like an el station up above the warehouse, running from one side to the other.

He saw me at the same time, opened the door at the top of the stairs and shouted, "You looking for me?"

"Are you Tommy Gagliano?"

"*Benvenuto*," he said. "*Stella dice che parli italiano molto bene*," Then he repeated himself in English, just in case: "Stella says you speak good Italian."

"*Si*."

"*Vieni*." He waved me up and we continued in Italian for a while. "You've never seen a red-headed Italian before?" he said as I climbed the stairs. "Testarossa! Like the car," he said. "Ferrari Testarossa," he explained. "Call me Tommy. I think we're going to be friends."

"Is that a car?" I asked. "Testarossa?"

He laughed. "Is that a car?" he said in English. "You're kidding me."

I shook my head. I was glad I'd had my hair styled. I wasn't really dressing my age, but I didn't care. I was wearing faded jeans and a white blouse. Almost no makeup.

"A lot of southern Italians have red hair," he said. "From the Normans, the French. In the Middle Ages."

"Southern Italian," I said. Even the chest hairs that spilled out of his open collar were red, or reddish.

His face was full of freckles and sunshine, his arms, too.

We sat in the office for a while, trying to find common ground. He'd never been north of Rome and I'd never been south of Rome. And by Rome we meant two different cities. My Rome was the climax of the two great foundational stories of Western civilization—the story of the Roman Empire and the story of Christianity. His Rome was the old produce market on via Ostiense, where he'd gone with his grandfather to peddle bergamot oranges, and the Baths of Caracalla, where he and his sister had seen *Aïda* performed with elephants. Trastevere we had in common. His mother's brother had once lived in a lovely apartment on via della Lungaretta, near Santa Maria in Trastevere, where I'd made my last confession, where I'd lived free from sin for more than two weeks. Trastevere was where I'd gotten pregnant with Stella. But these details I kept to myself.

"Stella already called from the edge of town," he said, looking at his watch. "Another fifteen minutes. She's very reliable. Always got the log book up to date. She's got a good head on her." He looked at his watch. "We can wait on the street."

The "street"—the market—was his life. "It all depends on trust," he explained. "No time for written contracts. It's self-regulating. Sort of like the sciences. You have to be able to replicate your results. Or others do. You don't keep your word, nobody's going to do business with you anymore. And yet it happens all the time. People lie, cheat. But they always claim there's a reason, a special exception. No one will ever say, I don't give a damn what's right. I'm just going to do what I want. No, everybody appeals to a higher court.

"We mostly do business with the chain stores. Roundy's, Red Owl, Trader Joe's, Safeway, Kroger. But I got a soft spot for mom-and-pop corner groceries. Not many left. I charge them same as I charge the chains. Otherwise how they going to compete? That was my dad's business—a hamper of beans here and a bushel of cukes, ten baskets of tomatoes . . .

"Now it's all changed. Strawberries. They come into O'Hare on the same day they're picked. Flying Tiger Express. I'm the biggest importer in the Midwest. Bigger than Becker in Detroit; bigger than LaMantia in Chicago."

"Good for you," I said.

He laughed. "Sorry."

"Who eats all the celery?" I asked, pointing at two men unloading crates of celery that were coming down a roller out of the back of a straight truck, covered with ice.

"Celery?" he said. "Italians consider celery to be primarily an herb, and use it, with carrot and onion, in the *battuto*, the mixture of chopped herbs. The French call it a *mirepoix*."

"But there's so much of it."

We continued the conversation over coffee in Nachmann's Market Bar on the corner. The coffee was brought by Julius Nachmann's daughter, who had one brown eye and one that was half-brown and half-green.

"So you want to buy a truck?" Tommy said.

"Not especially."

"*Neanch io*," he said. *Me neither.*

"What do you know about the truck? Other than it's got over a million miles on the odometer?"

"The truck is all right. The truck isn't the problem."

"What is the problem?" It was a delicate subject, and we tiptoed around it while we waited.

"I'm willing to help Jimmy," he said, "but I don't want him living in my house, if you know what I mean. I keep thinking he'll step up, give me a hand with the business, I was hoping . . . He says that's what he wants, but I can't get him to spend more than a day or two in the office. He don't want to learn. What I'm hoping is that your daughter, your wonderful daughter, can turn things around for him. Maybe it'll happen, maybe it won't. Stranger things have happened. She is very reliable. She's where she says she's going to be. She calls when the truck is loaded. She calls from the edge of town. I don't have to wonder. She's lots of fun."

I hardly recognized the woman he was describing. "But it *would* be strange?" I asked.

"So I can see setting them up with a truck, maybe. Provided Stella's part of the package. But that's as far as I can go for Jimmy. I did the best I could after my brother died. He's a nice kid, lots of fun, good at games. He even learned to play cricket. You can see the fields—they call them 'pitches'—three of them, from my apartment, down by the lake. I don't know how he did it because it's so complicated and he lacks patience. Can't wait for anything. Besides, they weren't his kind of people. He did some shoplifting as a kid, nothing too much, got off with warnings. Not till the assault and battery.

"My wife and I looked after Jimmy like he was our own. Then after she died . . ." He shrugged.

Tommy's office phones kept ringing and one of the secretaries kept shouting messages at him from the top of the stairs and he kept shouting back.

Someone came up to him on the street to complain about tomatoes. Six baskets. "Irving, I'll tell someone to make it right, okay?"

"You know better," he said to someone. "Give Irving whatever he wants. Let him pick them out himself."

Someone came in to say that they'd unloaded more celery from a boxcar. Did he want it in the cooler or was it going out right away?

"The whole thing goes out to Godfrey's. I don't know what they're going to do with it all, but they want it. But check with Nick first."

"Nick," he explained to me, "handles the celery account. I saw that certificate your daughter got. Truck-driving school. What put it in her head to go to truck-driving school? She's such a little bitty thing."

"She's five-six," I said. "Almost as tall as you are."

He laughed. "You know what I mean."

"I know what you mean. I grew up on a farm. My dad used to let her drive the tractor. But it's hard for me to accept it as woman's work."

"They've got their own organization, you know. It's called Women in Trucking. Headquarters right here in Wisconsin, up by Stevens Point."

"Women truck drivers?"

He nodded. "Stella grew up on a farm?"

"Not really. My dad and my uncle kept my grandfather's small farm. They raised some sweet corn and some corn for the pigs, and a big kitchen garden."

Tommy was an easy person to talk to, especially out on the street, with all the noise made by the flat trucks, dollies. I found myself telling him about Paul's death. "How do you make things right again? After death: too late, too late."

"It's sort of like reconsecrating a church," he said, "after it's been desecrated."

"Sort of," I said.

"Are you a religious person, Mrs. Godwin?"

"No."

"*Neanch io.* So this is it," he said, waving his arm at the market, at the double doors that opened into the warehouse, at the produce stacked on the broad sloping sidewalk. "It's good, isn't it? Avocados, cherries, plums, grapes, artichokes, potatoes, broccoli, Brussels sprouts, celery . . . You name it. God's plenty. Is it enough?"

"It's good," I said. "It's wonderful. But it's probably not enough."

"No, I suppose not. But it's what there is."

A sawhorse was blocking a spot for the truck, between a Leshinsky Potato Company truck and a semi that said James T. Wilkins, Tacoma, Washington, on the side. The back of the Leshinsky truck was open. It was stacked up with six tiers of hundred-pound sacks of potatoes. A big burly man took hold of two corners of one of the sacks on the bottom, jerked it out, and threw it over his shoulders. Bushels of green peppers from the James T. Wilkins truck were being loaded onto flat trucks and pushed into the warehouse. There wasn't a lot of room between the two trucks.

"Gonna be tight," Tommy said, "but Stella's a good driver. They really taught her some tricks in that driving school, or probably she's just got a knack. Myself, I learned the hard way," he said. "My dad gave me the key to a truck and told me to figure it out for myself. So I started making deliveries. Around the city, you know. Kohl's, Safeway, Roundy's, Godfrey—that used to be IGA. Used to be A and P and National Tea. Those were the big ones. I had some real problems. But those were straight trucks. The semis I could never manage, turning the wheel to the right when you want the back of the truck to go left. I never was too good at it."

But when the truck finally pulled around the corner, by Nachmann's Market Bar, Jimmy was driving, not Stella. He was wearing a baseball cap and big sunglasses. Stella was sitting next to him. She'd rolled down the window, though it was cold. She'd let her hair grow. She was wearing sunglasses too.

"Going to be tight," Tommy said again.

Broadway was a one-way street. South to North. If you looked north you could see the traffic on Wisconsin Avenue. If you looked south, you'd see more of the market. And beyond that, warehouses.

I was nervous. I hadn't seen Stella since Paul's death. I always had plenty of forgiveness for Stella, but there was a limit. Now she wanted me to help finance a truck with a sleeper, so she and Jimmy could have some privacy.

"Jimmy had a lot of adventures, you know," Tommy said. "I'm glad to see him settle down."

I didn't ask what kind of adventures.

I've watched a big furniture truck backing up the alley behind the lofts. Pretty amazing. All the way from Mulberry Street, around the corner into the alley that divides the parking lot, through the lot in front of the loft garages, and then angling into the furniture dock, always leaving me enough room so I could get my car out of the garage.

Jimmy waved from the cab, even tipped his cap. I could see Stella, but I couldn't see her face. I wanted to run to her, climb up on the running board. But I didn't.

Jimmy pulled across the space and then started to back up. But there wasn't enough room on the opposite side of the street for him to get even a forty-five degree angle. I thought he was going to back into the Wilkins truck—the one with the load of peppers—but he stopped just in time, pulled up, and tried again. But he couldn't get the cab—the tractor—to follow the trailer into the space. Tommy had his eyes closed. Jimmy tried three more times. People were starting to watch, and they weren't gentle people.

"Jack it in," someone shouted. Someone else laughed. I could see Jimmy through the open window, his head jerking as he looked from one mirror to another. I thought he might be looking for help. Finally he got out of the cab.

"Somebody's got to move this goddamn truck," he shouted, banging on the side of the Leshinsky Potato Company truck. "There's not enough room to get in."

"You just got to jack it in," somebody shouted again.

I wasn't sure what this meant.

"Fuck it!" Jimmy shouted.

The big burly man who was unloading potatoes laughed.

"Move the fucking truck," Jimmy says. "You can see I don't have enough room."

"Let your girlfriend back it in."

"Go shit yourself."

"Who you talking to?"

"To you, Polack asshole."

The burly man pulled a produce hammer out of his back pocket and started for the Jimmy. At least it wasn't a knife.

Jimmy whipped off his belt, which had a heavy buckle on the end, and whirled it around his head.

What was it Keats said about a quarrel in the streets? More exciting than a poem?

But Tommy intervened before things went any farther. *"Basta basta basta.* Take it easy. Put your hammer away, Leo," he said to the Leshinsky driver. And to Jimmy: "Put your belt back on before your pants fall down. Stop acting like a punk and I'll buy you a drink." He put his arm around Jimmy. And led him off toward Nachmann's Market Bar.

I stayed to talk to Stella, who was out of the cab now, looking over the situation. The truck was blocking the entire street. "Later, Ma," she said, glancing at me.

She climbed into the cab and made herself comfortable, then pulled forward till the back of the trailer was near the opening between the two trucks and then adjusted the back wheels, the tandems, all the way forward so she could make a shorter turn. I could understand the principle, but I couldn't imagine turning the wheel left to get the back of the truck to go to the right. And vice versa.

She started to back up, and I thought she was going to back right into the Wilkins truck. I could see her talking to herself, bending the truck to her will, and suddenly the back of the trailer swung around into the opening.

I could see her checking her mirrors and pulling on the wheel, a white light behind her, filling the cab. All of a sudden the angle changed again and it looked as if she were going to back right into the Leshinsky potato truck. And then the trailer magically straight-ened out and the cab followed it into the hole.

Later, in the bar—we were sitting in a booth—she said, "Sometimes when I'm in a tight spot I tell myself that there's a perfect line to follow. That's what they taught us in truck-driving school. If I could find that line, a line that would put the truck straight into the hole the first time . . . That line's the line you'd follow if you were pulling *out* of the hole, right? So you just follow the line that you take pulling out of a space and sink the trailer right *into* the hole. But you have to visualize that line.

"Sometimes there're going to be two lines . . ." She went on to explain how the two lines worked, and I knew then that Jimmy was going to kill her if I didn't do something to stop him. But what could I do? The waitress brought out coffee.

"You keep the temperature at sixty degrees?" Tommy asked Stella.

"All the way."

"They're hauling black-market tomatoes," Tommy said, turning to me.

"Black market?"

"Florida tomatoes. Not exactly black market, but I got a cousin in Pompano Beach figured out how to grow tomatoes that taste good in the winter. Like real tomatoes, not cardboard. But they don't look too good. Like those tomatoes with all the bumps and cat faces on them you see in Italy. So the Florida Tomato Growers Association decides he can't sell them out of state because they don't meet minimum beauty standards. Because of the bumps. I can't sell them to the chains without making a stink, but restaurants, they're another story. Not just Milwaukee, Chicago too."

That night Tommy made sauce with some of the black market tomatoes. Paul would have loved it. He cooked some garlic in olive oil, then cut the tomatoes in half and squeezed the juice into the pan with the oil and garlic. He cooked the juice down to concentrate it and then added what was left of the tomato halves. So the juice was concentrated, but the meat of the tomatoes cooked for only a short time. He put the tomatoes through a food mill and served the sauce on spaghetti. No Parmesan cheese. "Parmesan cheese is the emperor of cheeses," he explained, "but every dish is a little drama. Parmesan cheese is a strong actor. You don't want Parmesan cheese to upstage the lead."

Jimmy disagreed. He wanted Parmesan cheese.

"Grate it yourself," Tommy said, but Jimmy couldn't find it in the refrigerator and Tommy had to help him.

Jimmy couldn't let the truck-backing-up business rest. "Old man Leshinsky and his fucking potatoes," he kept saying.

"Don't talk like a punk," Tommy said, but Jimmy was determined to be disagreeable.

"He could of moved the fucking truck."

I could see where things stood. But could Stella see? Had she waded in too deep to turn back?

"I could of backed it in, but it just made more sense for that fat-ass Leshinsky driver to move his truck."

For a second course Tommy served thick pork chops, browned in olive oil and then baked with fennel seeds, followed by a salad. Later on Jimmy and Stella went out to a club.

"Stella knows how to drive," Tommy said. "That school must have been pretty good."

"What *I* want to know," I said, "is if she's going to be all right."

"You mean, is she going to turn things around for Jimmy. I'm glad to see him with a good woman. She stuck by him all that time he was in prison. Visiting every week."

I didn't say anything.

"Love," he said. "What do they know that we don't know?"

"There's more than bed to marriage."

He laughed. "You got that backward," he said. "That's what *we* know that they don't know." And for a while we explored the mystery of love. We didn't disagree about anything, but we didn't take the argument very far beyond the obvious.

"He did good work on the house," I said, not mentioning the chandelier.

"He's not afraid of work," Tommy said.

"What happened to his parents?" I asked.

"My brother was killed on the back loading dock," Tommy said. Crushed by a truck backing up. His wife couldn't manage on her own, died a year later. "He's my brother's son. We took him in, treated him like he was our own. My wife . . ." He crossed himself. "I promised my brother I'd look after him. Blood is blood. You've got to understand that. You look after your own."

And I thought he'd just told me everything I needed to know.

But it turned out there was more. Isn't there always more? A lot more?

"I'm going to put the dishes in the dishwasher," he said, "but let me put something on to lift the spirits. He had a fancy stereo system that could handle LPs as well as cassettes and CDs. I recognized the overture to *The Marriage of Figaro*, which Paul and I had seen in the Arena in Verona. And I experienced a peaceful easy feeling, like the old Eagles song, as if we were not doing anything special, as if we just happened to be walking along side by side, heading in the same direction.

We met twice, in Chicago, to see *Turandot*, at the end of February, and *Norma*, in the middle of March (at the end of the season). Both times I took the Illinois Zephyr from Galesburg, and Tommy, who took the North Shore down from Milwaukee, was waiting for me in Union Station. We took a cab to the Lyric Opera and sat on the mezzanine. Tommy was a subscriber.

We had a recording of Joan Sutherland singing "Casta Diva"— *Joan Sutherland's Greatest Hits*—but hearing June Anderson live was heartbreakingly beautiful. More than beautiful. It was like being seasick or coming down with the flu, but somehow wonderful, as if our limited physical responses had to do double duty, had to stand for the flu or for joy, the way the same notes on a piano score can sometimes represent the flute and sometimes the violin.

We stayed at the Palmer House, in separate rooms after *Turandot*. That was the first step. The second step was easy. After *Norma* we shared a room, and a bed. No one wants to imagine the sexual desires of an older woman. But let me tell you something, they're the same as yours: to be touched, stroked, embraced, to be held.

That's the long and short of it. To feel the earth rolling under your shoulder blades, to share a glass of wine, one glass for the two of you, to drink a cup of coffee together in the morning. That's what we did. Coffee and eggs Benedict in the hotel.

Inside I was as dizzy as a teenager who's just lost her virginity, as unsteady as a drunk trying to walk a straight line, but outwardly I remained calm as we walked north on Wabash to the river, leaned against the railing, looked down at the tour boats. I felt flirtatious, in command, still able to surprise a man. Myself too.

We talked about *Norma* from every possible angle—the difficulty of staging, the difficulty of coordinating the words and the music, the difficulty of finding a balance between carnality and spirituality.

"I never thought it was a problem," I said.

He laughed.

June Anderson's performance—I started to hum the aria—was the most beautiful thing I'd ever heard. Tommy explained bel canto singing, and opera singing in general.

"It's totally different," he said. "You got to link your different registers, and you got to do it with no microphones, no amplification. You got to make yourself heard. It's a kind of controlled screaming. It takes years to learn. You got to sing pianissimo over the orchestra and be heard in the back row of the top balcony. What you do is you make a column of air in your body and then ride it like a wave, like you're on a surf board."

I took a deep breath and tried to form a column of air deep within my body and then jump on that one word at the top, which I recognized as *pace* and ride it down to the end. I wasn't worried about anyone hearing me. Too much noise. Too much traffic on Michigan Avenue, too much traffic on the river.

Tommy put his arm around me. "Careful," he said. "You need to do some warm-ups first. You don't want to ruin your voice."

We ate a late lunch in one of the new restaurants underneath the station, and I left on the California Zephyr. I could have stayed longer and taken the Illinois Zephyr, but I was still shaky and I thought I'd better get home. Tommy saw me off. The California Zephyr is a big train. When it leaves the station it's more like an ocean liner leaving the port than an airplane taking off.

I walked home. The apartment's only a block from the Amtrak station. I'd had an unsettling glimpse of a new life. But what stayed with me was not so much the possibility of a new life, but the music, the aria. *Casta diva.* Chaste goddess. Like first love, it promised to vindicate life, or at least point toward what's important in life.

I went down to the garage, which was full of banker's boxes full of books. Some labeled. Some mislabeled. Some not labeled at all. But I found what I was looking for: our old *Scribner Music Library*, ten volumes of folk songs, popular songs, piano classics, and two volumes of opera excerpts. I took them upstairs and looked up the piano score for *Norma*—excerpts from *Norma*. The music for "Casta Diva" wasn't difficult. I sight-read my way through it without stopping. Then I played it again. Then I started to sing. The beauty was overwhelming. Not the beauty of my decent alto voice, but the way the melody holds its breath at the top and then pulses its way down to the tonic. I tried to sing the words, an octave low, but it was like trying to sing when you're seasick: "*Pa-a-a-a-a-a-a-a-a-a-a-a-ce . . .*"

I played it again, tried to form a column of air deep within my body, but I didn't know what it would feel like if I succeeded. But I recognized the experience now. It wasn't seasickness, it wasn't the flu; it was homesickness.

The doorbell rang. It was Lois, in her bathrobe. And Camilla. "I thought you might want your dog back," she said.

"Thanks, Lois," I said. "Sorry. I got carried away."

"You can tell me about it tomorrow," she said. "I'm going back to bed."

7

―――――――――― ❧ ――――――――――

"Truth Comes in Blows"
(April–June 1997)

Paul's memorial service, held on Shakespeare's birthday, was everything a memorial service should be. If you're part of a small liberal arts college, you don't need religion. You don't need a church. The college will provide all the things the people used to expect from a church: a sense of community, an active interest in the large questions about the meaning and purpose of human life, and even a memorial service when you die.

It was a lot of work. I sorted out photos for a slide show, and one of Paul's students put it on a computer. I even included one of Paul and his first wife, Elaine, who came all the way from New York to the service.

The slide show was impressive, and as people were filling Kresge Recital Hall they could listen to the third movement of Bach's sixth Brandenburg Concerto as pictures of Paul appeared and disappeared on the big screen at the front of the stage—pictures of Paul in the classroom, pictures of Paul at various Shakespeare parties

(Paul as Falstaff, Paul as Juliet, as Lear, as Hamlet's mother), Paul clowning at the Bernini Fountain in Piazza Navona in Rome, Paul and his first wife on Little Cranberry Island in Maine, Paul at the Blüthner grand, Paul at the head of a dining room table covered with dishes and bottles of wine, Paul and me in our tomato garden, Paul and baby Stella, Paul and Stella at Stella's various graduations.

Paul's colleagues were eloquent. They took turns at the microphone on the side of the stage and reminded me—reminded everyone—how much Paul had been loved. I wasn't the only one who would miss him. Father Viglietti spoke too, reminding us that Paul's insights into Shakespeare were insights into our own lives as well.

The college provided the food, but I had to pay for the wine. I didn't want to use up the rest of Paul's Barolo, still in the closet, so I bought a good Sicilian red wine that Tommy Gagg had recommended when I called him, trying to reach Stella.

Stella showed up at the memorial service. I hadn't seen her since the trip to Milwaukee, and then I saw her coming out of Kresge Recital Hall after the service. She'd been sitting in the back. *How many times could I forgive?* But she looked so terrible I could have made it to seventy times seven without breaking stride. I wanted to take her home, put her to bed, take her temperature, bring her a cup of bouillon, but she said she couldn't stay. We walked across the campus without talking. Finally she said, "'Like a long-legged fly upon the stream,' I thought Pa wanted someone to read that poem when he died."

"Ed Wilson read it at the graveside," I said. "When we buried the ashes."

"In my first class at the workshop," she said, "Professor Roberts tried to tell us that Yeats was being ironic. I almost walked out."

"You want to walk to the Fourth Street Bridge?" I asked.

She shook her head. She had to get back. I walked her back to her car, Ruthy's pickup, which she'd left on Cherry Street. I knew better than to argue with her. I knew better than to start crying. I watched her drive off and went back to Kresge, where people were still drinking wine in the lobby, and when it was all over I called Ruthy at TruckStopUSA. I was a little high, a little drunk, and I vented.

"How can she want to be a fucking truck driver? She was going to be a poet. She had so much talent." This question had been festering for a long time in my subconscious.

"I don't know any poets," Ruthy said. "Do you know any truck drivers?"

"No," I said. "That makes us even."

"Depends," she said. "Tell me about poets."

I thought about all the poetry readings Paul and I had sat through in the Common Room in Old Main. Names you've heard of. Distinguished names. I thought of W. H. Auden, so drunk that at the reading in Kresge Recital Hall he kept pushing the podium over to the edge of the stage. Almost pushed it off. Paul and Bill Young were ready to jump up from their seats in the front row to push it back, but Auden always caught himself just in time.

I thought of living poets, poets whose names you see in the *New York Times Book Review*, and *The New York Review of Books*. I thought of Poet A, who stopped to kiss his student girlfriend in the middle of his reading. More than once. I thought of Poet B, who boasted that he was the highest paid faculty member at the University of X. I thought of Poet C, who came as an external examiner for three honors projects and bedded all three honors candidates. I thought of Poet D, who brought a coterie of adoring students from Maharishi

University, students who crowded at his feet while he read and asked him to read every poem twice. I thought of E, who propositioned me after a dinner party at our house, and Poet F, who read so long that Paul had to bring the reading to an end by standing up and starting to applaud.

"All men?" she asked.

"I didn't mention the women."

"Were they jerks too?"

"No. But one of them talked on her cell phone while the department chair was introducing her."

"You want me to tell you about truck drivers?"

"Never mind," I said. "I'm sure they're the salt of the earth."

"Let me explain something to you, Ms. Godwin. You have to understand that I love your daughter too. You're going to have to get used to that."

"You make it sound like a threat." I could feel the strength in her voice, like a flower splitting a rock.

"Maybe it is. Up to you."

I could hear the sounds of the restaurant in the background, the clatter of dishes and silverware. I thought that whatever I said now would determine who I was going to become, but I didn't know who I wanted to become.

What I said was, finally, "Ruthy, I'm sorry." And I was sorry. Sorry that I didn't understand my own daughter any more than I understood the boy who delivered our morning paper. Sorry that I had never accepted her choices. Not really, not deep down.

"It'll be okay," Ruthy said. "Everything's going to be okay. But Stella has to figure it out for herself first. People can beat the love out of you, even unconditional love, if there is such a thing. That's what's happening now."

*   *   *

About a week later Stella called from TruckStopUSA. Every time I heard her voice something with sharp edges twisted around inside me. She and Jimmy were on their way to Anna, Illinois, that evening to pick up a load of peppers.

But I wasn't listening to her words. I was listening to the sounds in the background.

"Why are you calling from a bathroom?" I asked.

"How do you know where I'm calling from?"

"I can hear toilets flushing and water running and the sound of an electric hand dryer."

"I'm using Ruthy's cell phone."

"Why don't you go outside?"

"Jimmy doesn't want me to call . . . He gets pissed . . ."

"Jimmy's pissed? Jimmy's pissed? Your father's dead and Jimmy's pissed? Excuse me."

"Ma, calm down. I think I'm in trouble . . ."

Drugs, I thought. Pregnant? "Stella," I said. "Every morning when I look at the advice columns, I think one of those letters is from you. It used to be Dear Abby and Ann Landers, now it's something else. What's the matter with these women? I'm really in love with this guy, and he can be real sweet, but he's got a temper—"

"Ma," she interrupted, "you already said that. You don't understand."

"I understand all right," I shouted into the phone. "You need professional help. You need to get the hell away from Jimmy. It's as plain as the nose on your face. You need to come home."

"Ma, I've got to go. I'll be okay. It's just—"

"Just what?" I asked. But she'd already hung up.

I called Tommy Gagg, in Milwaukee, but he'd gone to Italy for a funeral and wouldn't be back for a week.

*   *   *

Ruthy called on Wednesday morning just after midnight. Jimmy had pushed Stella out of the truck as they were pulling out of the TruckStopUSA onto I-80. "He wanted her to go down on him. Suck him off, you know, while he was driving. She wouldn't do it. He started punching her, grabbing her by the neck. She got the door open and he pushed her out. Somebody picked her up, another trucker, and brought her back to the truck stop. She doesn't want me to call the police, but she wants to come home. She's afraid. She wants to be far away. I'm going to bring her to Galesburg."

I felt the thing with sharp edges twisting my stomach, something between anger and grief and joy, too. *At least she was on her way home.*

"Truth comes in blows." Paul liked that passage in *Henderson the Rain King*. Henderson is chopping wood and a chip of wood flies up and hits him in the head.

I got the bed in the guest room ready and put clean towels in the bathroom next to the guest room. Stella'd have a space all of her own, where no one could touch her.

I opened up the big couch in the living room for Ruthy. It made a comfortable bed. No bar to kill your back.

Then I got Pa's old .38 out of a banker's box in the garage. I noticed a little rust on the trigger. I spread out newspapers and cleaned it at the harvest table. The new gun, also a .38 with a long barrel, was in the drawer in a table next to Paul's side of the bed. I don't think he could have lifted it at the end.

Camilla sat with her head in my lap. Cammy. We had bonded, but I didn't allow her to sleep on the bed. At least not when I was at home. She was good company and sang softly when I played the piano. She was partial to Chopin.

The gun had been clean when I put it away, but I tied a strip of cloth around the rear cylinder opening and ran a brush through the barrel, then a patch with cleaning solvent, then two dry patches. I cleaned the cylinders the same way and then rubbed the gun with a light coating of oil, wiped it, and put six bullets in the chambers.

I didn't expect Stella and Ruthy for another hour. Camilla and I went to the small park by the depot and waited for a freight train. I was wearing a new pair of shoes. Vigotti Salla. Boot-type shoes. Very comfortable. The parking lot was always full on weekends. People going to Chicago. But there were plenty of spaces tonight. The depot was closed. The first Amtrak train would come at seven the next morning, but there were freight trains all night long. Paul had complained. Everyone complained. Except me. People were agitating for a quiet zone, but I liked the sounds of the trains.

We were standing where Carl Sandburg had once stood to see William Jennings Bryan. Near the huge old steam locomotive that had been given to the city by the Chicago, Burlington and Quincy. The beautiful big Burlington depot had been torn down, of course— I'd bought Paul's railroad desk at the auction—and replaced with a smaller modern depot, which would soon have to be torn down and replaced with a larger depot.

I wasn't up on Galesburg's railroad history, but I knew that the CB&Q trains had run on these tracks, or at least on this road bed, as had the Toledo, Peoria and Western. The old Atchison, Topeka & Santa Fe tracks ran by the house on Prairie Street. Now all the tracks are owned by BNSF, but they're used by Amtrak, TP&W, and Union Pacific trains, too.

I let Camilla loose. She sniffed the earth, returned, as she always did, to investigate a spot where someone had dumped some cat food a couple of weeks earlier. She never set foot out of the park. Maybe that's because I started to scream if she even looked like she was going to step outside. She pooped and I picked it up in a plastic bag and dropped it in the trash can by the station.

Once she helped the police with their inquiries by herding another dog that was loose in the park. I expected the policeman, at the end, to say, "You know, you're going to have to keep that dog on a leash." But he didn't. She herded everything herd-able, including the other dogs in the loft apartments. She was friendly enough, but given a chance she'd herd them into a corner of the deck and wouldn't let them out.

We didn't have to wait long for a train, coming from the south, out of the yards. It made a hell of a noise at the Chambers Street crossing: federal regulations now required a long pull at 110 decibels. The train wasn't going very fast, so the pull lasted a long time.

Standing at the back of the car rental place, I fired two shots into the ground. I picked up the casings and used my trowel to recover the bullets. Camilla came running to investigate. She was interested in the gun. I couldn't wave her away.

"You don't have to be afraid," I said. We'd had this conversation before, not about the gun, but about abuse. She was afraid of men with beards and it had taken her a while to warm up to Paul. The crows, startled by the gun, had started an unnerving racket. Black shadows in the branches.

"I need your help," I said. I let her sniff the gun. "Good dog, good dog. Now you can understand better. Maybe not everything. But something."

I wanted to walk to the Fourth Street bridge, but I didn't want to carry the gun around with me, and I wasn't sure I'd have time. I put the gun in my purse and went back to the apartment.

What was I feeling? Maybe I was feeling like Caesar in his tent, the maps spread out before him, about to take a fatal step. *Alea iacta est*, he said. The die has been cast. Except what he really said, according to Plutarch, was Let the die be cast. I had not yet crossed the Rubicon, but I was about to, and not for the first time in my life.

The crows had settled back down in the big ash tree in the park and in the locust trees at the side of the Packing House Dining Company.

I had my night vision by now. Orion was long gone, but Boötes the Herdsman was overhead, and I could still see Spica in the west.

I thought about Stella's telescope. It was very complicated and Paul got angry at the instructions, but we had got it to work, focusing on one bright star after another. It was still in the garage.

Clouds drifted overhead, covering a waning gibbous moon like strips of gauze.

I pushed the ejector rod and dropped the four remaining rounds into the palm of my hand.

I was back at the harvest table when Ruthy called from the parking lot, downstairs, about three o'clock. Stella didn't want a doctor, didn't want the police.

Ruthy's long red hair was darker than Tommy's. When she tossed her head you could see a little white birthmark on the side of her neck, shaped like a sock. She stayed in the guest room with Stella. Shared the little half bath. They had to shower in the big bathroom off my bedroom. Stella turned away from me when she came in to take a shower in the morning. Her hair was caked with dirt.

"How is she?" I asked Ruthy, out in the kitchen.

"Able to sit up and take nourishment."

"That's what her dad used to say."

Ruthy was a lovely woman. Beautiful. Tough. Alive. Jaunty. Her hair was still wet from her shower. Her jeans were too long and formed a puddle around her shoes. She acted like a woman who wanted to be seen and heard, acknowledged.

"You remind me of my husband's first wife," I said.

"Is that good?"

"Good but complicated," I said. "She came all the way from New York to the memorial. She was very kind to me. She was a good woman, but she couldn't stand the Midwest."

I drove out to Thrushwood Farms to get some pepper bacon. Stella's favorite. Pepper bacon and poached eggs. Stella stayed in her room. Ruthy took her breakfast to her.

"Why can't she come out and eat at the table?"

"Give her some time," Ruthy said.

We were sitting out on the deck. Ruthy was wearing some of my clothes. She was peeling an orange. I'd brought up the Italian flower pots from the garage but hadn't planted anything. The pots were plastic, not terra-cotta, but they looked real, and they were beautiful. Different colors.

"I haven't gotten around to planting anything yet," I said. "I haven't been up to it."

"It's not too late," Ruthy said.

Jimmy called from Milwaukee about ten o'clock.

"What happened?" I asked.

"She jumped out of the truck. Crazy bitch."

"You pushed her, Jimmy."

"She tell you that?"

"Jimmy," I said, "you made things miserable for my husband at the end of his life and you've made life miserable for my daughter. For your uncle, too. You're lucky you're not back in jail right now. And you will be if you touch Stella again. She's done with you. Through. Finito. Basta."

I was standing in the kitchen. Ruthy was making signs: "Stella's got to tell him herself," she mouthed. I handed Ruthy the phone and she took it to Stella, in the bedroom, and closed the door. I couldn't hear.

A few minutes later Jimmy called again. "You're going to bring her to the truck stop tonight," he said. "You don't want me to come up there, do you?"

"You're right," I said. "I don't want you to come up here. I don't ever want to see you again."

"Tell that bitch dyke Ruthy she's starting to repel me."

"I think she already knows that."

"Eleven o'clock," he said. "Tonight. Be there. Bring my wife, you hear, or I swear to God . . ." He didn't finish swearing.

I didn't say anything.

"You hear?" he said. "I want to hear you say it."

"I'll be there," I said.

I was glad that Ruthy was with us. For both moral and physical support. We took Stella to the hospital in the afternoon. It turned out she had a ruptured spleen and a cracked rib. And she'd also, the doctor told us later, had a miscarriage after she arrived at the hospital. She was not going to need surgery, but she'd have to stay in the hospital for a few days.

Back at the apartment Ruthy and I did the dishes. Two women in the kitchen. We let Camilla lick the plates before we put them in the dishwasher.

"I know a couple of guys at the truck stop who'd be happy to put Jimmy in the hospital," Ruthy said. "More than a couple. But I wanted to talk to you first. He'll be there tonight. He'll have to sleep for a while, fill in his log book."

I put a hand on Ruthy's shoulders. "I'm glad you're here."

"Me too," Ruthy said. "We should plant some flowers tomorrow."

What would Scipio Africanus do with a punk like Jimmy? Scipio, Scipio who defeated Hannibal. What would Pompey do? Pompey the Great, who rid the Mediterranean of pirates in three months.

What would Caesar do? Caesar . . . Well, Shakespeare got Caesar all wrong. Caesar was a real jerk. He walked around with a body guard of gladiators. No question about it, though, guys like Scipio and Pompey and Caesar wouldn't have put up with Jimmy.

But going back a little farther. Remember Cato the Elder: *Carthago delenda est.* Carthage must be destroyed. That's what I was feeling: *Giacomo delenda est.* Jimmy has to be destroyed. Or at least warned off.

Camilla rode shotgun during the ninety-minute drive. I left her in the car at the truck stop.

It took me a while to find Jimmy's truck—GAGLIANO BROS. PRODUCE— which was parked between two refrigerator trucks— reefers—in a long line of semis. Big rigs. They were making a lot of noise, emitting blue petroleum fumes. Their engines were running, making the ground tremble, and the refrigeration units were running.

I waited for Jimmy. I had to pee but I didn't want to go into the restaurant, so I squatted and peed by the truck. The .38 was tucked in my purse, like a good luck charm.

I gathered my strength, my nerve, while I waited, wiping my hands on my shirt before touching the pistol in my purse, holding my nerves tighter and tighter, crouching mentally, crouching in order to spring forward, like a sprinter with one foot on the starting block. Wanting to see Jimmy before he saw me, before he knew I was watching.

He finally showed, coming around the cab. High on something. He didn't see me at first. And then he did.

"What the hell are you doing here?" Had he forgotten? "Where is she?"

"Nice to see you, Jimmy. Let's just sit in the truck for a few minutes. We need to talk."

"Where's that crazy wife of mine?" We got in the truck.

"You mean my daughter?"

"Your crazy daughter, then."

"Jimmy, tell me what happened. I want to hear it from you."

"You got a lot of nerve messing in my business, you know."

"Just tell me what happened."

He hesitated, as if he'd just changed his mind about what he was going to say. "She jumped out of the truck, you know. What the fuck did she think she was doing? She just opened the door and jumped out. Good thing I was only going about forty. On the ramp."

"That was really lucky," I said. "And lucky that somebody stopped and picked her up."

"I figured somebody would. No way I could stop. The next exit isn't till Mendota. By the time I got back she'd of been gone."

I shook my head. "Jimmy. That was my daughter you shoved out of the truck and left on the highway. My daughter."

"She really knows how to push my buttons."

"What does that mean, 'push my buttons.' What buttons are you talking about? I never saw any buttons on a man."

"You've got some nerve. That woman you're talking about is my lawful wife, and if you think—"

"She was my daughter before she was your wife, and she'll be my daughter *after* she stops being your wife."

"Fuck you."

"Jimmy, I'm not here to negotiate. I'm here to tell you what the score is. Stella's going to file for a divorce, and you're going to say yes to everything she asks for. And don't forget the chandelier. That chandelier was worth sixty thousand dollars. I took photos. I kept the dangles with your fingerprints on them. And I'll tell the police how her spleen got ruptured. It was a blow to her lower left chest.

"One way or another you'll be looking at some serious prison time. You're a convicted felon, out on parole. You never would have gotten your commercial driver's license if it hadn't been for your uncle."

"What the fuck's a spleen?"

"It's a Greek word, Jimmy. If you were big-spleened, that meant 'big-hearted.' She was big-spleened. She had to be to put up with you. And she was pregnant. She miscarried, so you'll be looking at a murder charge, too. 'Murder one,' isn't that what they say on the cop shows?"

Jimmy was having trouble speaking. It was as if he had run out of words. I knew how he felt. There was nothing more to say. I'd been planning to threaten him, to scare him, but now I was hoping he'd lunge at me. But he just sat there, dumb as a stone. And then he recovered himself and said, "You are so full of shit I can't believe it."

"Jimmy," I said. "I have something to show you." I took the long-barreled .38 out of my large purse in one smooth motion, one I'd practiced.

The sight of the revolver revived Jimmy. At least he started to laugh. More like honking than laughing.

"Jimmy," I said, "put your hands on the steering wheel and keep them there."

"You know what," he said. "You haven't got the nerve, and I don't give a fuck."

"You're looking at murder one, Jimmy," I said. "Now tell me about the chandelier."

"Hey," he said. "If your stupid dick of a husband hadn't been so uptight about the fucking car, none of this would of happened. He couldn't drive it himself, and so he couldn't stand to have anyone else drive it."

"Did you use a baseball bat on the chandelier?"

He laughed. "I pulled that fucker out of the ceiling with my bare hands and then I stomped all over those little dangly things. It felt good."

"That's what I wanted to know. Now keep your hands on the steering wheel."

"Mrs. G," he said, "I'm going to count to ten, and we're going to get out of this cab and we're going to walk over to your car and get Stella. And if you give me any grief you'll be sorry for the rest of your life. You'll find out that what Stella went through was like a Sunday school picnic. Like a walk in the park. Like going swimming in a lake when the water's just right, real still and a little bit cold, not too cold, but cold, you know what I mean?"

"This was my dad's gun," I said. "He used it to shoot hogs. After we got married Paul used to do the shooting . . . Hogs, Jimmy. One shot, right behind the ear. Once a year for fourteen years. He put those hogs right down. One shot."

"One," he said. "You can just get out of the cab. We'll go over to your car and get Stella and you can head back home, and Stell'n I'll be on our way. I had a couple of pills a while ago. They'll get me to Milwaukee, but I don't want to fuck around here too long."

"Jimmy," I said. "Stella's not in the car, she's in the hospital."

"Two."

I no longer felt like the director of this drama; I was one of the actors, and we were improvising. I was a swimmer who'd been caught up in a strong current that was carrying her out to sea.

"Three."

"And then I want you to leave her alone. That's what it's going to take right now. You've got to give me your word that you're going to leave her alone. No telephone calls. No showing up in Galesburg."

"Four. She's got too much of a hold on me for that. All I got to do is touch her and she's ready to go, you know what I mean? Maybe you still remember what it was like?"

"She's not here," I said. "She's in the hospital."

"Sometimes it's like the cars coming at me on the other side of the highway are animals, wolves. You know what I mean?" He paused and held up five fingers. "Then I'm sure she's getting looked after okay. Tell her I'll be coming for her soon as she's out."

"She'll be there a week, Jimmy."

"Six. You gonna shoot me or what?"

I cocked the hammer to let him know I was serious. "I'll shoot you when you get to 'nine.' How's that? Either that or you give me your word that you'll never see her again."

"Seven. Right here," he said, touching his forehead with the tip of his middle finger and sticking his head forward.

"Eight."

I kept my eyes open and didn't argue with myself before squeezing the trigger. The hammer was already cocked. I didn't want to wait for "nine." I could see him tensing up to make a move, and I didn't think he'd wait for the full count. As I squeezed the trigger I could feel every moment of my life leading up to this point. (Of course, whatever point you're at, every moment of your life has been leading up to it.) I shot him in the chest the first time, because I didn't want to take a chance on missing, and because I didn't want to get spattered with blood. And then I put a second bullet in his heart. The reefers on either side of us were generating so much noise no one could have heard the shots.

Afterward I couldn't breathe and I thought for a minute I'd been shot myself. I put my hand on my heart and kept it there while I wiped the door handle with a handkerchief that I clutched in my other hand. I didn't take a breath till I got back to my car and put my hand on Camilla's head and my heart started to slow down.

I looked her in the eyes, wondering what she was thinking, would think if she knew. I looked up at the sky, but there was too much light pollution in the parking lot for star gazing.

I realized with a shock that I'd left the gun in the cab of Jimmy's truck. I went back for it, put it in my purse, and put a handkerchief over my finger and locked both doors. Jimmy hadn't moved. I tried not to look at him through the window as I wiped the door handle on the passenger side.

I pulled over at the next rest stop on I-80 to let Camilla out to pee. I could hear the grass growing, the trees leafing out, creating a dark canopy, blocking the stars. An owl hooted, and I thought of the owl that Camilla hears in Book XI of *The Aeneid*, as she prepares to kill herself. I could smell the dampness of the earth. I could hear Camilla (the dog) sniffing, then disappearing for a moment behind a tree. For a minute I couldn't see her, and then I did see her, sniffing another dog, a little white border collie on a long lead. On the one hand I didn't want anyone to see me; on the other, I needed some human contact, if only for a moment. Contact with another dog person. It was very dark; I couldn't see this person, but the dog itself stood out against the darkness.

I talked briefly with the owner, trying to keep my breathing steady. She had the dog on a retractable lead. A woman my age. She was crying.

"I didn't see you pull in," she said. "But I always feel safe with dog people."

"I just stopped to let the dog out," I said.

"He doesn't run away?"

"She," I said.

"She doesn't?"

"No. At least not yet. Are you all right?"

"Not really," she said. "Sometimes I just need to cry."

I felt like crying too, but I was too keyed up.

"Toby's started jumping the fence," she said. "And then he's off. The neighbors are wonderful, but sometimes he goes pretty far afield. And crosses some pretty busy streets. I tried tying him up, but that just makes him miserable. I probably need to get a higher fence."

"You might try spending more time with him out in the yard. You can't play with him when you're inside and he's outside." This was something I'd read in the dog training book that Paul ordered from Amazon. It seemed like good advice. "I know it's a pain, but you don't want him to get bored. If stuff's going on at home, he won't be so eager to run away."

"Thanks," she said. "Come on, Toby." The retractable lead made a ratcheting sound as Toby came running and jumping. "Have a good trip."

"Safe home," I said.

I stayed in the rest area for a while. It was very dark and the stars, which you could see from the side of the road, where the trees had been cut back, were very bright. *Praeterea tam sunt,* I said out loud, *Arcturi sidera nobis.* I made the students in Latin 2 memorize this passage from Book I of Vergil's *Georgics: Praeterea tam sunt Arcturi . . .*

The star of Arcturus, and the days of the Kids, and bright Draco the Serpent, are as much ours as theirs, who sailing homewards over stormy seas, brave the Pontic sea, and the straits of oyster-rich Abydos.

It was two o'clock in the morning. Arcturus was low in the west, and I, Frances Godwin, was sailing homeward over stormy seas.

Instead of getting off I-80 onto I-74 and heading south, I kept on going west to Rock Island, then crossed the Mississippi into Iowa on the Centennial Bridge, which had low railings on the sides, so it was easy to pull over and drop the gun off the bridge into the middle of the main channel. I followed 67 east on the Iowa side till I got to 74 and then headed south, back across the river and home to Galesburg. I still had a quarter tank of gas.

8

Vigil (June 1997)

I woke up in a panic. Everything had changed. I couldn't imagine a future, couldn't even see ahead to the end of the day. I didn't want this one act to define me for the rest of my life, perhaps forever. The blood pouring out of Jimmy's chest. On the other hand, I couldn't deny that I was glad that Jimmy was dead, and when I heard Ruthy in the kitchen, making little clicking sounds, the vision of blood faded. She'd made a pot of tea and was holding a large blue cup in her hands when I came into the kitchen. Or I should say kitchen area. Small, but designed very cleverly. I'd already disposed of my clothes, even though they weren't spattered with blood, and was in my pajamas.

"I see you found the tea pot," I said, "and the tea cozy." I was looking for a sign that she knew I'd gone out in the night. She was wearing a blouse that had been washed so many times you couldn't tell what color it was.

"Sleep all right?" she asked. Did she know something, suspect something? I was feeling hung over, confused, disoriented.

"I got up once to take the dog out," I said. "She doesn't usually need to go in the night, but I forgot to take her out before I went to bed. Just down to the courtyard."

We ate soft-boiled eggs and toast and then went to see Stella in the hospital. I was too tired and too overwhelmed with anxiety to think about the murder, if that's what it was. I thought that if I pretended not to be anxious, after a while I wouldn't be anxious.

Stella was doing okay, but she was going to have to stay in bed for a while. She spoke mostly to Ruthy. She wouldn't look at me, and she flinched when I tried to touch her.

The police didn't come to notify Stella till the next day. They hadn't found Jimmy's body for a while, and then they hadn't known where to find Stella.

What Stella told them was that they'd been arguing and she opened the door to get away from him, and he'd pushed her out onto the highway. What she didn't tell them, till Ruthy prompted her, was that Jimmy had been trying to force her to go down on him.

The police detective, Detective Landstreet, questioned me at the apartment afterward. He knew that I had bought a gun and had been taking shooting lessons. He knew that the gun that had killed Jimmy was a .38, the same caliber as the gun I'd bought at the gun shop across the street. The police had recovered two bullets.

"Jack Ruby used a Colt .38 to kill Lee Harvey Oswald," he said. "You remember that."

I indicated that I remembered.

"That was a little one, though. A Cobra."

By the time he was done he had a pretty good understanding of the way things stood between Jimmy and me, but the more he questioned me, the stiffer became my resistance, my resolve not to be pushed around. I told the truth about everything—all the little things—knowing that little lies point toward larger truths. I didn't want to be caught out. That left one big lie, of course, at the center, like a big arrow pointing right at me. Detective Landstreet thought he could see it, but he couldn't see it clearly. He kept coming back to the gun I'd bought at Collector's, which I produced for him, nestled comfortably in its wood-grained box.

"Are you sure you don't have anything to add right now?" he kept asking. "You know, Mrs. Godwin, no one would blame you for plugging that lowlife. I might have done the same thing myself, someone did that to my daughter, you know what I mean?"

"I know what you mean," I said, "but I'm sure I don't have anything to add."

Ruthy was sure, too. She held up under intense questioning. Detective Landstreet was determined to break my alibi for the night of the murder.

"Could Mrs. Godwin have gone out in the night?"

"Anything is *possible*."

"You were here the whole time?"

"I was at the hospital till about nine o'clock."

"And Mrs. Godwin was here when you came back?"

"Yes. We had a cup of tea."

"You would have heard her go out?"

"The dog makes a tremendous racket every time she goes out. She whacks her tail against the wall."

"And you didn't hear anything like that?"

"Not at all."

"You're sure about that? Because if you're not . . ."

"Look," she said. "There are a lot of truck-stop guys who've got beefs with Jimmy."

"We're looking into that, too," Detective Landstreet said.

The police took the gun with them, the new gun, not the one I'd used to kill Jimmy. And that's the way it ended.

Stella came home on Saturday morning. In the afternoon Ruthy and I filled the window boxes on the railing of the deck with geraniums; we filled five of the seven Italian pots with petunias and two more with basil and parsley.

Stella sat in a deck chair, a recliner, and watched me watch her. She didn't seem to have anything to say, and she didn't want me to touch her.

Later she took a nap, and Ruthy explained, "She's ashamed of herself. Shame can be very powerful. Give her time. She's not ready to face you."

"I'm her mother," I said.

"That's the problem."

"Oh."

"How can she feel that she has to 'face' me?"

"She's embarrassed. She knows she's in the wrong. She didn't come home when her dad died. She barely made it to the memorial service and then she left right away. She wants to make it right, but she doesn't know how. Just don't fuss at her."

"How come I've learned more about my own daughter from talking to you than I do from talking to her?"

"Because you're her mother."

I didn't return to the scene of the crime—TruckStopUSA—but I drove by it on my way to Milwaukee on Sunday afternoon. I had to push aside involuntary memories—the bullet wounds, the weight of the gun in my hand, peeing by the side of the truck. Leaving DNA evidence on the tarmac.

I was still glad Jimmy was dead, but it would have been better if he'd simply gone away, disappeared. And I was dreading the vigil. I didn't see how I could face Tommy. It was not impossible, of course, that Tommy was "glad" too. Or, rather, relieved. But I doubted it. I didn't think Tommy was that kind of person.

I was thinking of the bed in the Palmer House. All those pillows, and the chocolates on the pillows when we came in that night. The awkwardness. The false starts. The goodwill. The final uncomplications of bodily desire.

The vigil was held in Tommy's apartment. The funeral would be in the morning at a church. I didn't want to go to either, but as Jimmy's mother-in-law, I had no choice.

I had crossed a line, of course. Another Rubicon. There was no end of Rubicons. No going back. Not that there's ever any going back. But what was the nature of this line? I'd committed a mortal sin. I'd known it was wrong to shoot Jimmy. It was an act of free will, I knew it was wrong, but I'd gone ahead and pulled the trigger.

Actually, there was a way to go back. I knew the drill: contrition, confession, satisfaction. But I was in no mood to turn around.

I left my car at the hotel, the Knickerbocker Hotel, where Paul and I had stayed a couple of times, about half a mile from Tommy's apartment. I walked—I needed the exercise—down Prospect, a tree-lined street on a bluff overlooking the lake, but the view of the lake was blocked by apartments, and large houses (mansions, actually), including the Wisconsin Conservatory of Music.

I rang the bell, was buzzed in, and took the elevator to the eighth floor. The top floor.

There wasn't much drinking at the vigil. Not like the Polish wakes that I remembered where people banged down potato schnapps and vodka. The apartment was full. Some people were sitting in a corner with a priest saying the rosary. Out loud. In

Italian. Fingers active. I didn't join them. I was surprised to see the coffin, on a stand or dais in front of the windows, which looked out over the lake. I was glad it was closed.

People commiserated, asked about Stella. How much did they know? I wondered. I was going to have to talk to someone. Not at the wake, but later, sometime. Maybe a shrink. Would a shrink have patient confidentiality? But shrinks didn't do talk therapy anymore. Just pills. Maybe I could take a pill.

I could see a car ferry going out. An ore boat coming in. Ships passing in the night. Pictures of Jimmy on a table in front of the coffin. Stella too. Jimmy and Stella together.

Most of the people were older. The vigil had an old-fashioned feel. An old aunt sat by the coffin. She was crying seriously. In black. She was from another world. Unembarrassed. She hugged me, wouldn't let go, spoke to me in Italian. "My daughter, now my grandson. He used to . . . come by my house . . ." She spoke with such a strong accent that I could hardly understand the words. But I could understand the grief—unembarrassed, unrestrained.

Everyone asked about Stella. I said she'd been in an accident. I hadn't prepared my lie very carefully and didn't know what Tommy had told them. I said that she'd gotten banged up in the parking lot at TruckStopUSA. A friend had brought her to Galesburg. It wasn't a very good lie, but it was the best I could do.

Some of Jimmy's high school friends were there, and some of the men from the market. *Nil nisi bonum.* No one was speaking ill of the dead. There was some talk, among the friends, of going down to the truck stop to find out exactly what the hell had happened and take care of it themselves. But mostly people circulated happy memories, turning Jimmy's life into a string of anecdotes. The consensus seemed to be that Jimmy had been a little wild, a good kid, but wild. Even Tommy, who should have known better. Tommy, who didn't want Jimmy to live in his house. Dubious pranks were turned into humorous escapades: Jimmy drag racing down Broadway (the market) with one of the trucks; Jimmy's first car, a 1975 Mustang; his string of accidents with both cars and trucks; the drum set he bought from Goodwill and set up on the sidewalk one night in front of the warehouse; stealing the night watchman's little house, taking it up in the elevator to the second floor; shooting rats in the alley with a .22; hiding in the banana cellar under the sidewalk and pretending to be trapped; stowing away on the car ferry and getting tossed off the boat in Ludington. Tommy had to wire him money to get home. Then instead of buying a return ticket on the car ferry, he hitchhiked up through the Upper Peninsula and then down to Milwaukee. Wearing his blue leather jacket and wraparound sun glasses in church on Good Friday, and the priest refusing to serve him the wafer at communion. The time he forgot to close the door on a car of corn and somebody called Tommy, and by the time he got down to the freight yard a hundred crates of corn had gone missing.

I had a sense of living in a different world. Not just from the people at the vigil, but from the whole world. I had become invisible to all these people. And to my daughter, too. And to Ruthy (probably). I suppose everybody is invisible in this sense. Maybe my problem was that I'd become invisible to myself. I needed a drink, a snort of potato schnapps or Irish whiskey, something stronger than a glass of red wine. Something to turn myself into a different person, at least for one evening. But who?

I stayed till the end. The old aunt—Tommy's mother's sister, Jimmy's grandmother—was planning on spending the night in front of the coffin. Tommy tried to send her home with her niece. "I'll stay up," he said. "I got to talk to Frances a little anyway." But she refused to go.

This was a talk I didn't want to have. I poured myself another glass of wine.

"So what do *you* think happened? Jimmy told me she jumped."

"He pushed her, Tommy. On the exit ramp."

"That's what she told you?"

I nodded.

"Go figure," he said. "She was the best thing that ever happened to him. How's she doing? Does she know about Jimmy? I mean, what happened?"

"The police notified her on Saturday. They came to the hospital. She was two months pregnant. Miscarried in the hospital."

Tommy put his arm around me, and it felt good.

"How's she taking it?"

"She's pretty upset."

"In Gounod's *Romeo e Juliette*," he said, "Juliette forgives Romeo for killing Tybalt."

I was startled, more than startled. I thought for a minute Tommy was offering to forgive me for killing Jimmy, and, caught off guard, I almost said I was sorry.

"It's the morning after their wedding night," he went on. "He's still in her room. The sun comes up. Romeo knows he's got to leave, but Juliet begs him to stay just a little longer. The prelude's scored for four cellos. She forgives him and they sing the third love duet. They sing in thirds: '*Nuit d'hymenee . . .*' And then he leaves."

Tommy started to sing, "*Va, je t'ai pardonne . . .*" but soon broke down. "You speak French?" he asked.

"I can read French," I said, "but I can't speak it very well."

"You don't need to. It's the music that creates the character, it says what the words can't say. Would you like to hear it?"

"I don't think so, Tommy. It's too sad, and too late."

"It's not very long," he said.

Tommy put the CD on and found the track. The cellos began to swell, and after a few measures Romeo and Juliet began to sing. I couldn't understand the French, though I recognized, or thought I recognized, the famous lines about envious streaks lacing the severing clouds in yonder east. But Tommy was right. I didn't need to understand. The music created the characters. Romeo and Juliet on their wedding night. The morning after, actually. But what was I supposed to make of this?

"You know, when you first meet Stella you think she's a supporting character, somebody's friend, a *comprimaria*, like Flora in *La Traviata*, or Susanna in *Figaro*, but she turns out to be a leading lady, a real diva, but not so temperamental. A nice person, like Mirella Freni. It's Freni on the CD, by the way. And Franco Corelli. Two Italians singing French. A studio recording. Freni did Juliette at the Met in 1968. That was the last time she sang in the U.S."

"Paul had a DVD of Verdi's *Otello* with Mirella Freni and Placido Domingo," I said. "He used to show it to his Shakespeare class."

"They did it again at the Met in 1991," he said. He took the CD out of the player, put it in the sleeve, and handed it to me. "Play it for Stella."

The old aunt said something in Italian that I couldn't understand. "In just a minute," Tommy said. *Due minuti.* Holding up two fingers.

"I'm taking my aunt back to Italy in January. Right after Christmas. I go every year. I told Stella and Jimmy I'd take them, too. Maybe you and Stella would like to go. My treat. You got some vacation at Christmas, don't you? They're doing *Tosca* at the Teatro Cilea in Reggio Calabria. That's my hometown. Not Maria Callas, but it'll be good."

Aunt Tina wanted another candle to replace one that had burned out. Tommy got another candle and lit it. He held the lighted match for a few seconds. I could see his red hair. I was standing at a cross-roads, or perhaps a fork in the path. I could see a long way down one road, could see all the way to the end of my life: ten more years of teaching Latin, if they didn't drop the Latin program first; a retire-ment party; a stack of detective novels on the table next to the bed; crossword puzzles; maybe another trip to Italy, to Verona. But I couldn't see very far down the other road. I could see Tommy light-ing the candle, but I couldn't see all the way to Reggio Calabria. When I looked up at the window, I couldn't see the lake. Just the reflection of the coffin, and Tommy's aunt, Jimmy's grandmother, watching Tommy light a match and hold it to the candle. The coffin was blocking the way. All brass and dark wood, reflected in the windows. Heavy as lead.

"Think about it," he said.

He covered his face with his hands, and I could see that he was crying, and I was sure he didn't want me as a witness.

"Tommy," I said. "I'm sorry. Can I get you something? More wine? Tea?"

He shook his head. "Sit with me a minute."

He led me into the bedroom, off the entryway. The bedroom offered another view of the lake. The drapes were open. The moon was full.

He lay down on the bed with his clothes on and asked me to sit next to him. I sat on the edge of the bed and put my hand on his forehead. He put his hand on mine and moved it to his chest.

"Would you lie down next to me?" He moved over to make room.

"Tommy," I said. "This is not a good time. Your aunt . . ."

Tommy said something in Italian that I didn't understand and pulled me toward him and tried to kiss me.

I pulled back. He pulled harder, and I pulled harder too. Enough. I could feel the balance of power shifting, not just physically, but spiritually.

"I thought . . ." he said.

"Go to sleep," I said.

Aunt Tina was still sitting by the coffin when I walked over to say good-bye to her. She said something in Italian that I couldn't catch. She took my hand in hers and repeated herself. *Niente da fare?* I think she was saying. "Nothing doing?"

"*Non stasera,*" I said. Not tonight."

"Started out Polish," Tommy said. "Then Italian. Then hippie. Now gentrification. Sciortino's Bakery's still here, but it's not really an Italian community anymore." We were standing on Brady Street in front of Saint Hedwig's, while the bell tolled slowly, summoning the mourners. It was an old-fashioned Catholic funeral with no nonsense about sharing memories of the deceased. Just the basics. Once the preliminaries were over the priest, his hands joined together over his black chasuble, made a profound bow and recited the confession: "I confess to Almighty God, to Blessed Mary ever a Virgin, to Blessed Michael the Archangel, to Blessed John the Baptist, to the Holy Apostles Peter and Paul, to all of the saints, and to you brethren, that I have sinned exceedingly in thought, word, and deed."

He struck his chest three times and went on: "Through my fault, through my fault, through my most grievous fault. Therefore, I beseech Blessed Mary ever a Virgin, Blessed Michael the Archangel, Blessed John the Baptist, the Holy Apostles Peter and Paul, and all of the saints, and you brethren, to pray to the Lord our God for me."

It was the first time I'd heard the Confiteor in English. I was tempted to strike my own chest three times, but I was distracted by thoughts of Paul. Maybe I'd made a mistake with Paul. Just sending him off with no ceremony. Till later, of course, when we put the ashes in the ground in Hope Cemetery, and then the memorial service.

And then somebody died during the funeral! Jimmy's funeral. Right at the beginning of the Kyrie. I could see that something was wrong. An elderly woman three or four pews in front of me tipped over, disappeared except for an arm sticking up over the back of the pew. I could see her hand, fingers moving, as if she were waving good-bye. Another woman, younger, was kneeling beside her, whispering into a cell phone. The priest finished the Kyrie and kept right on going. The hand stayed in place above the back of the pew, but after a few minutes the fingers stopped moving.

By the time the ambulance arrived people were lining up to receive holy communion and the paramedics had trouble wheeling the gurney down the aisle. By the time the priest got to the Dies Irae the old woman had been hustled out on the silent gurney.

Afterward, back on Brady Street, Tommy started to laugh as he was getting into the limo to go to the cemetery. I laughed, too. Even Stella and Ruthy laughed. Later. When I told them the story. Everybody laughs when I tell that story, and I'll bet you're laughing, too. What are we talking about here? Cosmic irony? Some kind of irony for sure, but I've never figured out exactly what kind. The woman had come to the wrong funeral.

"You want to ride in the limo to the cemetery?" Tommy asked.

"No," I said. "I've got to get back."

He put his hand on my arm and I felt an involuntary response, a deep-down drum beat. "I'm sorry about last night," he said. "I was out of line."

"It's all right," I said.

147

"But I meant what I said about going to Italy after Christmas. You got some vacation after Christmas, don't you? They're doing *Rigoletto* at San Carlo in Naples—maybe I didn't mention that before—and *Tosca* at the Teatro Cilea in Reggio Calabria. Maria Callas did *Aïda* there in 1951. I was twelve years old. It'll be good. Think about it."

I've been thinking about it ever since.

9

Virgo (June–July 1997)

I was eating a soft-boiled egg and reading the Sunday supplement of the Galesburg *Register-Mail*, which was still sitting on the harvest table. Ruthy, who'd taken a few days off, had gone back to work. I was glad for her support, but I was also glad to have Stella all to myself for a few days. I'd been reading to her, but she'd fallen asleep. The house was quiet. It seemed to me that we were living in a house where all the furniture had been covered with sheets to protect it from the light. Jimmy's death was a grand piano. Stella's miscarriage was a sofa on which no one sat. Stella's lesbian lover was a barrister's bookcase. I didn't mind. Better Ruthy than Jimmy. Besides, Lois and I had experimented when we were rooming together for our freshman year in Belmont House at Knox. Stella going to mass on Sunday as if it were the most natural thing in the world? I saw going to mass as a big armoire. And Stella's failure to call me after Paul's death? This was huge, like a four-drawer lateral filing cabinet or a big stand-up desk, like Paul's railroad desk. The question was, how to uncover these large pieces of furniture, pull off the sheets so that we could move around the apartment comfortably instead of on tiptoe.

Stella had been making her presence felt by being cranky. She didn't want to be left alone, but she didn't light up when I came into the room and sat on the edge of the double bed she'd been sharing with Ruthy. I kept probing for an opening, but talking to her was like playing tennis against myself, which I hoped was a good sign. She wanted coffee, then tea. She wouldn't drink either coffee or tea unless it was in her special cup.

"We could paint your room," I said. "I'm thinking the opposite walls eggshell white and the front wall coral." The fourth wall, the outside wall behind the bed, was brick, like the outside wall in the living room. There was no window, so legally the room was a "den," not a "bedroom," but there was a large double closet.

"Is there any tea?" she asked.

"I can make some."

"I'll have some if it's already made," she said.

I started to clear off the small desk that had been Stella's in the house on Prairie Street—putting books, papers, pens, mechanical pencils in a banker's box. The desk was an odd shape—small, but fat, deep. It wouldn't fit through the door to her bedroom on Prairie Street. "You remember how your father had to take this desk apart to get it *into* your room?"

"Yes, Ma, I remember."

"The movers had to take it apart to get it *out* of the room."

"Right."

"I've made some space in the closet," I said. "Ruthy bought some underwear, socks, jeans, and T-shirts for you at Target."

She rolled over onto her stomach, her head turned away from me.

"Would you like another chapter of *The Wind in the Willows*?"

But she was already asleep. I could see a pulse along her neck. A lock of hair had fallen over the side of her face. I pushed it aside. Her face was warm. After a few minutes she kicked off the flannel sheet. She wasn't wearing anything but panties. Her face was pale, washed out, but I could see the young girl in her profile. I could see Paul's face, too, and the funny faces he used to make when he was shaving, and Stella's own funny faces, and I could see her history inscribed on her body. The large mole on her left arm that she tried to shave off with Paul's razor. The long scar on her leg from jumping off the balcony into the spirea bushes when they were in bloom and looked like big pillows. The small scar on her forehead, just under the hairline, from falling out of the jungle gym on the playground at Hitchcock Elementary. The broken big toe from turning a cartwheel in the living room and breaking the glass on the tall bottom shelf of a bookcase. I pulled the sheet up over her legs. We never replaced the glass, but I sold the bookcase for nine hundred dollars to the people who bought the house. On her back were the marks where one of the kids from the Salvation Army (behind our house) shot her with an air rifle. They took turns shooting each other in the back till the commander saw them one day and confiscated the air rifle. The scar between thumb and first finger: a wine glass had broken while she was drying it. Standing in the kitchen, a mother-daughter moment.

I wish I could describe the sound of her breathing—or was it my breathing?—but I can't.

These were all stories with happy endings, and I hoped that the abrasions on her left side, where she'd hit the pavement on I-80, would have a happy ending, too. But how? We'd painted ourselves into a corner. Our story had nowhere to go.

I went into the kitchen and got an orange and then sat back down on the edge of the bed. I was peeling the orange when Stella woke up. She turned over and pulled the sheet up and asked for a section. I put it in her mouth.

"Ma," she said. "You know, I kept wishing that Jimmy was dead."

"And now?"

"But not like that, Ma. Not getting murdered. I told him I wanted a divorce. On the trip. Before I told him on the phone when he called here. I told him I wanted to be with Ruthy. He went crazy."

"Did he know you were pregnant?"

"I didn't tell him. I wasn't going to. I didn't really know myself."

"Do you want me to clean your face?" I asked. "With Noxzema?"

She nodded. "Have you still got my telescope?"

"It's in the garage," I said.

"I want to see something far away."

"I don't blame you," I said. "The farther away the better. How about two and a half billion light years?"

"That might do it," she said.

"I think these big distances liberate us," I said as I went into the bathroom to get the blue jar of Noxzema. By the time I got back she was asleep again.

The telescope was in its box—two boxes, one for the scope and one for the tripod—behind the Christmas boxes. It had been her Christmas present the year my father died and my mother came to live with us—and I was feeling some of that sadness now, and excitement, too.

Years earlier we'd seen a distant quasar through the big telescope at the old observatory at the college, which was no longer in use. Professor Davis had a viewing party on the roof of the new science building before packing up the telescope. Quasar 3C 273 was, according to Professor Davis, the most distant object that most

152

backyard astronomers were likely to see. I was glad to see Stella coming out of her shell, getting excited about something. I didn't blame her for wanting to see something really far away. I wanted to see it, too. See it again.

Professor Davis had read a poem from *The Spoon River Anthology* about Professor Alfonso Churchill, who'd taught astronomy at Knox and had become known as Professor Moon.

We set the telescope up on the deck. It was complicated enough, though not as complicated as assembling the three-burner gas grill from Menards. It was a Meade reflecting telescope with a German equatorial mount that had given us a lot of grief at first.

Once you get the mount properly aligned to the North Star, you can move the scope along two axes, right ascension (horizontal) and declination (vertical), till you locate what you're looking for through the finder scope. Then all you have to do is lock in the two axes and the motor will track your celestial object as it moves across the sky. Not as easy as it looks, but doable. It would be easier if the sky stood still.

We practiced looking at the post office windows, which were frosted. A single pane filled the field of vision, but you could see moving shapes behind it. We examined the upper window of the old Carson, Pirie, Scott building, where we once saw Dick Larson dropping old TVs out the window into the alley for a TV commercial they were filming.

The telescope was already set for 40 degrees and 57 minutes latitude, so all we had to do that night was get it balanced properly and lined up with the Pole Star.

In the evening we sat out on the deck till it got dark and we could see the constellations rising as the earth rolled into the night. Stella went online and found the poem about Professor Moon, one of the few poems in *The Spoon River Anthology* that didn't expose a life that had been petty, spiteful, and disappointing.

> They laughed at me as "Prof. Moon,"
> As a boy in Spoon River, born with the thirst
> Of knowing about the stars.
> They jeered when I spoke of the lunar mountains,
> And the thrilling heat and cold,
> And the ebon valleys by silver peaks,
> And Spica quadrillions of miles away,
> And the littleness of man.
> But now that my grave is honored, friends,
> Let it not be because I taught
> The lore of the stars in Knox College,
> But rather for this: that through the stars
> I preached the greatness of man,
> Who is none the less a part of the scheme of things
> For the distance of Spica or the Spiral Nebulae;
> Nor any the less a part of the question
> Of what the drama means.

Quasar 3C 273 is in the constellation Virgo, which would be rising in the southwest, so we wouldn't be able to see it from the deck. We opened the south window in the living room, took off the screen, turned out the lights, and waited. If I'd estimated correctly we'd see Virgo appear from behind the locust trees on Seminary Street, cross the street, and sink down between the spire of Saint Clement's and the building that housed the gun store.

You can't see Polaris from the living room window, so I had to line up the scope using Paul's old army compass and then wait for Virgo. Virgo is not an easy constellation to see, even though our own galaxy is part of a cluster of galaxies in Virgo. Spica, the brightest star in the constellation, is a binary star, actually, though the two stars can't be resolved through a telescope. A blue giant. It was Spica that enabled Hipparchus to figure out the precession of the equinoxes. But I'm getting carried away.

When Spica finally did appear I sighted on it and adjusted the setting circles so that the scope was aligned with the heavens. I turned on the motor, connected to the RA gear, that would move the scope on the east-west axis in time with the motion of the stars.

"Why is she a virgin?" Stella asked. She was sitting on the stool at Paul's desk.

"Not a virgin, really," I said, "but the mother goddess— ambitious, aggressive, demanding—Isis, Ishtar, Inanna, Demeter, spreading her legs in the sky."

"That's better."

"They probably called her a virgin because they were afraid of her."

I used the finder scope to navigate to Porrima, then Auva, then Eta Virginis. All this took some time. According to my star atlas, 3C 273 should be between Auva and Eta, between the virgin's outstretched arms, that is, or between her head and her outstretched left arm. We wouldn't be able to see it in the finder scope, but I moved the scope to the coordinates for 3C 273—Right Ascension 12:29.1; Declination: -02:03.1—and crossed my fingers.

"Ma," Stella said, "do you think the star of Bethlehem could have been a quasar?"

"Probably not," I said. "Might have been a nova, or a comet, or a conjunction of the planets. But there's no record of anything. The Chinese would have spotted it if there had been. Besides, quasars are too far away."

I knew it was there. But we couldn't see it even with the shortest eyepiece. I used the fine adjustment knob to explore the area.

Nothing. We took turns looking. Nothing. Given the amount of light pollution, even in Galesburg, Quasar 3C 273 was beyond the range of our six-inch telescope, a telescope that gathered enough light to reveal myriad galaxies, nebulae, and star clusters in stunning detail. But not 3C 273. Not from where we were observing. Not even with the window open and the screen off. Not even with the Barlow lens and the 12-mm eyepiece.

"Like the dead," Stella said. "Like Pa. Like the baby. Two and a half billion light years is nothing to the dead." She snapped her fingers. "We're not even getting close."

When Detective Landstreet came back the next day, he brought a woman detective with him. He let her do the talking. She could understand, she said, my feelings about someone who abused my daughter, could understand my fear. He mentioned the ADT home security sticker on the door, and the dog, who was making a nuisance of herself, and the car theft and the restraining order. "Sounds like this guy was a real bastard," she said. "Excuse me. A real jerk."

Then Detective Landstreet dropped a bomb: "The ballistics matched," he said, and then he didn't say anything.

I could almost feel the point of a knife at the bottom of my rib cage and thought I was going to have a panic attack. Was such a thing possible? I'd read an article in the *Register-Mail* that—popular wisdom to the contrary—lots of snowflakes were identical. Was it possible that two different guns could leave the identical markings on a bullet? Or (more likely) that the police could fudge ballistic evidence?

"Then I'm calling my lawyer," I said, "because if you think you can get away with fudging the ballistic evidence, you've got another think coming."

I thought that he could tell from my expression that he'd crossed a line, and knew that I knew that he knew. Now he tried to cross back. "Take it easy, Mrs. Godwin. We don't need to get the lawyers involved. This is all preliminary."

"Preliminary? You're telling me that my gun was a murder weapon and you call this 'preliminary'? Why don't you arrest me?" I was sure now that he was lying. I said, "You don't like coincidences, do you?"

"No, I don't."

"You don't like the fact that the murder weapon was the same caliber as my gun, both .38s. But that doesn't give you the right to falsify the ballistic evidence." I started to say something more, but stopped, not wanting to appear too knowledgeable.

I went to the phone to call my lawyer. The phone number was written on the back of the phone book.

"Put the phone down, Mrs. Godwin."

But I didn't put it down. I dialed the office of Greengold and Fletcher and spoke to the secretary. "Tell David that the police are here, tell him they're saying that I killed someone and they're doctoring the ballistic evidence to make it look like it was my gun that was used . . . No, he didn't *say* that they're doctoring the evidence, but they are. My gun hasn't left this house since the last time I went to the shooting range. Two months ago."

Camilla came to the phone and sat next to me, protecting me.

When David came on the phone I had to slow down and repeat everything. Detective Landstreet kept protesting, even admitting that the ballistic evidence didn't match.

"Now he says that the ballistic evidence doesn't match . . . So he was lying before . . . Now he even admits he was lying . . .".

I turned to the detective. "Is that correct? You were lying about the ballistic evidence matching?"

"It's called 'trying to elicit—'"

Now Stella jumped to my defense: "It's lying. How can you think that my mother would shoot someone. It's ridiculous." I was glad to have her on my side. "Tell David," she said, "that he says now that he was 'trying to elicit' and that in fact the ballistic evidence doesn't match . . ."

I told David.

"Yes, I know," he said. "It does sound like lying, doesn't it."

I was enjoying myself, but I was also shaking inside.

"I'm not going to talk to you," I said to the detective, "unless my lawyer is present. He says that if you're faking evidence, I should keep my mouth shut and save a lot of trouble later on."

The detective protested. "You're not charged with anything. We're just trying to sort a few things out."

I started to speak, but Stella interrupted. "Ma, don't say a thing. Not a word. Till your lawyer gets here." Then, to the detective, "She's not talking to you till her lawyer gets here. How many times does she have to say it? What is it you don't understand?" I sat in silence.

The woman detective tried to explain. "It's perfectly legal; the police do it all the time. It's perfectly legal."

I just sat there. Unresponsive, I think, is the word.

"We're going to have to talk to your daughter, you know," she said to me.

"Not now you're not," Stella said. "You're not talking to anyone in this house. Apartment. Either charge my mother with a crime or get out."

I was glad to see Stella take charge. I thought she'd turned a corner, or that we had turned a corner. And I was right. I thought this was the sign we'd been looking for without knowing it. At least the sign *I'd* been looking for.

*   *   *

We had no more hassles from the police, at least not for a while. They'd shifted the focus of the investigation to TruckStopUSA. I pretended not to worry, and then after a while I didn't worry, though I was always a bit uneasy when the phone or the doorbell rang.

Stella continued to make her presence felt. She wanted a ceremony for the fetus. The hospital had nothing to offer. She asked about the priest at Saint Clement's. "He's a pal of yours, isn't he?"

"Father Viglietti? We go for a drink sometimes, on Saturdays, after confession. We speak Latin."

"You go to confession?"

I laughed. "Not me. After Father Viglietti hears confessions."

"He gave a good sermon last Sunday." she said.

"You don't hear many good sermons these days," I said.

"How do *you* know?" she laughed.

"Just guessing."

"He wears trifocals," Stella said. "They make his eyes jump around."

Pause.

"You don't have to believe, you know," Stella said.

"Do you believe?" I asked. Nervous, as if we were about to have a sex talk, or about to enter a sacred space.

"Yes and no," she said. "It's just that there's something inside me that's got to come out, take on some kind of form, if you know what I mean. So you're not at the mercy of your own feelings all the time. Like Christmas and Thanksgiving, only all year. Like this week. The feast of John the Baptist's coming up. He's the only saint whose birthday is observed by the Church. He didn't take the name of his father. An angel gave him his name."

I didn't know what to make of this.

"He's like the Virgin Mary. Free from sin. Cleansed in the womb."

"Do you believe that?"

She laughed. "No, Ma, I don't *believe* that. But it's a good story. It names something, gives it a shape, externalizes it."

Awkward. But I was glad that she was opening up. Disclosing. Declaring herself. A door had been opened, and Stella wanted to walk through it.

"Is he homophobic?"

"Father Viglietti? Officially or unofficially?"

"Unofficially."

"No. You're not going to find a priest, any man, who's nicer than Father Viglietti. No, I don't mean 'nicer,' I mean deeply decent and understanding. He's not going to trouble the universe about . . . about his own problems. But don't you think you might find a church that's a little less . . . a little more open to . . ."

"Ma, things are changing."

"That's not what I heard. Pope John Paul's pretty hard-nosed."

"It's not going to happen all at once," Stella said. "Maybe you could talk to him."

"The Pope?"

"No, Father Viglietti."

"Me? What do you want me to say?"

"I'd like some kind of ceremony for the fetus. I called the hospital. Nothing. There aren't any remains. Nothing. It all went down the toilet. I didn't even know I was pregnant. Wouldn't have known I had a miscarriage if the doctor hadn't told me."

"I can talk to him. I don't know if there's a miscarriage ritual."

"Ma, there's a ritual for everything."

"I'll call him right now. But first let me ask you something." I laid it on the line. About Stella's string of lovers. "You've got to stop saying 'yes' to everything that comes around the corner. Look at Howard Banks, look at the writer you went to New York with, look at . . . Jimmy . . ." I was using the kind of voice you use when you're telling someone something for their own good. I didn't care for the tone, but it was what came out of my mouth.

"I'm going to pretend you didn't say that," she said.

"I'm your mother," I said. "It's something mothers have to say."

"But isn't she lovely," Stella said. "The first time I saw her I wanted to take her home with me. I never know who I am around her. She's unpredictable. I never know how she's going to respond to me, so I don't know how I'm going to respond to her. It's exciting. I give thanks for her every day. It's like coming out of a dark tunnel into the light."

"She seems pretty stable to me, down to earth."

"And I love her for that, too. I want all of her, everything she's got to give. Even the way she eats her eggs in the morning. And she wants all of me."

"And Tommy's never, uh, said anything?"

"Jesus, Ma. You're a piece of work. His sister's a Saffica."

"Saffron?"

"No," she laughed. "Saffica as in Sappho."

"Oh," I said, and allowed myself to slip into her happiness without asking any more questions. "Let's put this moment in italics," I said, thinking the conversation was over. Thinking that we'd said enough.

Ruthy came back on Friday night and on Saturday morning the three of us walked over to Saint Clement's for a little ceremony.

Father Viglietti was waiting for us in the side chapel. We sat on folding chairs that had been set up in front of a statue of the Virgin Mary.

"Our help is in the name of the Lord," Father Viglietti said, and Stella and Ruthy crossed themselves. I felt an involuntary twitch in my arm. Bodily memory.

"Who made heaven and earth," they said. I hadn't been looking at the printed sheet Father Viglietti had prepared for us. I glanced over my shoulder at the closet-confessionals at the back of the nave, and then back at the program: Romans 8:26–31—If God is for us, who can be against us?

Father Viglietti concluded with a blessing: "Lord, God of all creation, we bless and thank you for your tender care. Receive this life you created in love, and comfort your faithful people in their time of loss with the assurance of your unfailing mercy.

"We ask this through Christ our Lord."

"Amen."

Father Viglietti sprinkled Stella with holy water.

"May God be with you in your sorrow, and give you light and peace."

"Amen."

What had just happened, I wondered? What had been externalized, put into words, given a habitation and a name?

Father Viglietti came for supper. Stella peeled four giant artichokes, the way Paul had taught her. Bending the leaves back and snapping them off, trimming off the green outer layer, scooping out the choke, slicing them into quarter-inch wedges that she sautéed in olive oil and garlic, then a splash of balsamic vinegar, then white wine. She and Ruthy and Father Viglietti talked all the time, and it was a pleasure for me to see the girls so animated, so focused on Father Viglietti. A handsome man. And I remembered Paul flirting with the nun in Rome, Sister Teresa. The one who taught Latin at a *liceo* in Florence. I see now that he did it to make me jealous, and it worked.

Father Viglietti never defended the Church. But he never apologized, either. He just listened.

"It's the beginning of a journey," Stella said.

"For you or for the Church?" I said.

"Both. But I think we've got a head start on the Church."

Father Viglietti asked Stella if she'd talked to Pope John Paul lately.

"No," she said, "and he's Polish."

"Do you speak Polish?'

"Just a few words that I picked up by accident. My grandparents spoke Polish to each other, but I never learned. If I knew Polish I *could* talk to the pope."

"I think his English is pretty good."

I was happy to see them so engaged, to listen to them talk about an upcoming convention in Boston, about a meeting between a group called Dignity and Cardinal John O'Connor in New York, about a poll conducted by the *National Catholic Reporter*, in 1996, that revealed that most U.S. Roman Catholics support full rights for homosexuals in the Church, including the right to marry. About a proposed rewording of the catechism.

"We're coming on strong," Ruthy said.

"Come the revolution," Stella said, "and I'm the commissar."

Father Viglietti laughed.

I thought once again of my early experiments with Lois while we were waiting for life to begin. Hard to imagine now. Hard to remember. These memories were like shadows. Lois and I never spoke of them, never brought them into the light. When we died, they would disappear with us. In those days you couldn't have a man in your room. I'd pushed these experiments out of my imagination, out of my working memory. But now they came popping into mind, like distant but familiar stars as you start to get your night vision.

*   *   *

On Sunday morning, when Stella and Ruthy returned from mass, Stella and I and Camilla walked back to the cemetery for some mother-daughter bonding. Once again I felt I was intruding on a sacred space. Paul's grave. Stella broke down. It wasn't pretty, but it wasn't terrible, and I suppose it was what I'd been waiting for, just being near her and knowing that she was going to be okay.

"It's just you and me, Ma," she said. "Right now, I mean." We'd been alone together for several days, but there were still things that had to be said.

"And the dog."

"You should have called her Lesbia. That was Catullus's girl-friend, wasn't it?" I stooped to pet Camilla and unfasten her leash. She ran off to stretch her legs.

"It's good to have you home," I said. "We can repaint your room, if you'd like, clean out the closet."

"I'm not staying, I can't stay, Ma."

"You're going with Ruthy?"

She nodded.

"That's what I figured," I said, "but I was hoping . . . I was hoping you could stay for a while. Maybe till the first anniversary of your dad's death. In September. Lois says that the spirit of the dead person sometimes comes back on the anniversary of his death. Wouldn't you want to be here for that?"

"Ma, you can't believe that. Lois? That's crazy, Ma. I'm surprised at you."

"You never know."

"Yes you do. You know that's nonsense. Consider the source."

I nodded.

"I'm thirty-three years old, Ma. I can't come back home."

"You could if you wanted to," I said, but I knew she was right. The only thing worse than having her leave would be having her stay.

"What are you going to do?"

"I'm going to take it easy for a while, then maybe waitress at the truck stop for a while. Ruthy's the manager, you know. She's got a business degree from the Illinois Valley Community College in Oglesby."

"I didn't know that."

"Till Ruthy gets her commercial driver's license. Then we'll start driving as a team. Maybe for Tommy. We'll be okay."

I knew better than to ask if she was writing any poetry. But I blurted out the last lines of the poem on the refrigerator. "'I didn't know where he was going, but I was going to find out.' You find out?"

She laughed. "It's not where he thought he was 'going,'" she said, and then she said, "Ma, I'm sorry for everything." She started to go on, but I interrupted her.

"You don't need to explain," I said.

"That's as close as you're going to get to an apology," she said. "I'm ashamed, and I'm ashamed of being ashamed, and there's nothing I can do about it, nothing you can do about it. I don't know how you can stand having me around." She squeezed her eyes closed and I realized she was on the edge of tears.

"You're my daughter, Stella. I love you. But I'm glad you're sorry," I said, "because now I can stop worrying about you."

She laughed. "You don't have to worry about me, Ma," she said. "Not any more. It's my turn to worry about you!"

"Me?"

"What are you going to do with yourself?"

"I'm going to think about all the good times, all the happy times. All the stories. All the Christmases, all the Thanksgivings, all the Halloween costumes. They're in a box in the garage. The photos, I mean. Remember when you came to Verona and went dancing with the landlady's son, and we ate horse in the Caffè Romeo e Giulietta, and the landlady's brother gave you that stone-age flint knife he made himself, and the way he started a fire with chips he shaved off a prehistoric petrified mushroom? And we walked all the way to Porta San Zeno and found the sycamore trees from the first scene in *Romeo and Juliet*? I still have a pile of offprints of the article Pa wrote about them, proving that Shakespeare actually went to Italy, but no one paid any attention to it. You'd think it would have made a big splash. Pa was disappointed, but it doesn't matter now, does it. I'd like to go back some time. Would you like to come?"

"Don't you get tired of remembering?"

"Never," I said.

Stella and Ruthy left in the late afternoon, going back to Ottawa in Ruthy's pickup. There were so many partings to remember: Stella going off to Knox, which was only half a mile away; Stella driving off to Iowa City in the VW bug that we bought for her so she could live out in the country, with a group of poets. Then taking off for New York with the fiction writer, without telling us. Driving off with Jimmy in Paul's car.

Maybe I *was* tired of remembering, but I didn't know what else to do.

10

Colloquia (July–October 1997)

Tommy called. More than once. I put him off. What could I do? I saw him in Milwaukee when I was helping Stella and Ruthy move into their new apartment. We cleaned and painted and bought some furniture at Goodwill. They both had commercial driver's licenses now and were going to be driving for Tommy. It was a two-bedroom apartment on Farwell with a decent kitchen. Farwell runs parallel to Prospect, but has a very different feel, a big city–small city feel. Lined with shops and three-story walkups.

"You don't have to be afraid of me," Tommy said. We were in the kitchen. This was a conversation I didn't want to have.

"I'm not afraid of you," I said. "I'm ashamed."

"You *should* be ashamed," he said. "First you put me at ease, and now you won't give me the time of day. And for no reason. Well, I suppose you had your reasons. But after *Norma*, I thought . . . And not one word of explanation. That's what I don't understand. Not one word! What were you thinking?"

"If things had been different . . ."

"You mean Jimmy being killed?"

I nodded.

"And the baby," he said. "Maybe if Stella'd had the baby every-thing would have turned out okay. Between her and Jimmy, I mean."

"It was a terrible thing."

"I'm glad she found somebody else," he said.

"You're not bothered?"

"My sister . . ." He shook his head. "*Per niente.*"

"That's not what you were about to say."

"I don't know what I was about to say. I know it was a terrible thing, but *I* didn't push Stella out of the truck, Frances. That's what I don't understand. You act like *I* pushed her. It don't make sense. *Non fa senso.*"

I was too embarrassed to say anything.

"*Mi dica,*" he said. "Talk to me, Frances. Tell me what went wrong. You don't know how many times I've been over it in my own mind. *Norma.* Dinner at Spiaggia. You don't want to know what I had to do to get reservations. They were harder to get than the tick-ets for *Norma.* Didn't we have a good time? Didn't June Anderson do a wonderful job? You know, the critics were a little bit lukewarm about the first performance, but that was at the beginning of February, and it was her first *Norma.* By the end of the season she had it down perfectly. Well, you were there. You heard her. And now she'll be doing it everywhere. All over the world. She's put her mark on it."

"I heard her, Tommy. It was beautiful. I got out Paul's old Scribner Music Library and played through 'Casta Diva' on the piano. And I listened to it on a CD. Joan Sutherland. I'll never forget it."

"Let me be blunt, Frances. Some things a person doesn't like to say or hear out loud. But I got to say it anyway. Why humiliate me?

After we're together in the Palmer House with all those fancy pillows on the bed. Two old people, but pretty good. Maybe not for you. What do I know? Who knows anything about women? And then? That night after Jimmy was dead. After the vigil. You could have stayed with me that night. Maybe I was out of line, but you saw how much I needed you to hold me, and you walked away."

"I'm sorry, Tommy."

"Like I said, you don't owe me anything. Except maybe one thing: an explanation. You decided you don't like me? I can accept. You don't enjoy being in my company? I can accept. You got another man? I can accept. You don't want to come to Italy with me and your daughter and her friend? That's harder, but I can accept. But you won't explain yourself, you won't talk to me. That I can't accept. Most people live in fear, their lives are shaped by fear—fear of failing, fear of succeeding, fear of dying, fear of living. What are you afraid of, Frances?"

"I can't explain, Tommy, because I don't understand myself." Or maybe I just didn't want to explain. Maybe I just didn't want to know what would happen if I confessed, told him I'd killed Jimmy.

Sitting in a pew at Saint Clement's, on the corner of Prairie and South, I was contemplating a new board game—*The Roman Republic*—that I thought might be useful in the oversubscribed Roman Civ. class that Father Viglietti and I were going to team teach in the fall. It was Saturday afternoon. I was waiting for Father Viglietti, who was hearing confessions. The line was long. Well, longish. Longer than usual. But not as long as when I was a kid. I was a senior in high school when I made my last confession at Saint Clement's. Pa would bring me in, and Ma. Sometimes they'd go to confession too. What could they have had to confess, I wondered at the time. I still wonder about people's sins. Some sinners were sitting in pews or kneeling;

others had lined up in the center aisle. They all looked so ordinary you had to wonder. A couple of men in overalls, one with purplish lips, one with a blond toupee. A large woman in a cotton house-dress. A mother and father team with two sullen teenage sons, a farm family (I guessed). A handful of students from the college. A little girl on her own in a yellow jumper, her short blonde hair in a pixie cut. Surely no great sins here waiting to be confessed. No interesting sins. I couldn't imagine that God had any special plans in mind for this lot.

I looked back at *The Roman Republic.* It was a pretty hefty box, big enough to hold three or four *Monopoly* games. I hadn't opened it yet. On the cover: a picture of a Roman general in a purple and gold toga, striding forward wearing the sort of military helmet the presi-dent wears in the Doonesbury cartoons on my bulletin board. I was anxious to try it out, anxious to get back into the classroom after the long summer.

I checked the line. It wasn't moving. Someone was taking a long time in the confessional, which was nothing fancy, just a closet in the back of the nave. Three closets. The center one for the priest, the side ones for the confessants. But I was startled, because this time—maybe it was that the light had shifted slightly—all the people seemed vitally alive, full of life, the purple lips shining like garnets, the blond toupee like a flash of sunlight, the patterns on the woman's housedress like stars in the sky, the teenage boys like Greek *kouroi*, the college students like wandering mendicants in their slashed jeans and jagged shirts. And I was thinking that they'd have some interesting stories to tell, that God could have some fun with them.

I was trying to loosen the top of the box that held *The Roman Republic*, which was more than three inches deep, when I heard a voice behind me. Curious. Neither male nor female: *"Vidi quod feceris, et scio quis sis.*" I saw what you did and I know who you are.

I started to turn.

"*Et noli versari,*" the voice said. "*Nihil non videbis.*" Don't turn around, you won't see anything at all.

I realized that the voice was speaking in Latin. I thought it must be Father Viglietti, the only other person in town, as far as I knew, who spoke Latin. We'd both taken Father Adrian's spoken Latin course in Rome, though not at the same time, and we always spoke Latin when we got together on Saturday afternoons, and in front of the students, who seemed to think it was some kind of parlor trick.

I turned around, but I didn't see anything.

Whoever it was was using the classical pronunciation, not the ecclesiastical pronunciation we learned in Rome, which is closer to Italian—"she-o" rather than "skio."

"*Sta in acie,*" the voice said. Get in line.

"I've no intention of getting in line" I said, in Latin.

"Then what are you doing here?"

"Waiting for Father Viglietti. We're going for a drink. And to talk about *The Roman Republic.* It's a board game. I thought we could use it in our Roman Civ. class."

"Too complicated," the voice said. "Seventy-five percent of the rules don't really apply to anything, and the board itself doesn't serve much purpose, and Roman numerals on the coins . . . Come on. Cute, but they make it hard to add and subtract."

"I like Roman numerals," I said.

"Turn the game over to the students. They'll figure it out." I looked down at the box in my lap. "He's a whiskey priest, you know. Potentially. You shouldn't encourage him."

"Father Viglietti?"

"Yes."

"He's one of my oldest friends."

"Frankeska, the police may have forgotten what you did, but I haven't. I saw what you did."

"And you know who I am."

"Exactly."

"And I think I know who you are."

"Of course you do."

"Don't you have anything better to do than hang around Saint Clement's on a Saturday afternoon?"

"I have a lot of things to do. Do you have any idea how many galaxies there are, just in the visible universe?"

"No idea."

"Over one hundred twenty-five billion."

"And I suppose you have to look after each one?"

"And that's only on this side of the visual horizon. You know, the universe is expanding so fast that the light from the oldest galaxies can't travel fast enough to reach Earth. So you'll never see them."

"But *you* can see them?"

"Yes, I can see them,"

"*Probe tibi*," I said. Bully for you. "And you have to keep them all running?"

"It's like trying to regulate a piano and keep it in tune, keeping the four basic forces constant, for example."

"I thought they just ran by themselves."

"Yes and no. It's like concert pitch. It's varied over the years, you know, and it varies from one ensemble to another. But not too much. If the strong nuclear force were two percent stronger, for example, then hydrogen would fuse into diprotons instead of deuterium and helium. The physics of matter would be radically different. You'd have a preponderance of heavy elements; you'd run out of carbon. You'd have to revise the Periodic Table. Or rather, *I* would. Life as *you* know it would be impossible."

"What if it were one percent stronger? Or maybe just a teeny-tiny bit stronger?"

"Well, there are always some tolerances, but in this case they're very narrow."

"What about gravity?"

"Gravity's a little different. Gravity's very weak, you know. Ten to the minus thirty-eighth times that of the strong force. When you pick up that fancy fountain pen that you carry around, you overcome the gravitational force of the entire Earth with no trouble. You can fool around a bit with gravity."

"You mean we could get lighter or heavier?"

"Not so as you'd notice. But I do like to let things slide sometimes, just a little, to keep the physicists on their toes. That's why they keep getting different results for the Big G. It's a moving target."

"The Big G?"

"The gravitational constant."

"Astronomy One-o-one is about as far as I got," I said. "And Lucretius."

"Now there was an interesting chap. Everything explained in terms of natural phenomena. No room for intentionality. Nothing can be created out of nothing."

"I read Lucretius to Paul when he was dying."

"It's really marvelous, isn't it. And these astronomer chaps are quite clever. I have to get up early to keep a step ahead of them. You couldn't have made it up. *You* couldn't, I mean." *Made what up?* I wanted to ask, but God kept on talking: "Look, there's only one person left in line. You haven't got much time."

I looked. It was the little girl in the summer frock. "She doesn't even look like she's twelve. Not even old enough to sin. What kind of sins could she have to confess?"

"Don't you remember when you were that age?"

"Forget it."

"Go, go," he said, "before it's too late. The little girl's the last one. She's going in now."

The little girl entered the confessional. But I didn't get in line. I looked down at *The Roman Republic*. There were no women in the picture except a statue in the lower left corner of a woman carrying a small amphora in her right hand and holding out a bowl with her left.

"That little girl," I said, "always takes her time. What's she got to confess?"

"You don't want me blabbing *your* secrets," he said, "so I don't suppose she wants me blabbing hers."

"What secrets?"

"You had an affair in Rome, didn't you? With an Italian. Guido Bevilaqua."

"Are you asking me or telling me?"

"I'm putting it as a question. More polite."

"Yes, but that was ages ago. I thought you were talking about Jimmy."

"I am talking about Jimmy. Why do you think I'm here? You've got a lot to answer for. You should go to confession."

"You too! *You've* got a lot to answer for. *You're* the one who should be going to confession."

"You need to worry about yourself, not about me."

"And if I don't?"

"It will eat away at you."

"I don't think so," I said.

"There's something perverse at the center of the universe that wants to destroy goodness. Are you part of that something? Or are you going to take a stand against it?"

"I didn't want to destroy goodness," I said. "I wanted to destroy Jimmy." He was getting my back up.

The little girl finally came out and gathered up her books. She tied the sleeves of her sweater around her waist. Then Father Viglietti came out of the center closet and walked over to the side aisle, where I was sitting, in front of a plaster statue of the Virgin.

He took one look at me and saw what needed to be done. "*Esne parata potum habere?*" he asked. Ready for a drink?

I nodded.

"*Ego quoque,*" he said. Me too.

The Sportsman's Bar had been renamed the Seminary Street Pub, but it was still an old-fashioned bar that had once been a speakeasy. I didn't mind the stale beer smell, which a lot of people find offensive, any more than I minded the smell of manure in a barn. It was part of the atmosphere, the earthiness.

I was anticipating the taste of a Schlafly's dry-hopped ale as I slid into a booth. I'd have two bottles. Father Viglietti would have an old-fashioned, maybe two. It was four o'clock in the afternoon. I stretched my legs out on the fake-leather seat and leaned back against the wall.

Father Viglietti brought the drinks from the bar. "*Sperasne umquam ut ignis descendat in aliquem?*" he asked. He positioned our drinks on the table before sitting down. Do you ever want to call down fire on someone?

"All the time," I said. "Students, politicians, Donald Trump. Working on a sermon?"

"*Modo cogitans*," he said. Just thinking. "James and John want to call down fire on a Samaritan village that doesn't give Jesus a warm welcome."

"What does Jesus say?"

"He doesn't go for it."

"That's a surprise."

"*Tu eos progredi dixeris?*" You would have given them the go-ahead?

"Probably not. But tell me something. Do you suppose God speaks Latin?"

I was upset by the little colloquium in the church, but I was excited, too. Feeling that push was coming to shove. I thought I'd crossed a line when I killed Jimmy, crossed the border into another country. Now God was standing at the border, waving me back. "Turn back, O Man, forswear your foolish ways." Maybe I was still in my old country after all. Maybe I could still turn back. Go to confession, make satisfaction. Or I could tell God to go to hell, that I wasn't going to enter that confessional, certainly not with Father Viglietti behind the door.

"*Hoc est in manu hominis cui loqitur.*" Depends on whom he's talking to.

"Does he speak to you in Latin or English?"

Father Viglietti laughed.

"I'm serious," I said.

"It's not as if he uses words," Father Viglietti said.

"Hmm," I said. I pushed *The Roman Republic* across the table toward him.

We had our differences, of course. He used the church Latin pronunciation favored by Father Adrian. I used the classical pronunciation I'd learned in high school and at Knox. He preferred Horace, I preferred Catullus. He admired the Roman Empire, the Pax Romana. I regretted the fall of the Republic.

I got up to get more drinks. He had the game open and was look-ing at the instruction book when I got back to the booth. *"Iesu, Maria, et Ioseph,"* he said. "This is worse than the tax code."

Speaking in Latin slowed us down. We spent an hour looking over the rule book, forty pages of fine print with no clear explana-tion of how to set up the game, how to get started.

I'd finished my beer. Father Viglietti was nursing his old-fash-ioned. If I'd had a third beer I'd probably have confessed right there in the booth, but I didn't. We caught up on the events of the day. It was a good year for the USA: not much was happening; we weren't at war with anyone; people were coming off the welfare rolls; *Seinfeld* had launched a new season; the Bulls had won the NBA and were gearing up to do it again. We didn't talk about God or the meaning of life, though I did tell him my fantasy about the people standing in line for confession, how at first they seemed so ordinary that they couldn't possibly have anything interesting to confess, and then, when I looked again, how extraordinary they appeared.

We clinked our empty glasses.

"Trahens nubes gloriae?" he asked. Trailing clouds of glory?

"Aliquid tale," I said. *Something like that.*

A waitress came over to the booth and asked if we wanted more drinks. Father Viglietti said no, we were fine. I always felt safe with Father Viglietti. I admired him, and Paul had liked him, too. He was a man who knew how to affirm the value of human life without hitting you over the head with the promise of rewards or threats of punishments in an afterlife. But maybe that was just part of his strategy.

God's agenda was to get me to go to confession. His strategy, at least at the beginning, was to appeal to natural law. My agenda was to test my own strength, to measure it against, say, Raskolnikov, whose name came up more than once in our second colloquium. My strategy was to distract God by appealing to his enthusiasm for the cosmos, for the actual physical universe, which he loved the way a boy loves an elaborate model train layout that he has put together with great care on a Ping-Pong table in the basement.

The pattern emerged clearly in our second colloquium.

I got myself settled in a pew with my Oxford Catullus. I'd been working on a translation for several years, but sometimes I just liked to sit down without a pencil in my hand and just graze a little. I first read through all the *carmina* of Catullus in Professor Davenport's class on the third floor of Old Main, back in the spring of 1962. Sixty lines a day, three days a week. No attempt at literary appreciation. I see now that that was a good thing. Without the pressure to appreciate, our responses were genuine. If you liked it, you liked it. If you didn't, you didn't. No need to pretend. All you had to do was sort out the impossible syntax. I liked it, and I think I brought a lot of Catullus's passion to my affair with Paul.

"You've heard people arguing," God said, interrupting my thoughts. "You've read Plato's *Euthyphro*."

"Not since I took Professor Connor's Greek class."

I noted some of the same people in the line. I suppose they'd committed the same sins over again during the week. Masturbation, fornication, evil thoughts. The same little girl too, wearing a different dress, waiting for everyone else to finish.

"Do people argue about numbers? No. How many eggs are in that basket? You don't argue about it; you simply count the eggs. Do people argue about where the Empire State Building is? They might, but if you said it was on the corner of Fifth Avenue and Forty-Second Street, you'd be wrong. If by New York you mean an imaginary city in your own head, that's one thing. But if you mean the actual city of New York, then you can go there and see for yourself. It's on Fifth Avenue between West Thirty-Third and West Thirty-Fourth Streets."

"Where can you go to 'see' right and wrong?" I asked.

"You don't have to go far. Just look around you. Everyone knows the difference between right and wrong. You can't imagine a society in which people praise soldiers for running away in battle, friends for betraying friends, police officers for lying and murdering—"

"Excuse me, Pater," I said. I didn't know what else to call him. "Jimmy deserved to die. He threatened me. He threatened my daughter. He pushed her out of a moving truck! And did you hear what he said to me on the phone? I didn't tell Stella. I didn't tell anyone. He said that if I didn't take Stella to the truck stop that night, he'd make what happened to her before look like a Sunday school picnic."

"Sunday school picnics can get pretty rough," he said, "but I take your point. You could have gotten a restraining order."

"And the chandelier?" I said. I didn't know the word for chandelier in Latin, so I said *lucerne.*

"*Candelabrum,*" he corrected me.

"Thank you," I said. "That's even harder to understand, in a way. An inanimate object. Baccarat crystal. Totally smashed. I never told Paul. I never told Stella, but I think she knew. We were in Paris once—Paul and I—and a man tried to sell us a chandelier. '*Maison de Baccarat,*' he kept saying, '*le premier maison du monde.*' I looked up Baccarat on line. There was a Baccarat crystal chandelier like ours for sixty thousand dollars. I had no idea. Sixty thousand dollars."

"Yes, but yours was not put together by Baccarat. Yours was put together by sailors who bought crystal dangles and fitted them up on a compass frame. So it wouldn't be worth nearly that. It's worth about five thousand dollars, but you'd be lucky to get that. But forget the chandelier. Why do you think you have a legal system? Do you want to go back to a tribal revenge model?"

"An eye for an eye, and a tooth for a tooth."

"You ought to know, Frankeska, that the code of Hammurabi was a way of *limiting* damages, not *augmenting* them. If someone poked your eye out, you could poke his eye out, but you couldn't kill him."

"That's comforting, but how do you get from the Big Bang theory to 'Thou shalt not kill'?"

"You can *see* the Big Bang, you know. If you turn on your TV to a station that's not broadcasting, ten percent of the static that you'll see will be the microwave background."

"I don't have a TV. I mean, we have a TV to watch DVDs, but it's not hooked up to cable."

"Of course. I forgot. You're above the common herd."

"I don't have a microwave, either."

"You can hear it, too. Not the Big Bang—the Big Bang didn't make any noise. There was no air to vibrate, nothing—but the early universe had a series of overtones . . ."

"The music of the spheres? Pythagoras?"

"Not exactly, but close. Like a musical instrument. The early universe was like a tube with holes in it. If you blew through it, you'd get a sound and a series of overtones with shorter wavelengths. You can still hear them."

"Why can't I hear them?"

"The sound waves are too long for the human ear. Baryonic oscillations. The astrophysicists know they're there. They just haven't figured out how to detect them yet, but it won't be long. Another four years. You might tell that former student of yours, Alan Teitlebaum, that if he wants to get in line for some serious kudos he should leave Princeton and go to Carnegie-Mellon. That's where the discovery's going to come from. They've put a tenure track offer on the table. Give him a ring."

"Wouldn't that be cheating?"

"I like to stir things up every once in a while. I tipped off Penzias and Wilson at the Bell Labs and they scooped Princeton.

"Who were they?"

"They were the ones who discovered the cosmic microwave background. They didn't get the prize till later. They contacted Robert Dick at Princeton, and that's what Dick said to his team: 'We've been scooped.'"

"You intervened?"

"Get off your high horse."

"Alan's got some kind of big fellowship at Princeton, he's not going to want to go to Pittsburgh."

"He's a Lyman Spitzer Fellow. They're going to name a telescope after him. Lyman Spitzer, that is. Not Alan."

"Lyman Spitzer," I said, "Paul knew the Spitzers at Princeton. He and his wife, first wife, used to house sit for the Spitzers. House on Lake Carnegie. Really beautiful, but just cement block walls. No plaster. I have some pictures. Somewhere."

"They're in the garage, in a box labeled Princeton. But the box is turned, so you can't see the label."

"Thanks," I said. "I suppose you know exactly where the missing Catullus manuscript is, too."

"The one that was found under a beer barrel in Verona? The Verona codex? The priests hid it under a false catalog number in the Biblioteca Capitolare. Too steamy for them. That's why no one can find it. Then they moved things around and it got buried in the reading room under a collection of liturgical manuscripts. On the south wall, next to the door. Bottom shelf. Verona Cod. MS DCCLXIX (olim 765). It's in a solander box."

"They had a moonrise party . . . the Spitzers. Everybody drank a lot of wine and Paul and his wife—his first wife—jumped into the fountain . . . a lot of other people, too."

God interrupted: "The line is getting short, Frankeska."

I could see that the confession line was down to one person. The same little girl. I'd started to think of myself as *the* little girl. But my last confession was at Santa Maria in Trastevere. I was tempted, but I wanted to know what the music of the spheres sounds like.

"Hurry up. This is your last chance."

"I want to hear them, the oscillations. The music of the spheres."

"All right."

God made a sound. Not too loud, not too soft. Not a sound that's easy to describe, a sort of blatting sound, but musical, too. Somewhere between a major and a minor third, shifting from one to the other.

"That's it?"

"It's like a computer simulation. Otherwise you couldn't hear a thing."

Someone came out of the confessional on the right and the little girl, always last in line, disappeared into the one on the left.

"It's not too late."

"No way. Jimmy was a miserable piece of shit."

"So are most people. That doesn't mean you can just wipe them out."

"What about the flood?"

"The flood. If I'd known how much flak I'd get about the flood . . . Funny, because I never *used* to get flak about the flood."

"Make that sound again."

God obliged. I lost track of time. Father Viglietti was shaking my shoulder. "I'm starting to worry about you, Frances. You were making a funny noise, and I think you were talking to yourself. Are you all right?"

"*Sum excellens*, Father." *Just fine.*

"*Esne parata bibere?*" Ready for a drink?

"*Certe.*" Of course.

"*Ego quoque,*" he said.

Our little ritual.

That summer—the summer of 1997—God and I covered a lot of ground: the categorical imperative, natural law, existentialism, black holes, dark matter, dark energy, the expanding universe, the curvature of space. I was especially interested in the curvature of space because I simply couldn't get my mind around it. But it turns out that space is not curved after all, or if it's curved, the curvature is only local.

"The human mind," God said, "can imagine almost everything. It can imagine—by analogy, of course—temperatures of millions of degrees, and billions of light years. But there are two things it can't imagine: space-time curvature and quantum mechanisms. All the images are misleading. Real scientific understanding is based on mathematics. You can't visualize these things. But fortunately you don't have to worry about either one. Newtonian physics will do just fine. Imagine," he went on, "that you're standing on a flat plane, or plain, either one, in a dense forest. You walk out one hundred meters into the forest and then you walk in a circle around your starting point and count the trees. That will give you your circumference, right?" He spoke as if I'd disputed the truth of $2\pi r$.

"Two pi r," I said. "Yes, that's it."

"Now walk out another hundred meters and make another circle. Counting the trees."

"Okay."

"You should have twice as many trees in your circle, right?"

"I guess so."

"You don't have to guess. The radius is twice as long, so the circumference will be twice as long. *If* you're standing on a flat surface. That's how you *know* you're standing on a flat surface. If you're standing on a curved surface—the top of a hill, or in the bottom of a valley—the circumference of the second circle will be more than twice the length of the circumference of the first circle. Now you can do the same thing with the stars. Pick a point, any point. Go out a hundred million light years, make a circle on an imaginary plane, and count the stars in your circle. Do it again, two hundred million light years. Make a circle and count the stars. If you've got twice as many stars in your second circle as in the first, then you know that space is flat."

"Don't you have to assume that the stars are equally spaced?"

"You don't have to assume it. I'm telling you they *are* equally spaced."

To tell you the truth, I found this information very satisfying. I never liked the idea that space, or space-time, was curved. But God always brought the *colloquium* back to Jimmy, back to natural law and human nature, Aristotle's conception of nature, the Stoic elaboration of natural law theory, the Thomistic synthesis, Hobbes, Locke, Kant, the problems inherent in cultural relativism.

"You've read Cicero's *De Officiis*," he said.

"Of course."

"His son was off in Athens with a huge allowance, but he was drinking and carousing instead of studying. Cicero was trying to put him on the right track. That's what I'm trying to do with you. What's morally wrong can never be expedient. When the Republic needed Cicero to come back from exile, he came back. He condemned Marc Antony, right? And Antony had him killed. Whose side are you on, Cicero's or Antony's? I always thought you were a Stoic."

"The Stoics didn't go to confession."

"No? What about Seneca and Cicero? They reviewed their faults systematically in the presence of a respected philosopher. Now get in line," he said. "We're running out of time. I'm running out of patience."

I was starting to weaken. I'd always admired Cicero. The founding fathers had all admired Cicero. But why didn't he accept Caesar's offer of a job? He might have made a difference.

"Get in line," God said.

"The little girl isn't here today," I said. "Maybe she's run out of sins."

"Nobody runs out of sins," God said. "She's on vacation with her family. Now get in line."

But there was no line, and Father Viglietti was coming out of the center closet. I was sure he was as thirsty as I was.

God and I remained on more or less friendly terms till the end of the summer, and God even offered practical advice—before doing what tyrants always do, that is, resorting to threats.

Regarding *The Roman Republic*, for example. "Stick to the first scenario, the Punic Wars, so that it won't take ten hours. And don't try it with just you and Father Viglietti. You need at least four people, five or six is better . . ."

And my translation of Catullus: "Keep working on it. Work on it every day. Do the marriage poems first; get them out of the way. Save the epigrams for last. Before you know it you'll be done. Don't waste your time sending it to any of the big publishing houses; go to the small presses, that's where the action is anyway. Send it to Hausmann Books in Brooklyn, they've got an editor who knows her Latin. On the phone she sounds like a young girl, but actually she's about your age. They won't send you on a book tour, and they won't offer you much money, but they'll do a nice job."

"Will you write a blurb for me?"

He laughed. "And if you want to see 3C 273 you're going to need a bigger telescope. At least an eight-inch. A ten-inch would be better, but it would be too heavy to lug around. The eight-inch Celestron Schmidt-Cassegrain is probably a little better than the Meade, but I'd recommend the Meade because the manual is much easier to understand. With the built-in computer and the GPS all you have to do is tell it what you want to see and it will point right at it."

He warned me about a coming recession and advised me to get out of the market and buy gold before the dot.com bubble burst. "You've got fifty thousand dollars left from the sale of the house. Tell your broker at A. G. Edwards to put it in gold."

He told me to warn the mayor that Maytag, Galesburg's largest employer, was going to pull out. Despite all the promises.

"Why don't *you* warn him?" I asked.

"I have."

"Do you give everybody these warnings?"

"Everybody. In one way or another."

"Bill Clinton too?"

"I told him to keep it in his pants."

"He didn't listen."

"Nobody listens."

"Any more advice for me?"

"If you sold that car in the garage you could buy back your old piano. And you could afford a good telescope."

I didn't want to deal with the car. "My neighbor Lois says that the dead return on the anniversary of their death to say good-bye."

"She picked up that nugget at the funeral home," God said. "It happens, though. Not often, but it happens."

"Paul?"

"If I were you I'd wait for him in Verona, not Galesburg. That way you could go to the Biblioteca Capitolare and have a look at the Catullus codex. It won't be that useful. It's already corrupt. But it would be quite a coup to find it."

"I can't go to Verona in October," I said, "I have to teach."

"You *could* go," he said. "Take some time off. They can find a substitute. Father Viglietti would take your classes if you asked him."

"I couldn't do that. He's already doing an extra section of Latin 3. And he's got too much to do. The new curate doesn't speak English. Or Latin. He's got the Fall Fest to prepare for . . ."

"You can shoot someone in cold blood, but you can't ask for some time off?"

"Please."

"Father Viglietti's not going to be around forever, you know. The Clementines are starting to flex their muscles in Rome. They'll be looking for men like Father Viglietti."

"I guess that would be a good move for him," I said.

"He likes it here," God said. "He doesn't have the stomach for Vatican politics."

"Should I warn him?"

"He's aware of the danger," God said. "But Frankeska, time is running out. You need to get things sorted out before school starts."

"If I confessed to Father Viglietti," I said, "wouldn't he have to tell me to go to the police?"

"Of course he would."

"Then I couldn't go to Verona, could I? And I wouldn't be able to teach in the fall, either."

"Frankeska," he said, "you still think that because you've fooled the police you can fool me?"

"Is that a threat?"

"More of a warning."

"You're going to tip off the police?"

"I might. I might tell them where to find the gun."

"The police returned my gun. It's in the drawer of the little table by my bed."

"Frankeska, don't play games with me. The *other* gun. The one you used to shoot Jimmy."

"That gun is at the bottom of the Mississippi River. Probably halfway to New Orleans by now."

"I know exactly where it is. And it's not halfway to anywhere. The long barrel makes that gun fairly heavy; it sank right into the sediment. It's right where you dropped it. It might move downstream in a big flood. But not down to New Orleans. There will be a high crest in 2002. The gun will stay put till then. So what's it going to be?"

I didn't say anything. Nothing at all. Just closed my eyes and waited in silence for Father Viglietti.

"*Quomodo agis?*" I said when I heard him finally emerge from the confessional and heard his footsteps in the aisle. How you doing?

"*Paratus bibere*," he replied. Ready for a drink.

"*Me quoque*," I said. Me too.

Three days later I got a call from Detective Landstreet. "If we were to drag the river right below the Centennial Bridge, what would we find?"

"I have no idea."

"If I were to come to your house and ask to see your .38 again, could you put your hands on it?"

"Still in the drawer of the table by my bed."

188

"Are you sure?"

"Look, Detective Landstreet, you already checked the gun. You still can't believe in coincidences?"

"No, I can't. You see, we got an anonymous phone call telling us to dredge the river west of the bridge. It would be a bit of an invest- ment. Divers, a boat, a lot of time, a lot of things to consider. So I just want to make sure we can put our hands on your .38 again if we need to."

"You took my gun before. You kept it for two weeks. What do you think could have happened to it?"

"Would you please check?"

"You want me to look in the bedside table?"

"I'd appreciate it."

I got the gun. Bedside table drawer. "It's here," I said. "You want me to hold it up to the phone?"

"That won't be necessary. Just read me the serial number again."

I read the serial number. "Go ahead and dredge. You may find a gun, but you won't find my gun."

What was he doing? What was he thinking? He'd already seen my gun. He knew it couldn't possibly be at the bottom of the Mississippi. I suppose he was simply reminding me that I was still in the frame.

I was annoyed with God. I didn't buy gold, but I tracked down my former student, Alan Teitlebaum, at Princeton, and told him to take the offer from Carnegie-Mellon.

"Mrs. Godwin," he said, "Why would I do that? I just got married. And how did you know about the offer anyway?"

"You haven't bought a house, have you?"

"In Princeton? Are you kidding?"

"Then what's stopping you?"

"I'm a Spitzer Fellow, Mrs. Godwin. I don't want to move to Pittsburgh. I don't understand . . ."

I tried to explain, but I simply didn't understand it well enough, didn't understand what God meant by "baryonic oscillations."

I went to the mayor's office in City Hall to warn him about Maytag. I'd met him once or twice, and he knew who I was, or appeared to know. He appreciated my concern. "We've given Maytag everything they asked for," he said. "They're not going anywhere."

"Then they're lying through their teeth," I said.

I talked to my broker at A. G. Edwards where we had a little money, about fifty thousand dollars, from the sale of the house.

"Gold?" he said. "HA HA HA."

At our next colloquium I went on the attack: "Pol Pot, Laurent Kabila, Milosevic. Why not go after them?"

"You need to worry about yourself," he said. "Let me worry about Pol Pot and the others."

The more God hammered away, the more I stiffened my back. But the argument was running out of steam.

"They might decide to drag the river after all, or the woman from the rest area might turn up. The one with the white border collie."

"I can't believe you," I said.

"You need to put everything behind you except the most important thing. Now get in line. Clean out your attic."

"That's what my mother used to say: *Clean out your attic*."

"Your mother knew what she was talking about."

At the end of August Detective Landstreet turned up the woman with the dog whom I'd met in the rest area near Ottawa. He called and said he wanted me to drive up to Ottawa to be in a lineup.

"Excuse me," I told him, "Are you crazy? I'm calling my lawyer."

"This is a pre-indictment lineup," he said. "You don't have the right to an attorney unless you've been indicted."

"Whoa," I said and hung up.

I called David. He laughed, but he also asked, "Is there something you're not telling me?"

"David," I said, "do I have to go up to Ottawa and stand in a line-up?"

"Of course not. It's been eight weeks since that kid was killed."

"Jimmy Gagg," I said.

"A lineup would have to take place shortly after the crime. There's no way the prosecutor would go for it now. Just sit tight. You don't have to do anything and the detective knows it."

Detective Landstreet did not call back, but my relationship with God had gone sour. I was furious. The next Saturday I confronted him, and I didn't mince words. I called him a *canis feminae filius* (a son of a bitch) and told him his universe was more like a Rube Goldberg machine than an instrument of precision. I told him that nothing matched up, that none of the cycles were in synch, that if it were a clock, it wouldn't keep good time, that if it were a piano, it would be out of tune. I told him that his music of the spheres sounded more like a gigantic wet fart than heavenly harmony.

God didn't mince words either. He even quoted Catullus 43 at me, insulting my nose, my feet, my fingers, my mouth, my appearance in general, and even—and this is what burned me up, got my goat, ruffled my feathers—my command of spoken Latin. *"Nec sane nimis elegante lingua,"* he declared. He really was a *canis feminae filius*.

I did not darken the door of Saint Clement's again for almost ten years. I continued to have a drink with Father Viglietti on Saturday afternoons, but I waited for him in the Seminary Street Pub.

I did not go to Verona to wait for Paul on the first anniversary of his death. I stayed right in Galesburg, though I mentioned to Lois that I'd thought about going.

"Why would you expect him to show up in Verona?" she asked.

"Because that's where we were happy. We were as happy as any two people have ever been happy. Stella too. She was between boyfriends."

"Go ahead," she said. "If you're not here he might come over to my place."

"Lois, really."

That first anniversary, which fell on a Friday, I waited. Lois wanted to wait with me, but I wanted to be alone. I thought if I could just talk to Paul one more time . . .

I fixed Paul's favorite dinner: tortelloni from Hy-Vee and *costolettine di agnello fritte*—baby lamb chops in Parmesan cheese and egg batter—from Marcella Hazan's *Classic Italian Cookbook*. I set the table for two. I broke open a bottle of wine from Paul's "cellar" in the guest room closet, and a bottle of expensive mineral water. Perrier. Paul liked it, though it didn't taste any better than the cheap Hy-Vee seltzer, and he never noticed when I switched them on him.

The wine was very special, a very expensive La Morra Barolo. I don't know where Paul bought it, and he wouldn't tell me how much he'd paid for it. But he'd been very excited about it, and I'd opened a bottle for him the week before he died. I thought it might draw his spirit back. I was not very knowledgeable myself. But this was a cru, not blended. There were five bottles left. Too bad he didn't get to drink them all before he died. He wasn't supposed to drink wine at all. That was one of the things we argued about.

It was colored a vibrant deep red, and had an intense nose (smelled great).

I spread out the tablecloth Paul had given me one Christmas, beautiful, but much too wide for our long (eight-foot), narrow (thirty-inch) table. I'd cut out a swath and resewn it, but the borders didn't match at two of the mitered corners because I hadn't cut it quite straight. That was not okay, but nothing could be done about it now.

Two napkins, which I'd made out of the leftover material.

I set everything out the way Paul liked it: the jar of flake salt, the Magnum pepper grinder, the bottle of California olive oil (Paul said all the Italian oil was adulterated), balsamic vinegar straight from Modena.

Paul had died in the morning. But I didn't think he'd show up till suppertime. Maybe I was just postponing inevitable disappointment, but I wanted the whole day to anticipate.

What was I expecting? Nothing really. Not a knock on the door, or the rattle of the front door, or footsteps in the long hallway. I don't know, but something, anything.

I sat down at the electronic piano and played through a couple of Chopin waltzes and picked out the melody of an old blues song. "Good and bad times, Honey, well that's okay."

It was three o'clock in the afternoon, and everything was ready. I watched the minute hand on the old French clock touch the 3 and listened to the clock chime four. It had been an hour off since we'd moved and we'd never figured out how to reset the chimes. We tried various methods, but then the clock wouldn't chime at all. For a while. And then it would start up again, still an hour off.

The lamb chops I'd special ordered at Thrushwood Farms were ready to be prepped. The recipe said to ask the butcher to flatten the eye of the chops, but that American butchers wouldn't do it. Maybe, maybe not. I forgot to ask. I could do it at home with a cleaver, but I didn't know what this meant. Just flatten the chop? And I forgot to ask the butcher to knock off the corner bone and remove the back-bone. Oh well.

Now it was four o'clock.

I took Camilla for a walk. I let her run in the park, and then I hooked her leash on and we walked through a small crowd at the depot. Police were there with a police dog, to intercept dope coming in to the prison from Chicago. Camilla saluted the police dog, a tan German shepherd, and we walked south along the tracks all the way to Cedar Street, then up to the Knox campus. Then home. It was five o'clock.

I didn't start supper till seven o'clock. I drank a glass of the Barolo as I attempted to cut just the ribs out of four lamb chops. I grated the Parmesan and spread it out on waxed paper. I put the chops on the grated Parmesan and turned them. I dipped them in the beaten egg and then in bread crumbs, checking the recipe at every step of the way.

I poured a second glass of wine as I added the tortelloni to a pot of boiling water. I forgot the salt and had to add it at the last minute. Too many things were going on. Paul never had any trouble juggling four or five dishes, but I was getting a little confused.

I drank my third glass as I ate the tortelloni and the fourth as I sautéed the lamb chops. The bottle was empty by the time I ate my salad, but I was still functioning.

I managed to get the dishes in the dishwasher and wash the pans.

I was glad Lois wasn't with me. I didn't want her to see me in this condition. I was still functioning, but not at one hundred percent. More like forty percent. Not that she would have minded. She would have enjoyed it, in fact.

I hadn't expected Paul to come, of course, but I'd hoped that something would happen in me, that I'd see something, or hear something. Like Creusa returning to say a few words to Aeneas, though Creusa didn't wait till the first anniversary of her death. Something to ease the pain of the end of the preceding year. *Seinfeld* helped. We'd always rented VCRs at Family Video. I kept expecting to discover one I hadn't seen before, but it never happened. I'd rented one for that night. It hadn't been rewound all the way and started up in the middle of "The Pony Remark." Paul and I both loved that episode, and out of the blue Paul might say, "I hef pony, my sister hef pony, my cousin hef pony."

I started the dishwasher and went to bed.

I repeated this performance every year on the anniversary of Paul's death. I got very good at telling the butcher what I wanted him to do with the lamb chops. After a few years I started making the tortelloni myself, rolling the dough out with the *materello* that Paul had bought in Verona. And stuffing them with pumpkin and Parmesan cheese, ground almonds, and nutmeg. I became an expert on baby lamb chops in Parmesan cheese and egg batter.

Paul didn't show up, of course. The dead, like the horizon, are forever beyond our reach.

PART IV: 2005–2006

11

Ave Atque Vale (June–October 2005)

Father Viglietti was reassigned to Rome at the end of the 2004–2005 school year. He was going to teach at the Clementine Pontifical Academy. The new American cardinal, who had been in the Clementine seminary in Philadelphia with Father Viglietti, wanted to strengthen the Clementine presence in Rome, and the new pope had given him the go-ahead. The Clementine Pontifical Academy needed men like Father Viglietti—men of talent and learning who'd been buried in out-of-the way parishes, men who spoke Latin fluently, men who could be trusted.

Why was I surprised? Everything else God had foretold had come to pass. The dot.com bubble had burst in March 2001 and the market had tanked. Gold had gone from about two hundred seventy dollars an ounce to five hundred sixty. If I'd followed God's advice and bought gold . . . but never mind. Then in May of the same year scientists at Carnegie-Mellon and the University of Maine announced the discovery of acoustic oscillations in the primordial fluid of the early universe, oscillations that can still be detected in the cosmic microwave background, providing support for the Inflationary Hot Big Bang model of the universe. You can *hear* the sounds of the early universe. I'd already heard them, twice, in the back of Saint Clement's. This news did not make headlines in the Galesburg *Register-Mail*, but I got a call from Alan Teitlebaum at Princeton at the end of May. He couldn't stop asking questions that I couldn't answer. How could I possibly have known . . .? I couldn't explain. Three years later Maytag, Galesburg's largest employer, closed up shop and moved to Reynosa in Mexico. I did not get a call from the mayor thanking me for giving him a heads-up.

The news wasn't all bad. I'd followed God's advice and sent my translation of Catullus to Hausmann Books on Nostrand Avenue in Brooklyn. God had been right. The editor who called me three months later—I'd almost forgotten about it—sounded like a young girl on the phone. The first thing she said, in fact, was "You probably think I'm a young girl. But I'm not. I'm probably about the same age as you." The second thing she said was that she wanted to publish *Catullus Redivivus*. The third thing she said was, "We've got a lot of work to do."

We sponsored our last *Roman Republic* tournament in late May, the day after examinations ended. In one corner of the room the fragile Republic defended itself against Carthage. In a second corner the Republic consolidated its powers and absorbed more and more provinces. In a third corner powerful politicians tore each other apart—like crabs in a bucket, as Father Viglietti put it—and brought the Republic to an end. Father Viglietti and I moved from one table to the next, helping students through the various phases of the game, encouraging them to note the parallels between the decline of the Roman Republic into Empire, and the decline of our own Republic, though Father Viglietti still hoped the United States would step up to the plate and assume its responsibilities as the world's only superpower and impose a Pax Americana on the rest of the world. The botched election of 2000 echoed the irregular election of Pompey to the consulship in 70 B.C., though at least Pompey had demonstrated his abilities as a general. The attack on Iraq brought to mind Varus leading his legions into the Teutoburg Forest. But at least Varro had the decency to fall on his sword afterward. Hurricane Katrina brought to mind the eruption of Vesuvius in A.D. 79, though the massive relief effort in the Bay of Naples was headed up, and partly financed, by the emperor Titus himself.

At the beginning of September Father Viglietti and I met in the Seminary Street Pub for a last drink. I had my dry-hopped ale and he had his old-fashioned. We celebrated the results of the National Latin Exam, went over a couple of problems I was having with Catullus 68, apparently written in Verona, and commiserated with each other over Father Viglietti's departure. I wasn't only sad, I was afraid, because Father Viglietti had become, for me, a shield against the indifference of the universe, and I detected God's hand in his transfer to Rome. I was going to be on my own now.

It had been twelve years since we'd met at a fund-raiser for the public library and discovered that we'd both taken Father Adrian's spoken Latin course in Rome. Eleven years since we'd started getting together once a week to speak Latin. Ten years since he'd taken over Latin 3 at the high school—Sallust and Cicero in the fall, Plautus and Terence in the spring; nine years since he came over with a bottle of wine and sat with me on the night of Paul's death and told me that I was on the threshold of a new and abundant life; eight years since I shot Jimmy in the parking lot of the TruckStopUSA. I'd never told anyone about Jimmy, but over our second round of drinks I was tempted to open up to Father Viglietti, tempted to make my confession right there in the Seminary Street Pub. I wasn't *sorry* I'd killed Jimmy—I'd never thought for one minute that I'd done the wrong thing—but it was a burden, and I thought Father Viglietti could help me carry it. But then I thought it was too much to ask. Besides, I was driving him to the airport on Monday. I'd have one more chance.

I did have one more chance as we sat opposite each other in the airport coffee shop while we waited for his flight to Chicago to be called, but I kept putting it off, and then he looked at his watch and said that he needed to get through security before they called his flight, so we said good-bye in front of the 1940s Caterpillar tractor in the concourse, outside the coffee shop, and I listened to NPR on the drive home. Secretary of State Condoleezza Rice was back from Texas where she'd been defending the president's response to Hurricane Katrina. The senate was gearing up for hearings on the president's nomination of John G. Roberts to the Supreme Court. Three teenage girls admitted starting a fire in Paris that killed sixteen people. Two British soldiers had been killed in Basra. A previously unknown painting by Edward Munch had been discovered in Bremen. Photos taken through the wide-angle Burrell-Schmidt telescope in Arizona would help scientists reconstruct the last few billion years of the Virgo cluster of galaxies.

In October I celebrated the ninth anniversary of Paul's death, as I always did, with lamb chops coated with Parmesan cheese. After half a bottle of wine I told Paul about my students. I told him that Stella had taken over Tommy Gagg's citrus accounts and that Ruthy, who understood computers, was now Tommy's office manager. I told him that Father Viglietti had left for Rome and that I'd driven him to the airport. I told him about the challenges of translating and arranging the poems in *Catullus Redivivus*, that my editor wanted to abandon the traditional order and arrange the poems according to type: invective, friendship, love poems, epithalamia. It was a plan that appealed to me, though it was subject to all the ills that plague any taxonomy: overlapping categories, the difficulty of establishing categories in the first place and then of placing particular poems in particular categories, and so on. We did not agree on everything, but it was a happy collaboration. And exciting.

As I was filling the dishwasher I gave him my rendition of Catullus's farewell to his brother:

> I have wandered through many countries
> and crossed many seas, my brother,
> to say good-bye at your grave.
> Words cannot contain my grief,
> and your ashes cannot speak.
> Death has separated us, brother from brother,
> but take these old-fashioned offerings, wet with my tears.
> O my brother. Hail and farewell.

But I wasn't happy with it, didn't care for "old-fashioned offerings, wet with my tears," which hovered on the edge of sappy; and there just wasn't any other way to translate *"Ave atque vale."*

"Hello and good-bye"? I didn't think so, though actually "Hello and good-bye" was probably more accurate than "Hail and farewell."

I pulled my Oxford *Catullus* off the shelf on top of the railroad desk and sat down with pen and paper and set to work, determined to keep at it till I got it just right.

12

100 MPH (Summer 2006)

In June I completed the circle, came back to the place where I'd begun: *Do not resuscitate.* I had to laugh when I thought about it, and when I thought about the nurse telling me not to worry about my clothes. And then losing the clothes. I'd filled seventy pages of my Clairefontaine notebook.

I hadn't been worried about my clothes, of course, and I wasn't worried now. The hernia repair had been successful; Jimmy's murder had been in the cold-case file for seven or eight years. At least Detective Landstreet hadn't contacted me since he'd asked me to go up to Ottawa to see if the woman with the dog—the woman I'd met at the rest area on the night I killed Jimmy—could identify me in a police lineup; God had gone back to tending the galaxies instead of poking his nose into my business, though I have to admit that I'd steered clear of Saint Clement's; I had no classes to prepare, no papers to grade, no late-night teachers-union meetings; some of my students had loaded the boxes from my classroom into Jason Steckley's father's funeral van and stacked them in my garage;

Stella and Ruthy were no longer driving over the road, so I didn't have any reason to worry about them; Quintus Lutatius Catulus had been replaced by Gaius Valerius Catullus on the jacket of *Catullus Redivivus*; and three blurbs had arrived out of the blue, including one from the man who'd kept kissing his student-lover during his reading in the Common Room and one from the woman who'd talked on her cell phone while she was being introduced. I forgave them both.

All I had to worry about now was whether it was too late to find some decent geraniums for my window boxes on the deck.

All I had to worry about now was clearing out the garage, which was so full that I had to park the Cutlass Cruiser outside in the city parking lot.

All I had to worry about now was life itself. How to fill up the thirty blank pages at the end of the beautiful Clairefontaine notebook. I thought maybe I'd be able to add a page or two at most, but my plan was to lie low for a while.

Looking back I thought I could see things clearly, thought I could look down on my life as if I were standing on the Fourth Street Bridge watching it—my life—rolling down a track in the hump yard, rolling down to my destination track in the classifica- tion bowl. Of course you can't actually see the hump yard from the Fourth Street Bridge. To see the hump yard you have to drive out all the way to the bridge on County Highway 10, by Old Thirlwell Road.

But that's the problem with autobiography, isn't it? Especially spiritual autobiography. You can't quite see everything from where you're standing. You see a shape, you see ups and downs, conver- sions, turning points, reversals. But then you keep on living, you keep on driving from one bridge to the next, and every time you look down on your life, you see a different shape.

That's what happened to me. I kept on living, kept on driving, kept on glancing at my rear-view mirror, trying to discern the shapes, when I should have been keeping my eyes on the road. If I had, maybe I would have seen what was coming. But maybe not. Would I have done anything differently? No, I don't think so.

By the end of the month I was ready to tackle the garage, but the garage wasn't ready to be tackled. Fortunately Stella and Ruthy were driving down from Milwaukee to give me a hand, do the heavy lifting.

We hadn't had a garage on Prairie Street, but we'd had a big attic, and everything from the attic was now in the big garage at the apartment—Paul's papers and notes, old Latin tests and quizzes, boxes of letters and newspaper clippings, Stella's baby clothes, our bikes, the license plate from Pa's old Studebaker. Plenty of stuff to inflame memory. And the sports car, of course. I wanted that car out of there. I didn't even know what kind of car it was, but it reminded me of how helpless Paul had been at the end. Half a dozen trips around the parking lot was all he'd managed. And it reminded me of how Jimmy had stolen the car and all the repercussions of that theft.

But I couldn't pull it out of the garage because all the boxes from my classroom were piled up behind it, or in front of it, depending. Boxes of books, boxes with all the models of Roman buildings, boxes of posters and signs in Latin. I couldn't move the boxes because of the hernia. Besides, there was no place to move them *to*. I couldn't move the flower pots for same reason. The pots were plastic, but they were full of dirt, and I didn't think it was a good idea to lift them.

Stella and Ruthy arrived late that night and we got to work early in the morning. It was a sunny day, so they stacked the boxes from my classroom outside in the parking lot to clear a path for the car. But when we tugged off the heavy tarp, Ruthy started hyperventilating. "It's a Shelby Cobra," she said. "Do you know what you've got here? It's a fucking Shelby Cobra. Pardon my French, but this is too amazing. You didn't know? And Paul didn't know?" She kept shaking her head and laughing.

"It doesn't have any windows," I said. "And there's no top."

"No top," she said. "No windows, no door handles, no power steering, no power brakes—just the basics."

"What do you do if it rains?"

"You get wet."

What I knew about cars I'd learned from helping Pa tune up his Ford pickup with 250,000 miles on it, out at the farm, and his 1952 eight-cylinder Packard Mayfair, with interior leather that matched the cranberry top over a cream body, and the Studebaker he bought so someone could drive Ma around.

I closed the garage door, so no one would steal the car, and we went upstairs, booted up my computer, and googled "Shelby Cobra." The 427 Cobra was the first American car to beat Ferrari—the first time any car had beaten Ferrari—in the Fédération Internationale de l'Automobile World Manufacturers' Championship in 1965 at Reims. If it was an original, then we were looking at over three hundred thousand dollars. Probably more. Depending on the model. Ruthy wasn't sure ours was a 427. It might be a 289.

Dr. Palmer's widow had died years earlier, so I couldn't get any information from her. I called Larry at Jones and Archer, where I still had the Oldsmobile serviced. "Probably a kit," he said, "or a continuation car."

Stella and Ruthy had brought braunschweiger from Usinger's, and a loaf of dark rye, and we made sandwiches and ate them while we waited for Larry. Paul loved braunschweiger. I'd never cared for it, but today it tasted wonderful.

When Larry arrived and looked at the car, all he could do was shake his head. "You know," he said, "this used to be every boy's dream. When I was a kid we used to drive around and look in old barns, and behind them, hoping for something like this. We used to buy some old cars and sell them to the junk yard, but nothing like this. And it's been right here in your garage?"

"Ever since we moved in."

"What Shelby did," Larry said, "was put a high-powered Ford engine in a British chassis. Guy over in Knoxville's got one, you might want to talk to him. But his is a two eighty-nine. This is a four twenty-seven." He popped the hood. "You can't be sure from the VIN number," he said, "because Shelby counterfeited some of his own cars. He had a block of VIN numbers for a hundred four twenty-sevens, but they only sold about fifty. Then in the nineties when the price of Cobras skyrocketed, he put together some cars from old parts, seated them on new chassis, and used the leftover VIN numbers to claim they were 1966 Cobras. But that was in the nineties."

"This car's been sitting here," I said, "ever since they built these apartments. That was in the eighties, and Dr. Palmer probably had it a long time before that. I don't know."

Larry kept shaking his head in wonder. "You ever see Bill Cosby's routine about *his* Shelby Cobra? Shelby made it special for him. A Supersnake. It's on YouTube. It's called 'Two Hundred MPH.' There were only two of them. Shelby sold one to Bill Cosby and kept one for himself."

It was my turn to shake my head as we stood in silence, staring down at a powerful Ford engine that didn't look anything like the engine in Pa's Ford pickup. I put my finger on the new battery I'd put in myself. I touched the radiator, the carburetor, and the air intake values, which looked like silver drinking goblets.

"I don't suppose you want to sell it?" he asked.

"How much?"

"I could probably give you fifty."

"Fifty dollars?"

"Fifty thousand. It'd take a while to get the money together."

"Probably not, Larry, but let me do some checking first, okay?"

"Look up Bill Cosby on YouTube," he said. "'Two Hundred MPH.' He makes all the engine sounds. It's pretty convincing." Pause. "But it was too much for him. He was afraid to drive it. He took it back. Shelby sold it to another guy who drove it off a cliff into the Pacific Ocean."

It was three o'clock when Larry left. We watched the Bill Cosby routine on YouTube and then called Tommy for some advice, and then I started calling auction houses: Barrett-Jackson, Gooding, RM—but they were all pretty snooty. Tommy had recommended the Bascomb Summer Classic in Indianapolis as the place for muscle cars. When I told the Bascomb customer rep that I had a 1966 Cobra 427, Mr. Bascomb himself, Lloyd, got on the phone—a rough sounding character, but very helpful—and explained everything I needed to know and everything that needed to be done before the July deadline: VIN, registration, photos, position request. They needed photos right away, and Ruthy spent the rest of the afternoon taking pictures from every angle with a new digital camera.

The insurance office was closed, but I called Connie at home and she told me I couldn't put a Shelby Cobra on my insurance policy. I'd have to go to Lloyd's of London or someplace like that.

"Lloyd's of London," I said. "Are there other places like that?

She gave me some names—Hagerty, Classic, Voyager—which I wrote down in the back of the phone book. My hand was shaking. She said she'd get the numbers for me on Monday. "Just don't drive it around tomorrow."

We put the tarp back on the car so that if thieves broke into the garage, they wouldn't see it.

And then we celebrated.

I made a big salad and cooked spaghetti alla carbonara using a recipe from a cookbook we'd brought back from Verona. "It's simplicity itself," I explained. "I don't know why Paul always had so much trouble. Some cookbooks tell you to leave some of the cooking water on the spaghetti, so the water will cook the egg, but the water just dilutes the egg and makes it runny. What you've got to do is use one medium egg for exactly one hundred ten grams of pasta. That's a quarter of a pound."

Ruthy grilled a steak on the deck and we ate the spaghetti while the steak rested. The deck was barren, but on Sunday we were going to bring the flower pots up and look for some geraniums for the window boxes.

We opened the last bottle of Paul's Barolo—which I'd saved for a special occasion—and stayed up drinking and talking and eating strawberries. We talked about our good fortune, and Stella ragged on me about going to Italy in January. "You're rich now," she said, "and you're retired. You haven't got any excuses."

"Is that young woman still coming to see Tommy every Wednesday?"

"Every Wednesday, Ma, and Tommy cooks supper for her."

"I'll bet he does," I said. I wondered if she was beautiful.

"Of course she is, Ma," Stella said, as if she'd read my mind. "I already told you, she's a graduate student at Marquette."

"That's doesn't mean she's beautiful. It just means she's young."

"I've only seen her once," Stella said. "She's definitely beautiful. But what's your point?"

"What's my point? You don't get my point? Let me put it nicely: so why doesn't he invite *her* to go to Italy?"

"He could. He could invite anyone he wanted to, but he invited you. Figure it out. I guess he wanted *you* to go. You don't have to go, but you don't have to cold-shoulder him when he comes to dinner. Ma, I don't understand you. You could come to Italy with us. Why not? It would give you something to look forward to."

"Enough, Stella. I've got plenty to look forward to. I've got to auction off a Shelby Cobra four twenty-seven in August and I've got a book coming out in September. I'm thinking about taking up the piano again. I've still got all my music. Most of it's in a box in the garage."

I hadn't been able to avoid Tommy, of course. He'd taken both the girls to Italy in 2003 and again in 2005 and they'd come back committed opera buffs. Stella insisted on inviting him to dinner when I went up to Milwaukee for a visit, and one night Tommy had brought a DVD of the Marx Brothers' *A Night at the Opera* and had sung along when Harpo inserts the sheet music of "Take Me Out To The Ballgame" into the conductor's score of *Il Trovatore*.

I hadn't forgotten Tommy's invitation, of course. An invitation conveyed through Stella. But what could I do? I'd killed the man's brother's son, his heir. I didn't see how I could sit next to him on a flight to Italy. Not even in a first-class seat. Or at the opera in Naples or Reggio Calabria. Not even in a couple of boxes on the mezzanine. I could see that saying no was the price I'd have to pay for killing Jimmy. I thought I could see God's hand in this, just as I had seen it in Father Viglietti's transfer to Rome. Everything had become clear: I'd been outmaneuvered.

I sent the paperwork off to Bascomb on the first of July—Ruthy's photos and a thousand-dollar payment for the "Star" entry, which gave us special covered parking, individual national ads, a scheduled run time, and Bascomb Web Marketing. I put down five hundred thousand dollars as the expected selling price! Why not? Estimated reserve? Hmm. Would I be willing to settle for—what? Four hundred thousand? Three? Bascomb's title search revealed that Dr. Palmer had bought the car from a Ford dealer in the Quad Cities in September 1966 for $5,995.00. I settled on four hundred thousand, which sounded pretty good to me. And Larry helped me put together a list of key points.

- Documented in Shelby American World Registry
- Original invoice (in the glove compartment) from A. C. Cars to Shelby American.
- Under 10,000 miles from new.
- Original 427 engine.
- Unrestored.
- No accidents, no "stories."
- No metal fatigue, no bowing, no cracking.
- Starburst wheels.
- Dash-mounted rear-view mirror.
- Brake fluid and oil have been changed.
- Original dual 4-V manifold and carburetor in original configuration.
- Carburetors and starter checked prior to shipment for sale.

The auction opened on August 10. The Cobra 427 would go on the block at 2:35 on Saturday the twelfth. We—Stella and Ruthy and

I—stayed at the Hampton Inn, generic but comfortable. Two double beds, big screen TV, mini-bar. The car had been picked up by a car transport company, Reliable. Another eight hundred dollars with insurance.

I'd never been a car buff, but the cars that we looked at during the preview brought back memories: lots of muscle cars from the sixties and seventies, a host of Chevy Bel Airs from the fifties, a 1946 half-ton Ford pickup like Pa's, and a 1950 Nash Airflyte with a reclining "airline" seat, the car in which several of my high school classmates had lost their virginity. I wasn't happy to see a total of three 1966 Shelby Cobras, but two of them were 289s. Mine was the only 427. In January Barrett-Jackson was going to auction a 1966 Cobra that was expected to bring over three million, but that was Shelby's personal car, the Supersnake. Like the one that had belonged to Bill Cosby, the one that wound up in the Pacific Ocean.

I enjoyed *Car Talk*, but my own personal car history was not very exciting. Paul had wanted a Mazda Miata, but we both drove Oldsmobiles. We sold the Alero when Paul couldn't drive any longer. I was still driving our Cutlass Cruiser when Oldsmobile went out of business in 2004. In fact, I was still driving it.

At the auction, which was held in the Pepsi Coliseum at the Indiana State Fairgrounds, I did a brief television interview, live, in which I managed to conceal my ignorance by focusing on preservation versus restoration. The two other Cobras coming on the block had both been restored. And of course I emphasized the "barn find" aspect of my story, which I'd rehearsed. The car was every collector's dream: you go into an old barn and there's a Shelby Cobra, or a 1950s Jaguar, or a 1955 Aston Martin that's been sitting there forever, preferably covered with a tarp.

The first Cobra, a 289, was pushed down the runway at 10:30, the second, another 289, at 1:00. The bidding for both topped four hundred thousand dollars, but neither met the reserve. When Paul's Cobra, a more powerful 427, appeared at 2:35, I saw it, really saw it, for the first time. Saw what Paul had seen. Like an Impressionist painting. The original deep red paint had faded, but you could still look through it, like looking through a slight disturbance on the surface of a sunlit pond into the depths. Smooth lines directed the eye from one surface to another without interruption.

As they were pushing the car down the runway the announcer began his spiel: a car is "original" only once. "This is it. Under ten thousand miles. Preserved. Not restored. The history of the car has not been removed. Everything original except the battery."

The bidding started at 2:40. We had a very good position. Two Cobras had already failed to meet their reserves. A Bascomb rep whose job it was to allay anxiety was at my side. "Those were two eighty-nines," she said. Yours is a four twenty-seven."

The Pepsi Coliseum was huge. The cars came down a lane in the front against a background of yellow panels with BASCOMB on them. The bidders sat on folding chairs, but some of them came right up to the front and chatted with the sellers, asking question during the bidding. A big screen on the left of the auctioneer's podium showed a photo of the car, the lot number, and the current bid. Auctioneer at a platform. Like a big podium, or a pulpit, like the one the high school principal stands behind at commencement.

Mr. Bascomb, Lloyd, was not the auctioneer. But he put on quite a show, mock fighting with his employees, shouting, haranguing the bidders. Guy stuff. Testosterone stuff. "This is a great barn find," he shouted. "One of the greatest. You take the cookies when the cookies are passed. You've got a chance to bid on a dream."

The bidding on Paul's car started slowly and stalled at $375,000. Bascomb started shouting at me to cancel the reserve.

I shook my head.

The bidding moved, but only slightly. If the auctioneer brought his hammer down short of the reserve we'd have to start all over.

I was getting used to the auctioneer's chant. Steady rhythm. Two-four time. Then three-four when he accepted a bid. He was saying something between the numbers. The numbers rang out clearly, but I couldn't tell what he was saying in between. There were several bidders at first, mostly in the reserved section in the front.

One of the bidders, however, stood next to me the whole time. A very handsome man—tall, bald, mustachioed. Not a dealer, a bidder's badge pinned on a black suede jacket.

By the time the bidding got serious he was up against two men in the front row of folding chairs. One of these men looked like Einstein. He was on a telephone, taking instructions from someone over the phone. His wife sat next to him. Another bidder farther down wore a canvas hunting jacket with the collar turned up. Also with wife. The third bidder: Ron, standing right next to me. I knew his name because Bascomb himself had called him by name.

One of the ring men—the auctioneer's assistants—ran back and forth between the two front-row bidders.

"Drop the reserve," Ron said.

"What if people stop bidding?"

"They won't."

"I don't care," I said. "I want you to have it."

"Don't talk like that."

"Did you bid on the first ones?"

He shook his head. "This is the one I want," he said. "No modifications. Nothing. Original tires. Original paint. You can't drive it on those tires, of course, but . . ."

I was afraid to look at Stella and Ruthy. But of course I did look. They seemed to glow. They were looking at me, encouraging me. "Do it, do it." I dropped the reserve. Mr. Bascomb started shouting and pounding his arm up in the air. "Somebody's going to drive this car home," he shouted. "This is the car that put Corvette in the trailer. This is the car that beat Ferrari at Reims," which he pronounced *rems*. "This is the only American car in a class with Ferrari, Bugati, Maserati. This is an American icon. It's your patriotic duty to keep bidding. What are you afraid of? You've let two of them get away. You're embarrassing me. You should be ashamed. You're embarrassing your country."

The auctioneer was going breath breath . . . four hundred, breath breath . . . four fifty, breath breath, four seventy-five, breath breath . . .

"Don't embarrass your country again," Bascomb shouted.

"Five hundred . . . five twenty-five . . . five fifty . . ."

"This is a real original. Not restored. Not repainted. Original tires. Original paint," he said, as if he'd been listening to Ron, next to me.

I had to look at the screen to understand the bid. I could hear the numbers, and I was starting to understand the auctioneer's filler words, which were like one of those prayers that some monks repeat all day long. *"Lord Jesus Christ, Son of God, have mercy on me, a miserable sinner."*

I started to feel faint. Looking at the car. Seeing it. It was like seeing Paul for the first time, like walking into his classroom for the first time, or like walking along the Janiculum with Sister Teresa and seeing him sitting on a bench feeding the pigeons. Like opening my eyes and seeing him sitting on the couch after the Shakespeare party, touching my hair to wake me up, though in fact I was wide awake, telling me it was time to go home. Or like seeing Stella for the first time, the doctor holding her by her feet.

I started remembering all the times Paul and I had sat in this car, in the cockpit, Paul with his portable oxygen supply. His hands on the wheel.

"I used to sit in the car with my husband," I said, "when he was dying. He drove it around the parking lot a few times. That was it."

"Five fifty."

"I reread almost half the *Aeneid* in the cockpit of that car. We'd open the garage door so we could look out on the parking lot, people walking by, stopping to wave."

Ron bid five seventy-five. I shut my mouth.

The auctioneer asked for six hundred. Over and over. Bascomb went into a frenzy and seemed by the strength of his enthusiasm to push it past six hundred thousand. Two ring men huddled with the bidders in the front now, one on Einstein and one on the man in the hunting jacket. Bascomb himself kept hammering away at Ron. Talking to him the way he might talk to an old friend.

After a couple of dramatic pauses the bidding edged up to seven hundred thousand and change ($720,000) before the hammer came down. I wasn't sure what had happened, but Ron put his arms around me and Lloyd Bascomb was pounding me on the back, pounding Ron too.

The instant the gavel came down, the car was no longer mine. That's the way it works. It now belonged to a tall bald man with short, straight mustaches that matched his short, straight eyebrows. Ron. We walked out together next to the car, driven by one of the Bascomb agents. By the time we got to the Bascomb office I was crying.

"I'm sorry," Ron said. "I'm sorry."

I couldn't stop crying, even though a check for $720,000, less commission, was waiting for me at the Bascomb office.

"Where did the money come from?" I asked.

"They know me here," he said. "And I have a line of credit."

"Must be a long one," I said.

I'd already surrendered the title, along with the car, so all I had to do was show some ID and pick up my check. I folded the check in half and put it in my purse. You'd think a check that size would take up a lot of space, but it fit comfortably between a twenty dollar bill and a little single-use floss envelope that I carried for emergencies.

"Look," Ron said, "how about a cup of coffee."

"I'm all right," I said.

"I know how it is. I sold a four twenty-seven just like this one four years ago and I've never gotten over it."

"You know why I'm crying?" I asked, surprising myself. "I'm crying because I never drove it. All these years it was sitting in our garage. My son-in-law was crazy to drive it. He stole it once, and my husband called the police. He had a pretty serious record—my son-in-law did—and spent some time in jail. After my husband died—I never really saw it after that, maybe two or three times. We kept a tarp over it. But I'm sorry. I shouldn't be bothering you with this. It doesn't matter."

"Would you like to drive it now?" he said.

The Bascomb driver got out and shook Ron's hand.

Ron held the door. "Get into the cockpit," he said.

"Do they really call it a 'cockpit'?" I asked.

"You'll see when you get it."

"I couldn't do that," I said.

"Yes," he said, and "Of course you could." He took my arm and maneuvered me into the cockpit. "Sit tight. I'll just be a minute.

I've got to call my insurance agent and tell him to put the car on my policy."

"I won't know what to do," I said, thinking of the Bill Cosby show, which I'd watched several times on YouTube.

"You know how to drive a stick shift?"

I nodded.

"Then there's nothing to it. You need to brake with your left foot, that's all. That's why the pedals are skewed to the left. But take it easy till we get some new tires."

The figures on the speedometer, I noticed, went counterclockwise, all the way up to 180 MPH.

"What about seat belts?" I asked.

"Wait till we get some insurance and some new tires."

He made the call on his cell phone. Once the car was insured, I turned the key and the car roared. I eased it out of the lot and we drove out a long diagonal street, Binford Boulevard, to a tire store near the beltway. "I already ordered the tires," he said. It was hard to hear over the roar of the engine, even though we were going only twenty-five miles an hour. At first the car leaped and bucked, but by the time we got to the tire store I had it more or less under control. "Cokers," Ron said. "Corky Coker bought up all the molds for the old fourteen-inch polyester tires. I had to order them online."

"What if you hadn't gotten the car?"

"Then I'd have four extra tires."

It didn't take long to get the new tires balanced and aligned. Ron got me hooked into the complicated five-point harness, hooked himself in, and we were back on Binford Boulevard heading out toward the Hampton Inn. When we came to the end of Binford Boulevard I started to follow 69 north toward Fort Wayne (and toward the Hampton Inn) but Ron told me to head west on the 465 beltway.

"Do your braking before you start the turn," he said as we approached the entrance ramp. "Use your left foot on the brake. Now find your apex, your racing line, halfway between the shortest possible turn or corner and the longest possible turn or corner. You want to minimize your time in the corner and maximize your speed at the same time. It takes a while, but you'll figure it out."

My apex? My racing line? I thought of the imaginary line that Stella used to guide the trailer into the tight spot between the Wilkins truck and the Leshinsky potato truck.

"As you let up on the brake, *push* the top of the steering wheel into the turn. Don't pull it. Hit the gas as you come out of the curve. You want to feel the center hold when you accelerate."

I was glad we were going only fifty miles an hour. I had a little time to think.

Pulling out of the curve. Speeding up. I could in fact feel the weight shifting toward the rear. Could feel the power.

"Aim high in your steering." He had to shout.

"What's that supposed to mean?"

"Look all the way down to the end of the road," he said. "And keep your eyes moving. Look in your mirrors."

I did what he said.

"Hug the centerline," he shouted, and "Relax. This is a sports car, don't hold up traffic." He laughed.

At sixty miles an hour it was getting harder to hear—over the wind, over the roar of the engine. But not impossible as long as we weren't accelerating.

"Now pass that big ugly Lincoln," he shouted. "Get his attention first, make sure he knows you're coming. Center yourself on his outside mirror."

I remembered my father teaching me how to drive in the cemetery—Hope Cemetery. A police car came into the cemetery and pulled us over. The cemetery, the policeman said, wasn't a place to teach someone to drive. I was never sure why not.

"Don't pull into the left lane and then slow down. Put the power on and keep it on till you've passed him. One smooth motion. When you speed up you throw the weight onto the back tires, and that gives you more traction. Keep the weight back there. Now doesn't that feel good?"

It felt very good. I pulled back into the right lane. And then we passed another car, and another, till we were passing everything on the road.

We got up to eighty when passing and then I slowed down to seventy.

We passed the exit for 31 north to Kokomo and South Bend, and the turnoff on 865 west, which cuts over to 65 north to Gary.

"We're going to take I-74 west to Champaign," he put his mouth up to my ear. "I want you to work on your cornering.

I thought we'd been on the road about twenty minutes, but I was going so fast now I didn't want to look at my watch. I cornered onto I-74, heading toward Galesburg, or was it Kentucky, I wasn't sure. I did my braking before the exit, looked for the apex, for the racing line, lost it in the turn, found it again as we got onto I-74. I could feel the rear tires balancing as we came out of the curve.

Ron was silent. Relaxed.

"Open it up a little," he might have said. I couldn't hear the words, but I could understand his hands. "More. More." He was making a rolling motion with his right hand.

We went faster and faster. It was unnerving at first. But then I got a sense of control.

At ninety miles an hour I was afraid to take my eyes off the road. The car shuddered and bucked, and my arms were getting tired, but Ron kept up the rolling motion with his hand and I kept my foot on the pedal till the speedometer touched 100. The tachometer, which was partially blocked by the steering wheel, was at 4,000 RPMs.

How many gears were there anyway? Was there still another gear? I couldn't hear Ron. And I'm sure he couldn't hear me. But he wasn't signaling me to do anything and I thought we'd reached the top of the gear chain. We flew past fields of beans, then small developments with young trees. We passed signs for Brownsburg, Pittsboro. The next big town was Crawfordsville.

I was aware of everything. We were up to a hundred and five now.

This was what Jimmy wanted, wasn't it? Had he pushed it up to a hundred miles an hour on I-80? Probably not. The original tires wouldn't have been able to take it. I suddenly remembered bringing him a sack of roofing nails when he was working on the porte cochere, handing him the sack out the window of my little study, both of us laughing at a squirrel that had jumped down on the roof and seemed to be admiring the new shingles. I remembered the animal vitality of his Caliban, a sort of natural man, uneducated, untrained, whose mother could control the moon. A man with a grievance: "This island's mine, by Sycorax my mother, Which thou tak'st from me." I remembered the way his muscles rippled under his tattoos. And of course how desperately he wanted to drive the car. And why not? If we'd let him drive the car . . . and for a minute or two I thought that the person sitting next to me was not Ron but Jimmy, and I wanted to explain, and then for a few minutes *I* was Jimmy. Jimmy in all his animal vitality. I was alive. I was flying.

Ron shouted something in my ear and started to make a braking motion with his hands. In the mirror I could see a flashing red light behind us. Ron had already seen it. Maybe some instinct had kicked in. He pointed at the mirror and made more braking motions with his left foot.

"The radar gun must have been in that disabled car on the shoulder," he shouted, when I'd slowed down to seventy. Then sixty, fifty, and so on.

I got a ticket, but the cop was very nice. He wrote on the ticket that I was doing ninety. Not one hundred. Over a hundred miles per hour would have been a felony. I handed over my license and put the ticket in my purse to show in lieu of my license. In case I got stopped again.

"See those crows over there?" the cop said. "Know how fast they're going?"

"No idea."

He pointed his radar gun at them. Took a while to get an accurate reading. "Twenty miles an hour," he said.

"Thanks," I said. He waited in his car for us to drive off. "You'd better drive," I said to Ron.

"You're doing fine," he said, "but keep it under seventy on the way back."

"My daughter's going to wonder what happened to me." I'd forgotten about Stella and Ruthy.

"It will be all right," he said, and I knew it would be. Stella pretended to be angry when we finally got back to the Pepsi Coliseum, but her anger didn't run very deep and didn't conceal a series of small smiles.

The ticket was expensive, but worth it. Later, back in Galesburg, I attended a traffic safety class at Carl Sandburg College in order to have the ticket expunged from my record. The instructor was a nice man with no sense of irony at all. He took his work seriously. We learned that by going seventy-five miles an hour instead of sixty, from Galesburg to Monmouth, a distance of 17.2 miles, you'd save only three minutes. Was it worth it? To save three minutes?

The class was one long session. Four hours. The instructor's day job was trainer at a truck-driving school. I told him my daughter was—had been—a trucker and was really good at backing a truck up. He said they spent most of their time at the school working on backing up. I filled out some paperwork. Later I got a response from the State of Illinois. The ticket had been expunged. As if it had never happened.

13

"Maiden Voyage" (August 2006)

O ne night in mid-August I drove to TruckStopUSA, where big trucks roll in day and night, traveling east and west on Interstate 80, north and south on I-39. Tommy had bought a new truck, a big Kenwood, and Stella and Ruthy were taking it for a test run down to Anna, Illinois, and back, just to keep their hands in. A little vacation from office work. I was going to meet them at the truck stop in Ottawa and ride with them up to Milwaukee.

It was two o'clock in the morning when I got to the truck stop. I drove around a little, my heart beating faster as I passed the spot where Jimmy had parked the truck. Where I'd shot him.

The restaurant had been turned into a Burger King, but the lobby was full of the same junk, the same offensive signs. IF WOMEN CAN LEARN TO FAKE ORGASM, MEN CAN LEARN TO FAKE LISTENING.

Men came and went. A few women, too. I had a sense of being invisible. I wanted someone to see me, especially when I went into the new Burger King and saw Stella and Ruthy at a table with a couple of truckers. Stella's dark hair was held back in a clasp; Ruthy's bright red hair poured out under her Cubs hat.

I joined them at the table and ordered a Whopper and listened to truck talk as I ate. It was a foreign language. Some other life was going on all around me. Stella and Ruthy ordered hundred-mile cups of coffee to go, and we said good-bye to the truckers, the other truckers, that is.

The new Kenwood was parked at a diagonal along with dozens of other "big rigs." It was running and the exhaust was blue. "Do truckers really say 'big rigs'?" I asked, but the trucks were making so much noise they didn't hear me.

It was three o'clock in the morning when we left TruckStopUSA. I had the bound galleys of *Catullus Redivivus* in my briefcase. Lying on one side in the big sleeper, I turned on a little reading light, like the reading lights in an airplane, and read one of the poems aloud to Stella and Ruthy. A loose translation of 97:

> I don't know which smells worse,
> Your farts or your breath.
> At least your asshole doesn't have any teeth . . .

"Ma," Stella interrupted. "That's disgusting." She turned her head to look up at me in the bunk. Ruthy was driving.

"I think it's pretty funny," Ruthy said.

"Maybe you'd prefer it in Latin: *"Non (ita me di ament) quicquam referre putavi . . ."*

"Enough, Ma."

"Catullus was the first poet to really grab me," I said. "My first love, so to speak.

"He freed himself from the impersonal objectivity of his Greek models. He responded seriously to the demands of love. There's a kind of intimacy that was just not there in earlier literature."

"Ma," Stella said. "You sound like you're giving a lecture."

"That's from the jacket copy," I said.

Ruthy asked for another poem.

> Let's live and love, Lesbia.
> Let the green-eyed ones go to hell if they don't like it.
> Let the sun set tonight.
> Another one will come up in the morning.
> But when our sun goes down,
> We'll go down with it,
> Extinguished in endless night.

The backs of their heads were silhouetted, outlined by light from the dials on the dash. Ruthy still wearing her Cubs hat.

> Give me a thousand kisses,
> A hundred.
> Another thousand.
> Another hundred.
> Thousands
> More than green-eyes can count.

"Not bad, Ma," Stella said. "Really. You should apply to The Writers' Workshop."

"Right," I said.

"That's nice," Ruthy said.

"I'm going to go to sleep now," I said.

"Before you go to sleep," Stella said, "we've got a proposition for you."

"So that's what this trip is about," I said. "I've been wondering."

What Stella wanted to do was to form a corporation. Tommy had never incorporated his business. Now was the time. I'd invest what was left, after taxes, from the sale of the Cobra—over half a million dollars. Tommy would hold fifty-one percent of the stock. Stella and Ruthy would each hold five percent. I would hold the remaining thirty-nine percent. "Gagliano Brothers" would become "Gagliano Produce, Inc."

"What's in it for Tommy?" I asked.

"With your five hundred thousand we could expand into the old National Warehouse on First Street, which has its own cold storage facility."

It would be a subchapter-S corporation. The corporation itself would pay no taxes. The profits would go directly to the share-holders. Roughly two hundred thousand dollars a year after paying salaries and the mortgage on the new warehouse. My share would be eighty thousand. Not bad on an investment of five hundred thousand. I did the calculations in my head: sixteen percent.

I was pleased and annoyed at the same time. "Tommy wants to do this?" I asked.

"He's still going to take three months off every year."

"Why don't you put this in writing and send it to me so I can talk it over with my lawyer, or with the broker at A. G. Edwards?"

"Because we've got you trapped in the sleeper so you can't get away till you agree."

"It's a good thing I didn't put that money in the stock market," I said. "Because the market tanked. Good thing I sold the Cobra when I did, too. The bottom's dropped out of the classic car market."

"Besides," Stella said, "if you don't do anything with the money you're going to pay thirty-five percent to the government, but if you invest it, I think you can get a better deal. You'll have to ask Tommy."

"I need to go to sleep."

"There's one more thing, Ma."

"That's what I was afraid of."

"We're going to Italy again, right after Christmas. I want you to come with us. It'll give you something to look forward to."

"I'm not dead yet," I said. "Maybe I'll put that on my tombstone. 'Not dead yet.'"

"Very funny, Ma."

"What about Tommy?"

"Tommy wants you to come. You don't have to *do* anything. I mean, you'll have separate rooms if that's what you're worried about. Naples. Then Reggio Calabria. The family's got a big house. You can see Mount Etna from the balcony."

"Mount Etna's in Sicily."

"I know, Ma. But you can see it across the strait."

"*Catullus Redivivus* is coming out in September, Stella. I'm going to be very busy."

"You going on a book tour?"

"No."

"Two weeks. Right after Christmas. That's what I'm asking. You can spare two weeks. We're going to see *Così fan tutte* at Teatro di San Carlo in Naples and then *Tosca* in Reggio Calabria."

"I thought Tommy said *Rigoletto* in Naples. But it doesn't matter. I'm too old for this sort of thing."

"I think it's *Rigoletto*," Ruthy said.

"Ma," Stella said, "I'd like us to be a family. It just seems so right to me. Tommy is such a good man."

"Better than your father?"

"You don't have to be snide. Not better than my father, but

different. He puts on a show, but down deep it isn't really a show. It's the real thing. He's kind and thoughtful and lots of fun."

"And rich?"

"Yes, rich too. So what?"

"And I'm refusing to cooperate with your fantasy? Why should I cooperate? Did you ever cooperate with my fantasies? Did you ever listen to me?"

"You just cut him off. You humiliated him."

"I think it's time to end this conversation."

"Ma, don't walk away from this conversation."

"Not likely. You've got me trapped. Like shooting fish in a barrel."

"I've never understood that. I mean, why would you want to shoot the fish?"

Silence.

"I told him about the miscarriage," Stella said. "I think that bothered him more than Jimmy's death. No biological immortality."

"He was Jimmy's uncle, not his father."

"Still, Jimmy would have pumped some of the same genes into the gene pool."

"Did you tell him Jimmy pushed you?"

"I told him that too. I told him everything."

"What do you mean 'everything'?"

"Taking the car, Pa calling the police. What I told the prosecutor."

"The whole works?"

"The whole works."

Silence. "It's been almost ten years, Stella. Besides, what about the young woman who comes on Wednesdays?"

"She got married. There's another one now that comes on Thursdays. Another graduate student."

"I wouldn't mind having a graduate student come by once a week."

"There aren't any graduate students in Galesburg."

"I can see Andromeda," I said. "Out the little window. Andromeda, Taurus, Orion. The light from Andromeda is coming from thirty-seven light years away. It started out in 1969."

"Thirty-seven light years?" she said. "That's pathetic. You told us that that quasar we tried to see was two and a half *billion* light years away. Two and a half *billion*."

We contemplated these enormous distances.

"Ma," Stella said, "I want you to do this for me. We could pretend to be a family, even if it's only for two weeks. You can see the stars, but you can't see what's right in front of your face."

"Enough, Stella. I've got to go to sleep."

"Good night, Ma. Do you want to listen to an opera? We've got *Norma* and *Le nozze di Figaro*. I know you saw both of these with Tommy."

"No," I said. "We saw *Turandot*, not *Figaro*."

"And I know you went to bed with Tommy after *Norma*."

"You don't know any such thing," I said.

"Well," she said, "he was singing Figaro's aria from 'The Barber of Seville' all week after that. It was like a musical comedy where the characters burst into song all the time. Or like an opera."

"I'm tired, Stella."

"If you don't want to hear an opera I'm going to put on the CB radio for a little while."

I listened to the chatter on CB radio: road work on 80 west of Joliet, which was behind us; big hats out in force in plain wrappers because of the weekend; a missing swindle sheet; a reefer hitting an underpass near the Dominick's warehouse in Chicago; a madam who'd lost track of one of her girls in the big parking lot at the truck stop. I imagined I was in a berth on a train or on a ship, and that I didn't know where I was going.

And then I was asleep.

I woke up at five o'clock. I had to pee, but there was no place to go. We weren't on the interstate. We were on a county highway, near a lake. Probably near the Wisconsin border, maybe Delevan. I thought of Goethe arriving on the outskirts of Verona and unable to find a bathroom. *Anywhere*, the porter tells him. *Wherever you want.* It wasn't the first time I'd peed behind a truck. Stella and Ruthy were skinny-dipping in a farmer's pond, separated from the highway by a fence topped with barbed wire. I could hear them before I could see them. Just their heads. Then nothing. Then coming out of the water. Popping up like balloons, or like two nymphs. No makeup, their faces their own. They put their towels over the barbed wire to protect their legs as they climbed over the fence.

I was tempted to join them, but it was too late. What I realized, suddenly, was that Stella and Ruthy were no longer girls, no longer young women, no longer nymphs. Stella was forty-two years old. Ruthy a year older. These were two middle-aged women. I could see it in their faces, in their bodies, could see the young nymphs they had once been, and the substantial goddesses they had become, the old women they would turn into. And it broke my heart.

Natalia Ginsburg, my favorite Italian author, says that old age is essentially the end of wonder. We lose the capacity to amaze ourselves and to amaze others. Having passed our lives marveling at everything, we no longer marvel at anything. But I couldn't agree. Love makes these moments indelible.

We drove past the cemetery where Jimmy was buried and twenty minutes later we were at the market. It was six thirty in the morning. The market was bursting with life. Tommy came out to greet us. He was older too. His red hair had faded, like the paint on the Cobra. He touched his cheek with his index finger. (A warning? Danger?) His sleeves were rolled up; his light skin was translucent; the freckles on his arms were starting to look like liver spots, or stars, constellations.

Stella and Ruthy had disappeared. Duh.

He held out a hand for me to shake.

"So," he said. "You want to start a corporation?"

"Not particularly," I said.

We were standing on the sloping sidewalk next to big crates of cantaloupe. You could see the cantaloupe through the slats of the crates. And you could smell them.

"You want to protect the girls. Protect yourself, too. You can't just sit on all that money."

"Protect against what?"

"Creditors, mostly. So they can't come after you personally, can't take your car, your house. If you're incorporated they can't touch you. Personally."

"I don't have a house. Stella and Ruthy don't own a house."

"Don't play dumb."

"Maybe I should give it all to the church, to Saint Clement's," I said. I was teasing him, but actually it didn't seem like a bad idea.

"Then you better do it this year," he said, "or you're going to pay taxes on the whole thing as income. Give it all to the church if that will make you feel better. Then nobody pays any taxes and everybody's happy. Except the IRS, I suppose. If you don't you can still take the seven hundred thousand as capital gains, save some money that way."

"What about Stella?"

"If you want to give the money to Stella, give the money to Stella. If you want to put a chunk of money in this new corporation, fine. You don't want to, that's fine too. It's up to you. If you don't, we'll make a corporation without you, but Stella wants you to be a part of it. You're lucky you got a daughter like that. You should hear her on the phone. She's buying oranges in Florida and California, she's buying grapefruit in Texas, she's buying avocados in Texas and California. She taught me to stop screaming. 'In this business,' I told her, 'you got to scream to get people's attention.' 'Try it my way,' she says. 'Keep your voice down. Then people have to shut up to hear you.'"

"Everybody knows that trick now."

"And I've even got a mantra that I say when I feel like screaming."

"What is it?"

"If I reveal it, it will lose its power."

"Does it work?"

"Sort of."

"Maybe I should get one."

"Do you scream a lot?"

"No, but I feel like screaming. At least I used to."

"And now?"

"I think I've turned a corner."

"And you should hear her trying to talk Italian to my sisters and my aunts and uncles and my cousins at home. She doesn't talk Italian too good, but she talks soft so everybody listens and she makes herself understood."

"You mean in Reggio Calabria?"

"That's what I mean. No air-conditioning, but from the balcony you can see Mount Etna across the strait."

"I'm sure it's very beautiful."

"Okay, Frances. I can see you don't want to talk to me like an old friend, that you haven't talked to me in a long time. What can I say? I had to ask. You want to invest in this corporation, fine. You don't want to, that's fine too. I already told you. As far as I'm concerned, between you and me it's strictly business, because I don't know how else it *can* be."

"Strictly business," I said. "I'm sorry, but I think that's best."

The conversation was over. Tommy had said his piece, and I'd listened. Dumbly. How could I have explained? What could I have said except "I'm sorry." I was sorry, and I was even sorrier later in the evening at Tommy's apartment when I thought I detected a woman's touch and was immediately overwhelmed with jealousy. Jealousy opened my eyes. I could see clearly. Everything was in order. There was a new picture on the wall over the sofa—two oil drums, not my idea of great art, but in fact the colors were astonishing—a deep, resonant, vibrant red that made my heart start beating faster and an orange so intense it might have been used to paint the sun. The furniture had been rearranged. A couple of new chairs faced each other in front of the window, where Jimmy's coffin had sat, or stood, whatever coffins do.

The woman, Simona, was not young but she was beautiful. Her hair was gathered at the back of her neck. She didn't speak English. She wore diamond studs. I didn't hate her; I didn't want to scratch her eyes out. I was happy for Tommy. Sort of. But I was glad to learn that she was his sister.

"So exciting, about the *società*," she said in Italian—*the corporation*, though in fact I hadn't agreed to anything yet. "The girls are thrilled. Tommy told me about the car. What made you wait so long before you sold it?"

"I don't know," I said. I was short of breath. "It was just there. It was almost as if I couldn't see it. Maybe I didn't want to see it."

She wanted to know about the time Paul and I spent in Verona, and I told her more than I usually tell people. Maybe because we were speaking in Italian. I didn't tell her everything, but I told her about waiting for Paul in the courtyard of the Casa di Giulietta, watching young lovers having their pictures taken on Juliet's balcony.

She took my arm and we crossed the room to the window, where the others were watching a car ferry and talking about the truck. Tommy opened a bottle of prosecco and poured it into a special pitcher. I experienced the sensation of calm and peace that I sometimes have when I enter someone's house and find everything in order, no clutter, everything beautiful. There was nothing fussy about the *caffettièra* and the bowl of fruit on the table, the flowers, the bottle of red wine, the light sparkling on the glasses. Like a series of still lifes by Chardin. I thought (not for the first time) that I was seeing things as they really are. Understanding, for a moment, that there's enough beauty to go around. Or at least pockets of it. Pockets of beauty, pockets of happiness. I had wandered into a little pocket of beauty. It was enough. At least for the moment, and I resolved, as I had often resolved before, to incorporate some of this beauty into my own life.

Tommy filled our glasses with prosecco and proposed some music. "What would be appropriate for this occasion?" he asked his sister. "Maybe something for Francesca. You know. Hard to find the right role for her. A *mezzo*, don't you think? She could do Lady Macbeth, of course, or maybe Isabella in *L'Italiana in Algeri*. Or Carmen, what do you think?"

"We don't want to listen to opera while we eat," Simona said. "Why don't we just sit quietly for a moment and concentrate on the prosecco." And that's what we did.

*　　*　　*

"You could stay here, Ma, you know," Stella said at the end of the evening. "You'd be more comfortable."

"Your apartment will be just fine, I said. "Let's stick with the plan."

"Ma," she said. "I don't understand you."

"Maybe it's time to stop trying," I said.

14

Verona (September–October 2006)

School started again in September, started without me. I was
planning to substitute teach, because I missed the students
and wanted to stay in the classroom, where I'd spent my working
life, but I had too much on my mind and didn't get around to filling out the necessary forms. On the first day of school, a Monday,
I went over the last of the paperwork for the corporation—the
"articles of incorporation"—with my attorney, who was still David
after all these years. The Bascomb check had cleared—seven
hundred twenty thousand less commission—and I now had more
than six hundred sixty thousand untaxed dollars in my checking
account at the Farmers and Mechanics Bank on Main Street.
People sat up and took notice when I walked in. I owed the IRS
about two hundred thousand, less if I could take the profit on the
car as a capital gain. David said yes but that I should check with my
accountant.

"I don't have an accountant," I said.

"Get one. Let me just finish this last article."

I waited a few minutes. "Hypothetically," I said, "what would happen if I confessed to a murder?"

David didn't look up. I had to say it again.

He looked at me. "Frances?" Rubbed his forehead. "Is this about your son-in-law?"

I nodded.

He took his glasses off and pinched the bridge of his nose. "Can't you just confess to a priest and leave it at that?"

"Because the priest would be obligated to tell me to go to the police."

"But you wouldn't have to go, would you?"

"No, but then the confession wouldn't take. You've got to offer satisfaction, penance."

"Like Hail Marys and Our Fathers?"

"Right."

"So? Say a dozen Hail Marys. A hundred. A thousand. A hundred thousand. How long would it take to say a hundred thousand Hail Marys?"

I had to laugh. "I could run off six Hail Marys a minute," I said, "but that's when I was in shape."

"That would be three hundred sixty an hour," he said. "What's three hundred sixty times twelve?" He got out a calculator from a desk drawer. "Four thousand three hundred twenty. One hundred thousand divided by four thousand three hundred twenty would be twenty-three point one five. So if you worked at it twelve hours a day, you'd be done in a little over three weeks."

"Do-able," I said.

"Better than twenty years."

"You think that's what I'd get?"

"Twenty to life."

"How long is that in light years?"

"Not long at all.

"Seriously, Frances, do you have a clear idea about what life in prison would be like? Passing messages in library books? Making weapons out of broken CDs?"

"I have *some* idea."

"Based on what? *Crime and Punishment*?"

"My aunt was a nun. I used to visit her at the Dominican convent in Sinsinawa, up near Dubuque."

"A convent. That sounds about right. You won't have to do hard time, you know, unless that's what you want. And there's room to negotiate. No one's going to be too eager to put you behind bars. You'll have some options."

"Negotiate? Options?"

"Right now you're holding all the high cards. All the cards, in fact. But once you sign off on the confession, it will get sticky."

"The way I think of it, David . . . It's like stepping out of the shadows into the light." (I was very attached to this phrase.) Right now I'm invisible. No one can see me. You're the only one. I've never told anybody. I thought Ruthy, my daughter's partner, might have suspected something. Maybe she did. But she was glad to have Jimmy out of the picture, so I can't really tell. She's never said anything."

"You could just tell everyone you want to know about it. Don't put it in writing. Just sit down with each person . . . and say, this is what I did, this is why I did it."

"What about Stella? And what about Tommy, Jimmy's uncle? Stella's working for him now, buying strawberries and blueberries."

David shrugged. "They're going to find out anyway if you go to prison. You're still in touch with them, right? They'll notice if you're not around?"

I nodded.

"The food won't be very good."

"That'll probably be the worst part. But I've heard you can cook in your cell with a stinger or a hot plate."

"Maybe in Italy, Frances. Not in Henrietta Hill."

Henrietta Hill Correctional Institution for Women was located on the edge of town. "I might be able to stay in Galesburg?"

"It's one of the things we can negotiate. But you might be better off in the women's prison in Decatur. Minimum security, and I think they've got a garden program. I'll have to do a little research."

"What will happen?

"We'll go to the police station on a Monday so you don't have to spend the weekend in jail. The police will contact the prosecutor for intent-to-file charges. After a charge is filed you'll be booked into the local jail and await your arraignment. Depending on your priors, your flight risk, the fact that you've been a model citizen for many years and were acting under extreme provocation—at least I assume you were—a bond will be set until your preliminary show of cause hearing where a plea is again entered. *Nolo contendere* will be the safest in this case. Then we'll have a pretrial conference and a trial. After which you will be sentenced. And yes, self-surrender does look better for you"

"Can I go to the police station here or do I have to go to Ottawa?"

"We'll have to drive up to Ottawa. We'll go in my car."

"Because I won't be coming back?"

"Right."

"It's that simple?"

"Well, no. Before we do anything I'll have to talk to the prosecutor and tell him I have evidence of a crime. That's when we do our negotiating, try to get the charge down to murder in the second degree. Maybe as low as seven years with time off for good behavior.

They don't have any evidence, so they don't have any leverage. *Until you make your confession.* And then they may not believe you. You'll probably have to submit to some psychological testing. And they'll want corroborating evidence."

"Like the woman with the dog I called you about when the police wanted to put me in a lineup? Or the gun? I dropped the gun in the Mississippi, off the Centennial Bridge."

"You better tell me the whole story, Frances."

I told him. Everything, from Jimmy's stealing the car to destroying the chandelier to Stella's bathroom phone calls to the telephone threats to shooting him at the truck stop.

"You say the lead detective has retired?"

"I didn't say that, but it's true. I called about three years ago to see if they were making any progress. He wasn't there anymore. I could probably teach Latin. In prison, I mean."

"Why not? People in prison will sign up for anything. They're desperate, but the courses are usually taught by professors from a community college. Maybe that's something we could negotiate."

"And we could play *The Roman Republic*."

"Slow down, Frances. What exactly do you want to happen? Have you thought this through? Before we do anything—"

"Contrition, confession, satisfaction."

"You need to think this through, Frances. You need to know your own mind before you sign a confession. You'll still have to plead. You'll have to stand before a judge and he'll ask how you plead, guilty or not guilty, and you'll have to say 'guilty.' Some people who confess change their minds at the last minute. Look at Zacarias Moussaoui. Said he was guilty, then at the arraignment he changed his plea, pleaded 'not guilty.'"

"Then what happens? I mean if you change your mind?"

"Then there's got to be a trial. And everybody, including your lawyer, will be thoroughly pissed at you because you've been wasting their time."

Instead of walking straight home, I turned down Prairie Street toward Saint Clement's. I was feeling very calm, as if I'd been diagnosed with a fatal illness and had come to terms with it, had been very brave and had accepted it as my cross without complaining. Or as if I'd taken up Zen meditation to calm my mind, or Qigong, or started on a twelve-step program. I kept this knowledge inside me. It sustained me.

I entered the church from the south side. Father Viglietti's wisteria had gone into overdrive, and needed a fall pruning. As I was climbing the steps I imagined that the church was the convent up in Wisconsin and that I was visiting my aunt and that we'd soon be drinking tea in the library with Sister Teresa from Father Adrian's class in Rome. At the same time I saw myself from the outside, as if part of me were standing in the parking lot, and thought, this is a picture of a woman about to enter a convent.

I was, I suppose, clinging to the idea that the universe itself cares, in some way, about our behavior. That the rules are grounded in something. Natural law. Plato, Aristotle, Cicero, Aquinas. Not just a Lucretian universe of swerving electrons. But something's got to care, doesn't it? There's got to be something at the center. You can't just do whatever you want. Everybody knows *that*. Don't they?

There was no midweek service. The church was empty, but I'd taken up the piano again, and the music rushing through my head—Bach, Brahms, Chopin, Dr. John—seemed to fill the nave and the side aisles and the little chapel where Father Viglietti had blessed the soul of Stella's unborn child. I sat quietly by the side exit for a while. Waiting.

"*Frankeska.*" Finally. A familiar voice: "*Non diu te vidi.*" It's been a long time.

It was good to hear Latin again, even though God mangled my name, as he always did, with his classical pronunciation. "*Paene decem annos,*" I said. Almost ten years.

"Nine years and three days," he said. "*Parata salire videris.*" You look like you're ready to jump.

"*Fere parata,*" I said. Just about.

"You're doing the right thing."

"Do you think so?"

"You remember what Father Viglietti told you after Paul died? 'You're at the threshold of a new and abundant life. You have to go forward or go back'? And he was right, wasn't he?"

"I suppose. In a way."

"In an important way, Frankeska. But instead of going forward you went back. Look at your life now. What have you been doing? You went right back to teaching a dead language. Even the Church has given it up. You and I are the only ones left in town who can speak it. You got a huge chunk of money for a car that someone left in your garage and what did you do? You drove the car a hundred miles an hour—you could have killed someone, you know. Someone else. You could have done some real good with that money, but instead you turned it over to your daughter so she could turn it into even more money. You've kept right on dabbling in Latin poetry that people read only for the dirty bits. How many people are going to read *Catullus Redivivus* anyway? You've been dabbling in astronomy. You can identify thirty major constellations, but you've never invested in a real telescope. And you've been dabbling at the piano. You can play a few simple Chopin preludes and a Brahms waltz or two, but you'll never play the Étude in C Minor, and you know it. You'll be lucky to get your fingers around "C. C. Rider." Have you ever really examined your life? Have you ever confronted the big questions head on? Have you ever paid attention to the inner religious life that wells up from the unconscious in times of disaster or of great joy? The inner life that began to emerge after Paul's death, and then after Stella was almost killed? After you murdered your son-in-law? Or did you turn away? Did you try to tamp it down? Murdering Jimmy may be the most important thing you've ever done in your life. It took real courage; it grew out of deep feelings. It meant something. But then you ran away from the consequences. You tried not to think about them. You fooled the police with your extra .38. That was clever. You wouldn't listen to me. But now you have a chance to change lead into gold. Now you're at a new threshold. You're standing right where Saint Paul stood when he was arrested and imprisoned in Rome. Boethius, too, and Hugo Grotius, Marco Polo, Cervantes, Bunyan, Sir Walter Raleigh, Dostoyevsky, Oscar Wilde, Arthur Koestler, Malcolm X, Martin Luther King, Nelson Mandela."

"All men," I said.

"Kate Richards O'Hare," he said. "Zarah Ghahramani, Malika Oufkir, Angela Davis, Nawal El Saadawi. You could add your name to the list of women writing from prison."

"Me?"

"You, Frankezka. Why not? You're at the beginning of a great spiritual adventure. Don't turn back. Don't let yourself get distracted. Go to Rome, if you need to. Make your confession to Father Viglietti. He'll know what to do."

"*Pater*," I said. "Make that sound again. The music of the spheres."

He laughed, and then he made the sound again. I could still hear it rumbling in my ears as I left the church.

*   *   *

245

I don't suppose anyone expects very much from a new translation of an old poet—I know I didn't—but before the classical journals had a chance to weigh in, *Catullus Redivivus* received a "briefly noted" review in the *New Yorker* that stunned me. *New Yorker*s continue to arrive, as they've done for years. They disappear for a while and then resurface, sometimes years later. So I didn't see the review until I got a call from my editor at Hausmann in Brooklyn, who read it aloud to me over the phone. But I wanted to see it with my own eyes. I couldn't locate my current issue, so I went to the public library. And there it was. "High-minded and fine," it said. I was blown away. I'd never thought of myself as high-minded and fine. Nor Catullus. "Everything about this translation is high-minded and fine, even the naughty poems, which snap off the page and sting like nettles . . . and Godwin breathes new life into the long epithalamia . . ." I made a copy. I didn't have any change, didn't have any money at all, didn't have my purse. I borrowed a dime from the reference librarian, who knew me, at least knew my face. I got the magazine positioned the wrong way on the copy machine and had to borrow another dime.

This good news did not distract me. In fact it strengthened my resolve. I was acting from strength, not weakness.

When I got home there was a bill from David in the mailbox. He was an old friend, but he charged me three hundred dollars. I hadn't realized we'd talked for two hours. I sent him a copy of *Catullus Redivivus*, inscribed with a line from number 49, originally addressed to Cicero: *"optimus omnium patronus,"* the best advocate of all.

I flew to Verona on my way to Rome. I left Chicago on the last Friday of September and arrived in Verona the next day, after a long layover in Frankfurt. I wanted to go back to Verona because Paul and I had been so happy in Verona. We'd been as happy in Verona as we'd ever been—as happy as any two people could ever be. Things were conspiring to make us happy—the success of Paul's book—*Shakespeare and the Invention of the Inner Life*—the publication of my own translation of Catullus 62 ("Vesper adest") in *the New Yorker*, the maturing of our love into a relaxed and companionable marriage, the bright promise of our daughter, Stella, who came to visit in December and stayed till we all went home together for Christmas.

I wanted to taste that happiness again. One more time, if only in memory. Before making my confession. In Catullus's hometown. Romeo and Juliet's hometown, too. I wanted to look for the Catullus codex in the Biblioteca Capitolare. No doubt I would find it where God had told me to look. I wanted to visit Sirmio, the Catullus family estate on Lake Garda. I wanted to sit on a bench looking out at the lake. I wanted to wait for Paul where we'd waited for each other so many years earlier: the bookstore at the end of via Capello, or at a table in Piazza delle Erbe, or in the Caffè Dante in Piazza Signori, or in the courtyard of the university library. I wanted to wait for Paul's spirit on the balcony of Juliet's house on the anniversary of his death, as I'd waited so many times in our own living room, eating lamb chops coated with Parmesan cheese and drinking some of the Barolo, and then saving some for later, to drink with Stella and Ruthy, though we'd already drunk the last bottle. And I wanted to say good-bye.

Goethe was thirty-seven years old when he arrived in Verona in September 1786, and he already felt at home in Italy. I was sixty-six when I arrived for my second visit, but I felt like an adolescent—insecure, anxious, inadequate, disoriented, unable to make a simple phone call from the airport because I couldn't get the new smart phone that Stella had given me to work. I was reminded every time by the newspaper headings that the global financial market was collapsing, taking Paul's TIAA-CREF and my TRS savings with it; I had to remind myself that I had sold a car for more than seven hundred thousand dollars and that I could expect to be earning close to eighty thousand dollars a year, in quarterly installments, from my investment in Gagliano Produce, Inc.

Looking back I realize that I always feel this way when I come to Italy, and I'm happy to recall that even the great Goethe was sufficiently concerned about fitting in that he stopped wearing his high boots in Verona when he noticed people staring; he was also concerned about the rate of exchange, about changing money, about paying bills, and even about finding a bathroom.

I took a cab to the apartment that Stella had found for me on the Internet, on via Vipacco, across the street from the university library, and sat on the steps for two hours, wishing I were someone else in some other city, Florence, Bologna, or Rome, or even Galesburg. How had I wound up on these hard steps? My bladder was about to burst by the time the *padrona* came home. The *padrona*, Samantha, was younger than I had expected. She was beautiful in a hard European way, and she was in a hurry, but not in too much of a hurry to collect the rent. In cash. Eight hundred expensive euros that I'd had to special order at the bank in Galesburg. Samantha was in a play that night, she explained. She had to leave immediately, but she promised to come by in the morning. All this in English. I was too tired to argue or to force the conversation into Italian.

Instead of taking a nap I walked down via Capello—the old Roman *cardo* or main street—to Piazza delle Erbe, which would have been the Roman forum when Catullus was a boy in Verona, and where Romeo undoubtedly killed Tybalt, and then over to the apartment where Paul and I had lived, on via Pigna, near the Ponte Pietra, the oldest bridge in the city.

On the way home I stopped at the Casa di Giulietta. I had to push my way through a crowd of young people who were scribbling messages to Juliet on the walls of the corridor that opened into the courtyard. Along one wall of the corridor people were listening to recordings on machines, holding receivers—like telephone receivers—up to their ears. The shop in the courtyard was full of unbearably cute gifts: dozens of little books on love, little plastic purses with Juliet or Giulietta printed on them, bright red aprons with I LOVE JULIET embroidered on them in white thread. Guide books. Postcards. Romeo-and-Juliet key chains. Romeo-and-Juliet earrings. Romeo-and-Juliet salt and pepper shakers. In the courtyard people were lining up in front of a large bronze statue of Juliet to rub her right breast. For luck, or for a new lover. Would-be Romeos stood in the courtyard and photographed would-be Juliets up on the famous balcony. Paul had taken my picture on that balcony, which had been added in the 1930s to look like the balcony in the George Cukor film.

I didn't go into the house itself—because it was getting late—but I bought an Italian translation of *Romeo and Juliet* in the gift shop.

That evening I was going to read for a while and then cobble together a dinner from some spaghetti and garlic Samantha had arranged on the kitchen table, along with olive oil, balsamic vinegar, salt and pepper, a packet of bread sticks wrapped in cellophane, and a large bottle of red wine. The table was covered with a bright yellow cloth.

But after a second glass of wine, sitting alone in the empty apartment on via Vipacco, my copy of *Romeo e Giulietta* unopened on the kitchen table, I began to fantasize that Paul's spirit *would* show up in Verona. I didn't want it to go to Lois's.

"Oh, Paul Paul Paul," I said aloud, surprising myself, as I peeled a clove of garlic. "What an adventure this would be if you were here. Not the way you were at the end, but . . ." I didn't finish the sentence, but I was thinking, remembering Paul at his sixty-third birthday party, before the cancer, when we first talked about returning to Verona. You couldn't see the top of the harvest table for all the dishes and wine bottles, but I could see Paul presiding at the far end: bawdy, Falstaffian. The whole department was there, and Paul was singing:

> No more dams I'll make for fish
> Nor fetch in firing
> At requiring;
> Nor scrape trencher, nor wash dish
> 'Ban, 'Ban, Cacaliban
> Has a new master: get a new man.
> Freedom, high-day! high-day, freedom! freedom,
> high-day, freedom!

"Oh, Paul Paul Paul," I said again, as if I were sitting on the edge of his bed again on the day that he died. "You know what I *really* want? I want to set things right again. All this time I've blamed you. Maybe Dr. Franklin was right. I should have been more understanding. I see now that there was plenty of room for the books and for the piano. But I'll have to leave that for someone else. And Jimmy. I killed Jimmy, you know. He had it coming, but I'm sorry anyway. I'm going to confess to Father Viglietti in Rome. He doesn't know it yet. You remember Father Viglietti, of course you do. He spoke at your memorial service at the college."

I tried to concentrate on the clove of garlic I was trying to slice with a dull knife. I poured a little olive oil into a saucepan that weighed about two ounces—the sort of saucepan you find in vacation cottages—and turned the gas on.

I tried again to call Stella, but there was no land line in the apartment and I still couldn't get the new cell phone she'd given me to work. There were too many options, too many buttons. I tried several times, following her written instructions, dialing the code for the U.S. number over and over again, but before I could enter her cell phone number, a voice in Italian would interrupt and explain why this call couldn't be made. My Italian is pretty good, but I couldn't understand the explanation.

I had brought with me a CD that Stella had made for Paul and me, a Christmas present, with recordings that she'd transferred from old cassette tapes to GarageBand and from GarageBand to iTunes and from iTunes to the CD. It contained a short version of the story of our life as a family, or at least one version of that story: Stella reading some of her early poems and playing the piano; me playing Chopin and reading my translations; Paul reading Shakespeare sonnets and playing the piano.

I inserted the CD into the slot on the front of my laptop computer and waited, while the computer made grinding noises, for the CD icon to appear on the screen. When it did, I double clicked it, and suddenly Paul's voice filled the room: "Th'expense of spirit in a waste of shame is lust in action."

I thought about Paul and Lois. "You always were a dark-lady guy, Paul, weren't you. Couldn't keep your hands off Lois when I went to Rome that summer. You thought I didn't know."

But I managed to stop myself right there. Who was I to talk? Besides, I hadn't come to Verona to scold Paul.

I added a handful of coarse salt to the pasta water and then a handful of thick spaghetti. There was no scale to weigh the spaghetti and no timer to time it, but I had an inner scale, and an inner timer.

I gave the spaghetti a stir with a wooden spoon. I was on my third glass of wine. Paul was on sonnet 138. I repeated the words along with him. "'When my love swears that she is made of truth, I do believe her though I know she lies.' It was a mid-life crisis," I said. "I was very understanding. I took a certain pleasure, in fact, in being very understanding. And I really was understanding. I wasn't faking it. That was twenty-five years ago, ancient history. And then one day I come home from school—the last faculty meeting of the year—and you're dead and Lois is sitting on the bed next to you.

"Ah, the hell with it . . . What am I doing here? Talking to a ghost? Not even a ghost!"

By the end of the evening, and of the bottle of wine, I had no idea.

I woke up with jet lag aggravated by a terrible hangover. I was still disoriented. I was confused and depressed. I'd crossed a line the previous night. Made a fool of myself. At least no one had been there to see me. I didn't see how I could go back, didn't see how I could go forward, either, couldn't think of a single thing I wanted to do in Verona. Or Rome. The prospect of confession to Father Viglietti now seemed like a foolish pipe dream.

I tried to make coffee in the espresso pot, but the espresso pot leaked from the center, where the top screws onto the bottom. The coffee ran down the side. The gas flame sputtered and went out. I turned off the stove. I hadn't unpacked my suitcase and didn't intend to. I was going home ASAP.

I tried again to call Stella but got the same calm voice explaining that this call was not possible. I tried calling from different parts of the apartment—from the balcony off the kitchen, from the window in the bedroom, on the north wall. Always the same voice explaining why the call couldn't be completed. I listened to the explanation, but I still couldn't understand.

I got some clean clothes out of my big suitcase, something suitable for confronting a *padrona*—a simple sheath dress, gathered at the waist, and a pair of flats. I was trying to get a brush through my tangled hair when the bell rang. I hadn't cleaned up the mess on the stove. I didn't care. I wanted my money back. Most of it, anyway. But there was no confrontation. Samantha returned the money, eight bank notes, which were still in her purse. Eight crisp one-hundred-euro notes, each with a picture of a Renaissance palazzo with receding arches. She agreed to help me change my return flight, and apologized about the coffee pot. It was a special pot, she said. You needed only a small amount of water.

"I'm sorry," I said, embarrassed. "I wanted . . . I thought . . . It's the anniversary of my husband's death. Next Tuesday. I need to be home. In case his spirit returns to say good-bye."

"I should have explained about the coffee pot," Samantha said. "I was in such a hurry yesterday afternoon."

"I'll clean up the stove," I said. "But maybe we should call the airline first."

Samantha started to wipe off the stove. "We need some coffee. Let me show you." She proceeded to demonstrate, using a little plastic cup to measure a small amount of water. Then she dipped her finger in a tiny jar of olive oil and rubbed the tip around the threads of the coffee pot. "You have to do this to get a proper seal," she explained.

She put the pot on a small burner with the lid up. We waited for the coffee, staring at the inside of the pot.

"You have to keep the lid up," Samantha said, "or it won't make the *crema*. And that's the whole point of this pot."

I knew because Paul had a pot like this that I was not allowed to touch. I didn't want to spoil it for her.

We waited. "It takes a while," Samantha said.

Finally a sheen of coffee wrapped itself around the stem and then suddenly the pot whooshed and Samantha turned off the burner. The coffee continued to bubble up through a special valve, or filter, and then Samantha poured two small cups with blue stripes under the rim, just like the ones we used at home. The surface of the coffee was covered with a rich crema. We sat down at the kitchen table.

"You know," Samantha said, "your husband's spirit is free to wander over the whole universe. I'm sure he'll find you right here in Verona."

"Do you think so?"

"Of course."

But then he could have found me in Galesburg . . .

The coffee was delicious. The best I'd ever tasted. Better than the coffee in the big machines in the bars.

Samantha, I learned, was from Bologna. We discussed Bologna. And after a while I realized that we were speaking in Italian, and that Samantha was calling me Francesca instead of Frances.

Samantha loved Bologna and had never wanted to live anywhere else, but she'd fallen in love with a Veronese.

"*Amore*," I said, shaking my head. "*Odi et amo*. Catullus 85. 'I hate and I love. How can I do both? I don't know, but I feel it, and it's a bitch.' I've just finished a translation of Catullus," I said. "I wanted to come back to his hometown. Maybe go out to Sirmio, the family place on Lake Garda."

"Sirmione," Samantha said, giving it its Italian name. "We could go together, but I couldn't do it this afternoon. I've got the play again tonight."

"It's a different kind of love," I said. "Not very romantic. Catullus and Lesbia weren't Romeo and Juliet."

She laughed. "The love impulse is irresistible," she said, "unstable. But so is the impulse to love one person with your whole heart. Have you been to the Casa di Giulietta?"

I looked her in the eye: "Fake fake fake," I said. "The balcony was added later to look like the balcony in the George Cukor film. But you know that."

"Yes, it's fake," she said, "but it's become real. A real shrine. People come here when they're in trouble, in pain. Like your shrine of Canterbury. Or Santiago di Compostella. They even write letters."

" 'Dear Juliet' letters?"

Samantha nodded. "There was a Russian woman who stayed three weeks in this apartment. She became the Russian Juliet. When we get a certain number of letters from Russia, we put them in a packet and send them to her in Moscow. She answers them in Russian and sends them back to us, and then we send them back to the people who wrote them."

"That's ridiculous," I said. But it turned out that Samantha was one of a dozen volunteers—all young woman—who answered the letters. Five thousand letters a year.

"Like Ann Landers." I shook my head. "I'm sorry. It's just that romantic love is nothing but trouble. It's all based on frustration. In the Middle Ages it was regarded as a disease. And there was only one sure cure."

"What was that?"

"Let the lovers live together for a while."

Samantha laughed. "Francesca," she said, "you're just like a window. I can see right through you. Tell me the truth, was that your experience? I mean really?" She touched me—a light touch on the wrist with her fingertips, and then a firm hand clasp on my forearm—and it had been such a long time since anyone had touched me that I broke down and started to cry, and by the time I was done crying, I'd told her about the end of Paul's life and about Lois and about Stella and Jimmy and Tommy (but not about the murder).

"What would *you* say to Paul?" I asked her. "I mean, *you* as Juliet?"

She looked into her empty espresso cup. "If I were Juliet," she said, and after a long pause she put her hand over her heart and started to speak. I didn't recognize the words in Italian: *La mia generosità è davvero sconfinata come il mare*.

"It's from the balcony scene," she explained. "Just before the nurse starts calling Giulietta to come in."

And then I put two and two together.

> My bounty is as boundless as the sea,
> My love as deep; the more I give to thee,
> The more I have, for both are infinite.

"That's what Juliet would say to Paul?"

"No. That's what she would tell you to say to Paul's spirit when he shows up. You don't need to be afraid. He's not going to scold you."

"What if he goes to say good-bye to Lois instead?"

"That's a risk you'll have to take."

She gave me a cell phone to use—she had three—and said I probably needed an Italian SIM card for my phone to work in Italy. I wouldn't be able to call the United States with her cell phone, but I'd be able to receive calls from the U.S., and I could make calls in Italy. I dialed her number. Her phone rang. The two of us stood in the kitchen and talked to each other on our cell phones.

"What about Juliet?" I asked. "What would you say to *her*? If *you* were Juliet?"

Samantha laughed again. "If I were Juliet, what would I say to Juliet? I'd say, 'Don't do what I did.'"

*　　*　　*

I didn't go home. I gave the eight hundred euros back to Samantha. I was no longer angry at Paul—I'd made a fool of myself—and it would have been too embarrassing to go home. How could I have explained? I didn't want to lose face. I wasn't going to taste the old happiness. That was out of the question. But I could get through four days before taking the train to Rome.

That night I went to see Samantha and her husband, Giorgio, in *Trappola Mortale*, a British detective story translated into Italian and adapted for the stage.

And on Monday morning, in the reading room of the Biblioteca Capitolare, the oldest library in the western world, I held in my hands the missing Verona codex, the one that had been discovered under a beer barrel seven hundred years earlier, the one read by Petrarch, the one that had disappeared in the fourteenth century. It was known to be corrupt already, but still, it was the source of all the other Catullus manuscripts. And there it was. In a solander box, right where God had told me to look for it. Hidden for centuries. Whoever had made the solander box had either not recognized the codex for what it was or else had deliberately miscataloged it.

I was too overwhelmed to interrogate it properly. There were a number of cruxes I was curious about, but I turned directly to the apparent gap between Catullus II(a) and II(b). Were these one poem or two? Many scholars thought there were some lines missing between the two. Now I knew that they were one poem.

I'd been over the poems so many times while working on *Catullus Redivivus* that they'd lost some of their pizzazz, but reading them in Gothic miniscule on leaves of parchment, reading them in the copy that Petrarch had held in his own two hands, reading them in the copy that had been discovered under a beer barrel seven hundred years earlier, reading them in the manuscript that had kept Catullus from disappearing forever, was such a thrill that I dropped my fountain pen on the floor, as I was writing a note to myself on the back of a receipt, and ink spattered all over the floor. I'd forgotten the first rule of rare-book rooms: no pens, especially no fountain pens. I had a Kleenex in my purse and was trying to wipe up the spill when a priest-librarian came rushing over. He didn't order me to leave, but he wasn't interested in my apologies. I slipped the codex back into its box and said I'd be on my way. He didn't encourage me to stay any longer.

In the afternoon I took a bus out to Sirmione—Sirmio in Latin—and walked out to the Grotto of Catullus. I'd taken a picture of Paul in the so-called "grotto," and he'd taken a picture of me. I had no idea where they were now. Probably in a box in the garage, which Stella and Ruthy and I had left more or less as we'd found it, though the car was gone and there was now room for the Cutlass Cruiser. I sat on the wall overlooking Lake Garda and declaimed Catullus 31: "Sirmio, eye of islands . . ." The wind was blowing off the lake. It was too cold to linger. I didn't go into the museum. I turned around and took the bus back to Verona.

In the evening I walked across town and shopped for myself at the little shops where Paul and I had shopped—near Ponte Pietra—and managed to e-mail Stella from an internet café on via Garibaldi, and recount all my "adventures." At least I had a story to tell. I wouldn't go home in disgrace. At least not this particular disgrace. I had not told her about my intention to confess to Father Viglietti.

On the morning of the anniversary of Paul's death I got up early, splashed cold water on my face, and went out without taking a shower. I was on the Ponte Navi when the sun came up and the tops of the Alps appeared on the horizon. I was standing outside our old apartment in via Pigna when the bells of the duomo began to ring and two priests scurried across Piazza Duomo, late for the first mass of the day. I was in Piazza delle Erbe when the *venditori* opened up their *bancarelle*, and I was the first one to order a cappuccino and a dolce in the little bar in Piazza Signori. I wanted to sit at a table outside in the piazza with my coffee and read *Romeo e Giulietta* in Italian and try to figure things out for myself.

By the time I finished Act IV it was almost noon. The sky was pale blue and the temperature was just right, and I was thinking about Samantha's advice, about what I'd say to Paul. I'd sat in this piazza, in this bar, with Paul, overlooked by statues, perched atop the Loggia del Consiglio, of Catullus and other worthies, including Pliny and Vitruvias. I folded *Romeo e Giulietta* around my thumb and wondered if I'd turned into one of the worldly cynical figures who surround the lovers in Shakespeare's play. I tried to conjure up the lovers' radiant inner experience, even though I knew then that I would never experience it again. I wasn't sure I wanted to.

While I was waiting for something to happen, I imagined Paul joining me, ordering one of those orange drinks that I saw on every table. Some kind of liquor, like Campari. Aperol. Something that would turn me into a different person. What would *I* say to him? What would *he* say to me? I couldn't imagine this conversation. In my imagination we sat there in silence. Till the silence became unbearable. You could have drowned in it.

"Paul," I said, just to hear the sound of my own voice. "Paul."

In the afternoon I took a nap. When I got up I took a shower and put on a decent outfit—a gray wool sweater that Paul had given me years ago, gray wool slacks, my black cloth coat. I wasn't trying to make a statement, just to fit in. Paul had died about noon, seven o'clock Italian time, and I wanted to be on the balcony in the Casa di

Giulietta by six thirty. The doors closed at seven thirty and everyone had to be out by eight o'clock.

I bought a ticket, expensive, and went up the stairs. The house itself, unlike the gift shop, was as uncluttered as Tommy's apartment. On the second floor I stopped at the computer station where four people at a time could send e-mails to Juliet! I was tempted, but thought better of it. On the third floor I admired Juliet's bed. I was suddenly very tired and was tempted to lie down on the bed, which was, I thought, the bed that had been used in the Zeffirelli film. A formidable looking *custode,* in a civic uniform, seemed to read my thoughts and moved closer. "You wouldn't be the first," she said.

"Olivia Hussey and Leonard Whiting," I said. "What a lovely scene. Olivia Hussey was only thirteen, you know. Same age as Juliet. She had to get special permission to see the film because she was under age!"

"In America, you mean. Not in Italy. But Leonard Whiting!" The *custode* touched her cheekbone with the tip of her finger and twisted her hand back and forth, as if she were drilling a hole in her cheek.

On the balcony lovers were taking pictures of each other. "Let me have the camera," I said to a particularly attractive young couple. "I'll take a picture of you together." I took their picture and then pictures of several more couples, and then Samantha's cell phone rang inside my purse, which I had slung over my shoulder. It was Samantha, who laughed when I told her what I was doing.

"Do you think I should warn them?" I asked her.

"What would you say?"

"That there's more than bed to marriage. One of life's hard truths."

"I don't think that's the kind of truth you can tell anyone who doesn't already know it."

What about you? I wanted to ask, but didn't.

I sat on a bench outside the balcony door. It was cold, but not uncomfortably cold. I hadn't told Samantha the *whole* story, hadn't told her the bits I'd been keeping hidden even from myself, the bits about Paul's first wife, who'd always been kind to me, and who'd flown out from New York for Paul's memorial service and talked to me afterward and returned Paul's old copy of *Henderson the Rain King*, which had gotten mixed up with her books when they separated. This was the woman Paul and I had deceived while I was still one of his students at Knox. Was it a transcendent vision that led us to the Super 8 motel out by the municipal airport? I shivered suddenly, as if I were confronting these hard truths for the first time. I still hadn't figured things out, and I didn't expect to now. I was just going to wait and see what happened.

It's the annual Shakespeare party and I'm in Paul's attic, a big old attic in a big old Victorian house. The rafters are exposed. Roofing nails stick through the roof boards like the tips of thousands of tiny arrows. A keg of beer slops on a pile of towels. Cases of pop are stacked next to the keg, and trays of cheese and cold cuts from the food service are laid out on card tables. Everyone is smoking. Paul smoked then. Everyone did. Old sofas, left behind by previous owners, overflow with students and faculty.

Paul and his wife, Elaine, have assembled a collection of costumes, which hang on hangers, from a low rafter, and a big box of hats. I try, as always, not to think of Elaine, who is in New York.

An ancient Shakespeare party custom dictates the reversal of gender roles in the balcony scene. My Romeo outfit is a red toque with feathers sticking out of it and a burgundy blouse, with gold-trimmed hanging sleeves, over a black leotard. Paul has pulled on a woman's bathrobe. I look up at him, a bearded Juliet, perched on a step ladder. "But soft," I say, "what light through yonder window breaks? It is the east, and Juliet is the sun." We play it straight, which is part of the fun, and suddenly

Paul is on the balcony with me. Or I am in the attic with Paul. My Juliet. Or my Romeo. At first I can't understand him, because he's speaking in Italian and because I'm too surprised. I've been pretending to be asleep on my back on one of the old sofas. I've had too much to drink and am, in fact, on the edge of sleep. Everyone has gone home. The attic is empty, lit by a single floor lamp. Paul, sitting on the edge of the sofa, leans over and kisses me. Suddenly I'm as wide awake as I've ever been.

Shakespeare leaves the night of passion to our imaginations. I've never believed that a thirteen-year-old, virginal Juliet, who's never been around the block, would in fact experience towering passion, sexual ecstasy. But who knows? In the Zeffirelli film, which Paul showed to the class, you see the young lovers on the morning after, looking very pleased with themselves. You catch a glimpse of Olivia Hussey's breasts and some very nice shots of Leonard Whiting's bare butt, the sight of which made me tingle when I saw it with the Shakespeare class. It's not my first time around the block, but it's my first time with a man who knows what he's doing. I can feel Paul's strong hands massaging the insides of my thighs. My whole body is on fire, radiating heat, and a young woman inside me is spreading her legs for her lover for the first time, leaving her old life behind her, waving good-bye to her mother and father in her old home, starting out slowly, taking the first tentative steps of a long journey, the sofa steady beneath her like firm ground, like the globe itself. She's not hurrying because there's plenty of time to get to wherever they're going. Her mother is calling her back, like Juliet's nurse. But she can barely hear her mother's voice.

In the distance a bell rang, and then rang again. I arched my hips to meet Paul's, and then . . . And then I realized that my cell phone was ringing. I managed to find it in my purse, but the little lights on the phone were backward. The green light was on the left instead of the right, and the red light was on the right. I pushed the red light and the phone went dead. I realized I was holding the phone upside down. A few minutes later the phone rang again. *Pronto*, I said. *Pronto*, thinking it was Samantha, the only person who ever called me, but it was Stella, calling from Milwaukee.

"Ma, Ma? Is that you? I can hardly hear you."

"Stella?"

"I can hardly hear you. Can you go outside or move to a window?"

"I am outside," I said, stepping out onto the balcony.

"Why didn't you call? I've been worried sick."

"I couldn't get the cell phone to work."

"We went over everything."

"I dialed all the numbers you gave me but nothing happened. And my landlady can't get it to work for the United States, and she's got *three* cell phones. Why didn't you call me?"

"Ma, did you put in the Italian SIM card? It's in the case with the phone. You just open the back of the phone the way I showed you and slip it in. And I didn't have the number of your landlady's phone till I got your e-mail. I got this number from her. You were supposed to call from the airport. Listen, Ma, I just wanted to know how you are, that you're all right. Today, you know. The anniversary."

"Everything's fine," I said. "I can't tell you how glad I am that you called."

The next morning I gave a talk at the Club di Giulietta to a dozen young women, Juliet surrogates, including Samantha, who'd made the arrangements. I entertained them with imaginary letters to famous tragic lovers: Dido, Francesca, Guenevere, Isolde, Norma, Aïda. Were they different from the young women who wrote to Juliet, to Ann Landers and Dear Abby?

Or is it the same thing over and over?

"The problem," I said, in Italian, "is this: these women haven't learned how to suffer, haven't learned how to translate their suffering into thought, their jealousy into self-knowledge, their unrequited love into a deeper understanding of love itself. Our task, as Juliets, is to teach these young woman to learn how to suffer like intelligent young women, not like dumb animals who can't articulate their experiences."

Not too bad, I thought, but at lunch with Samantha, I had my doubts. It was good advice, of course. But like a lot of good advice it's not really the sort of thing you can teach someone. Nor was it something I could apply in my own case.

The next morning I had coffee in a bar in Piazza Signori—the drawing room of Verona. This piazza, with its elegant Romanesque facades, was relatively quiet, unlike neighboring Piazza delle Erbe. Only the one bar, and the Caffè Dante. It was eight o'clock in the morning, early October and cool. The sky was pale blue. I was thinking about Samantha's advice, about Juliet's advice. I'd sat in this piazza, in this bar, with Paul. I read Catullus and drank more coffee till the waiter began to set up tables outside the Caffè Dante. It would probably be too chilly to eat outside, though I was warm enough in my cloth coat. The sky was gray now, like the piazza. I walked around the piazza. A sign in stone on the east side said: CI SIAMO, E CI RIMANEREMO. We're here, and we're going to stay here.

I had lunch at Caffè Dante as soon as it opened. Paul and I had eaten here. It was warm in the café and I pulled off my sweater. I was wearing a white blouse with a high collar tucked into a dark blue skirt that was pleasantly tight around my hips. Samantha had helped me tie my hair up in a French twist. I could feel it coming loose, but I didn't care. I wasn't looking at anything. I couldn't focus, and when someone walked by wearing a suit like Paul's, I had to take my glasses off and put them back on again.

The waiter brought my pasta, I don't remember what it was, and then thin slices of horse in a thick tomato sauce. I'm not really fond of horse, but it's a specialty in Verona. Not bad, but the sauce was too heavy, or maybe I was just too sad.

15

"Confession" (October 2006)

The next morning I took a very early train to Rome so I wouldn't have to change trains in Bologna. Samantha and Giorgio drove me to the station and we promised to write.

The train stopped in Florence, backed into the station. I wasn't scheduled to meet Father Viglietti till the next day, and I thought of getting off. Going to the Uffizi, or to the Accademia. There were friends I could call, now that I'd installed the Italian SIM card in my cell phone. But nothing called to me. Not "The Primavera," not Donatello's "David," not the "Portrait of Federigo da Montefeltro." I was too anxious to get to Rome. I had a copy of Saint Augustine's *Confessions* in my briefcase, but I hadn't opened it.

The sacrament of confession, I knew now, was instituted by Christ after the crucifixion when he appeared to his disciples, outside the empty tomb, and breathed on them and gave them the power to forgive sins, or not forgive them. Not as a personal prerogative, of course, but in their official capacity as deputy priests. This power has been handed down from one generation of deputy priests to the next through the apostolic succession and now rested in the hands of men such as Father Viglietti.

Contrition, of course, is part of the deal. The sacrament's not going to take if you're not really sorry for whatever it is you did and if you don't pay the debt you've incurred by sinning.

Hard to credit, but it externalized something, as Stella liked to say, gave it a shape and a name, gave bodily form to our conviction (mine and just about everyone else's) that in some mysterious way the universe, the totality, cares about our behavior, that a preference for torturing animals or small children is not the same as a preference for pistachio ice cream or Italian ices.

My heart was restless. This restlessness was something I could understand on an experiential level, in the body, along the pulse and in the heart. So to speak. It was like the tug of beauty I felt coming from the Chopin Étude in C Minor or "C. C. Rider," or "Casta Diva." The kite string again. Paul and I flying a kite, trying to let out a mile of string up at Warren Dunes on Lake Michigan. Letting the string out was one thing; reeling it back in was another. We pulled too hard, the string broke, and we never saw the kite again.

In the afternoon I walked along the Tiber, pausing in front of Carcere Regina Coeli—Queen of Heaven Prison—and trying to imagine what prison life would be like, but not getting very far. I was no longer agitated, as I'd been in Verona. But I was in a state of great excitement, too, as might be expected of a traveler about to embark on a long and dangerous journey.

That night in the hotel I browsed through the *Confessions*, thinking I might get a glimpse of my destination. But I landed on Book V, where Augustine describes his experiences in Rome. He was not a happy camper. He had come to teach rhetoric, but his students would skip out just before the end of his lectures to avoid paying his fees.

I was not going to meet Father Viglietti till one o'clock, so in the morning I walked from the hotel to the Vatican and located the Excavations office. I hadn't made the required e-mail reservation, but I paid my nine euros and was put in with a group of pilgrims from Lyon. Mostly women my age. Very well decked out. It was not too cold in Rome. I'd left my coat behind at the hotel and worn just a heavy sweater over a turtleneck. I could follow the French-speaking tour guide, but my mind was on other things, and it wasn't till Father Viglietti explained, at lunch, that I began to understand what I had seen. Like so many things in Italy the whole excavation below the Basilica of Saint Peter was wrapped in scandal. In a space below the high altar excavators had discovered not the bones of Saint Peter but the bones of sheep, oxen, pigs, and a mouse. One archaeologist had cut the electricity when he was gone so other archaeologists couldn't do any work. At first there was no evidence that Saint Peter had been buried there, but later a woman had discovered his bones, as well as a lot of inscriptions, but she had been completely discredited. In the seventeenth century archaeologists had discovered a number of erotic items that the pope of the day had apparently thrown in the Tiber, but Father Viglietti wasn't clear about these items, and apparently no one else was, either.

We were eating lunch in a restaurant in Piazza Santa Maria in Trastevere. We reminisced about the times we'd spent playing *The Roman Republic*, going for drinks in the Seminary Street Pub, arguing about the Republic and the Empire, but our hearts weren't in it.

After lunch we sat on the stone steps that circle the fountain. I kept the strap on my briefcase, which I'd almost forgotten in the restaurant, hooked under my arm.

"This is where I made my last confession," I said. "In the church. And then Paul came. I thought . . . It doesn't matter. I was thinking, I'd like to make my confession now. To you. We can just do it, right? Privately? An auricular confession. Well, not so privately, but just the two of us."

"What have you done, Frances, that can't wait till you get home?"

"You won't know unless . . . Please, Father."

Father Viglietti was very reluctant.

"You don't need any equipment, do you? Holy water?"

"No," he said. "No special equipment. It *has* been a long time, hasn't it."

"Bless me, Father," I said, "for I have sinned."

"How long since your last confession?"

"Forty-three years."

"Go on."

"Father, I've committed murder. I killed someone. In cold blood. Well, I was angry, but I know that's no excuse. You remember Jimmy, Stella's boyfriend. Her husband, actually. He wanted . . ."

I told him the whole story.

He didn't say anything for a long time. I kept my head down, but I was aware of the water splashing in the fountain, of the footsteps—high heels, flats, boots—on the gray paving stones; the waiters clearing the tables in the restaurants; the traffic on the via della Lungaretta; someone playing an accordion and singing.

"Frances," he said finally. "You know something?"

I waited. Keeping my head down, as if expecting a blow.

"It doesn't matter."

"Doesn't matter?" And I understood immediately that Father Viglietti was a step ahead of me. I'd been expecting him to hold his hand up and say "Turn back, Frances," but he was beckoning me to follow him into the indifferent Lucretian universe. I'd crossed one line after another, one Rubicon after another. I'd thought I'd gone as far as I could go, but now a new landscape was opening up before me, still another Rubicon. *'Tis but a man gone*, Roderigo says to Iago as he lies in wait for Cassio. Was that Jimmy, too? *'Tis but a man gone.* I didn't want to think so.

"That's not all, Father," I said.

I could see he was surprised.

"You've killed more people?"

"No, just the one. But I made a mess of things, didn't I? Stella was going to file for divorce. I didn't have to kill anyone. She could have gotten a restraining order. She could have gone to Jimmy's uncle. He would have protected her. And now she has, in fact. He's the one she looks to when she needs advice or affirmation. Not me. And Paul. Why was I such a naysayer? Why didn't we get new tires and drive the car around? He could have managed. Why did I put the kibosh on the telescope? It was too expensive, sure, but we could have managed, and he could have seen 3C 273 again before he died. And the piano. I shouldn't have sold it, I realized that, later—realized it as they were carting it down the driveway to the truck. I still could have tracked it down, bought it back. Maybe. And why didn't I listen to Dr. Franklin, who wanted Paul to start taking lithium? Maybe lithium would have calmed him down, helped him with his damned shoelaces. But instead I gave him a hard time every step of the way. He wanted new locks, an alarm system, a dog, a pistol. So what? Jimmy didn't come in the apartment, the way Paul thought, but he might have, and he did in fact come in the house on Prairie Street and trash the chandelier.

"What have I done with my life, Father? I taught a dead language for forty-one years. I've published a translation of Catullus that no one will read. I discovered the Verona codex and didn't say anything about it because . . . I dropped my fountain pen and spilled ink on the floor. I sold a car for three quarters of a million dollars and then invested that so I could make more money. What happened to the impulse that Paul and I had to give away all our possessions? Give the money to the poor. That was after we'd been drinking, of course, and we didn't know what we'd do next. I did give away one of Paul's pots, a copper saucepan, and he never got over it!

"I drove the car over a hundred miles an hour. How stupid was that? I could have killed someone, someone else.

"And what about Tommy? I lay down with him in the Palmer House and then killed his nephew and then I humiliated him. Couldn't face him. Couldn't do the honest thing.

"You know something, Father? I know now that the atoms in my fingernails were generated in the cores of distant stars. We're all stardust. But that's not enough. Not for me, anyway.

"You remember you heard a funny noise in church one Saturday afternoon? You wanted to know if I was all right? That was God making that noise. That's your music of the spheres.

"My life doesn't add up to anything, Father. More like the story of Troy—all in a day's work—than Rome, going in circles instead of moving forward. I've worn out all the roles I used to play—daughter, student, lover, wife, mother, Latin teacher. Now I'm just . . . I don't know what I'm doing. Every September, when school starts up again, it starts up without me."

I'd never experienced an awkward silence with Father Viglietti, but I thought I was about to experience one now as I was starting to sink into the implications of what I'd just "confessed." The music, the buskers—guitars, an accordion, even a double bass—all seemed far, far away.

"*Frankeska*," he said finally, switching to Latin. "*Non absolutione sed 'grappa' opus est.*" You don't need absolution. You need a grappa, and then a nap."

"Tonight?" I said. "Could we have dinner, sort it out over a glass of wine? We could have deep-fried artichokes at one of those restaurants near Campo de' Fiori. *Carciofi alla Giudia.*"

"I'm sorry, Frances," he said. "It's the rector's dinner tonight, a fundraiser for the Clementine Pontifical Academy. I might be able to get you a ticket for four hundred fifty dollars. A seat at the rector's table will set you back fifteen thousand." He laughed.

"I understand," I said. Though I didn't really understand.

"You have to go?"

"I'm the rector."

"I didn't realize that," I said. "You never told me."

"You're leaving in the morning?"

I nodded. "But I have something for you." I handed him the copy of *Catullus Redivivus* that I'd been carrying in my briefcase. "I've already inscribed it," I said.

He tucked the book under his arm and held both my hands in his. For a long time. We were both reluctant to let go.

"*Ave atque vale*," I said. Hello and good-bye.

"*Ave atque vale*," he replied. "Do you need a cab?" he asked. "Back to your hotel?"

"No," I said. "I think I'll just stay here for a while. In the piazza. And then I'll walk back. It's not far."

*　　*　　*

I sat on the steps of the fountain all afternoon. I did not go into the church. I did not feel that I was free from sin. But I felt free from something. I wanted to call Stella. To hear her voice. It was late afternoon, eleven or twelve o'clock in Milwaukee. By this time lots of young people had gathered around the fountain. I got out my cell phone, but instead of calling Stella, I decided to try my astronomy app in the daytime. Something I'd never done. It worked. Astonishing. I kept looking up at the gray-blue sky, but of course there were no stars. And then looking back at the little screen on the cell phone. It was October, but the little screen on the phone was full of spring constellations. Pegasus was rising over Testaccio, Virgo was setting over the Janiculum. It was disorienting. To see these constellations in the daytime. In October. I couldn't get my mind around it.

I sat on the steps till it started to get dark and the steps started to get crowded. A young couple with a baby that needed its diaper changed sat down next to me. I kept holding up my cell phone to see the stars and then looking at the sky itself, but I couldn't ignore the smell. Mamma and Papà were struggling with the baby's diaper. The baby really stunk it up. People—young people who'd never changed a baby's diaper in their lives—moved away. I stayed put. Mamma and Papà had run out of baby wipes. I offered them a packet of Kleenex from my purse.

The father disposed of the diaper.

"I have a daughter too," I said.

"Well," the mother said, "we should have asked you to change her."

"I'd have done it in half the time," I said, and we started chatting.

What was I looking at? they wanted to know.

"The stars," I said. They took turns looking at the stars on the screen on the phone and then up into the darkening blue sky.

I listened to the sexually charged banter of the young people sitting on the steps, touching and rubbing against each other. The lashing of the fountain, the gurgling of the baby, and the buskers scattered around the piazza.

"The Big Dipper," the man said, looking at the phone and then at the sky and then back at the phone. Only he called it *orsa maggiore.*

A man lay on his back near the church steps, knees up, supporting a young woman in a short checkered skirt who was spinning something on her fingers. Another man played a small accordion while another juggled three balls, then four, then five. I thought they were together but couldn't be sure.

We sat on the steps till it grew dark and the real stars began to appear. There was too much light pollution to see any but the brightest stars—Altair in the east, Aldebaran in the west, Deneb overhead. Rome is at about the same latitude as Galesburg, so I felt right at home. If she looked up, Stella would see the same night sky, though Milwaukee is a little farther north, and it wouldn't be dark for another six hours. Or seven. I could never remember.

I held the baby while her mother went to one of the trattorias in the piazza to get something to eat. She brought back a tray of salami and cheese, omelets, couscous, tarts and pizzas, pasta, crostini, salads, desserts. A half-liter of wine. Real glasses. Napkins.

I thought I could taste the stars, the food was so good, and the wine; and hear them too, in the sounds of the piazza, and even smell them in the faint smell of the baby's diaper that still lingered in the air. And hold them in my arms, like the baby, whose name was Gina. I could hear it, the music of the spheres. Well, I could hear something.

After they'd gone I was tempted to leave myself, but instead I sat on the hard steps till it was quite dark. The piazza wasn't empty, but it was quiet. I had put my hair up in a French twist, again, but I'd done it in a hurry and I could feel it coming loose. It always came loose, but I didn't care. I wasn't looking at anything. I couldn't focus, and when someone sat down beside me, I didn't recognize him at first. He was wearing his "Italian" suit. He was sitting beside me. The man who had once been the brightest constellation in my cosmos. His hair was still streaked with gray, his eyes set deep, his nose slightly beaked, his beard neatly trimmed.

"Paul," I said. "Don't scold me."

"Why would I scold you?" he said.

"You know something, I said. "In all the years we were married we never learned to read each other perfectly clearly, never solved the mystery."

He started to laugh and I started to cry. "Oh, Paul. I should have loved you better. Should have been more generous. There was room for all the books. Well, not all of them. And for the piano . . . We could have put the piano in the bay window. I didn't see it till it was too late, and the telescope, too. We could have afforded it. I don't know what I was thinking. I shouldn't have given you such a hard time about the locks, and the dog. She's staying with Lois."

"It's all right, Franny. You were always careful with money."

"You mean cheap?"

He laughed. "Don't you get tired of remembering?"

"That's what Stella wanted to know."

"You've got to let go, Franny. Move on. Get yourself an eight-inch telescope; and get the piano back; get it restored. You can afford it now. It's in a Pentecostal Church in Davenport. They haven't taken care of it. Go to Naples and Reggio Calabria with Stella and Ruthy."

"And Tommy?"

"Of course."

He stood up.

"Where are you going?"

"Back," he said.

"Wait," I said. I wanted to tell him about Stella and Ruthy, about Jimmy and about "Casta Diva." I wanted to ask him if he'd known that the car in the garage was a Shelby Cobra; I wanted to ask him about the joke he used to tell. It had a great opening: "Confucius's Superior Man and Aristotle's Magnanimous Man walk into a bar . . ." But I couldn't remember the rest of it.

But by this time I was sitting by myself by the fountain. The buskers were gone; the restaurants were closed. But I could still hear the music. Stars like daggers, tips touching my chest. Lingering smell of the baby's diaper. Taste of the wine on the back of my tongue.

"Paul," I said aloud, remembering Samantha's advice.

> My bounty is as boundless as the sea,
> My love as deep; the more I give to thee,
> The more I have, for both are infinite.

I stayed on in Rome for a week. My hotel—Hotel Antico Borgo di Trastevere—was near the river. Every night I walked across the Ponte Cesto and ate in the same trattoria, Sora Lela, on the Isola Tiberina. I didn't call Father Viglietti. I didn't go to the Sistine Chapel or the Vatican Museum or the Borghese Gallery. But every evening I sat in the piazza, and every morning I walked to the French church to look at the Caravaggios, and every afternoon I climbed up the stairs to the Capitoline Hill. I tried to remember the passage at the beginning of *Civilization and Its Discontents*, which Paul used to teach in the Freshman Preceptorial program at Knox, in which Freud compares the human mind to the Eternal City. Had Freud himself stood here on the Capitoline Hill, looking down at the Forum Romanum? Did he create his elaborate analogy with his Baedeker open on his desk, or did he simply have an extraordinary memory? All the traces of the Republic had disappeared, like the traces of our early lives, but in his imagination Freud could see the different strata of the city superimposed upon each other, Renaissance churches superimposed on ancient temples at every turn, the palaces of the Caesars superimposed on the earliest settlements on the Palatine Hill, Michelangelo's Campidoglio, where I was standing, superimposed on one of the most sacred sites of antiquity.

And in my own imagination I seemed to be looking down at the strata of my life, superimposed one on top of another: the Knox campus superimposed on the farm, the house on Prairie Street superimposed on Old Main, my classroom at the high school superimposed on the house on Prairie Street, Samantha's apartment in via Vipacco superimposed on the apartment in via Pigna, a dozen piazzas superimposed on top of each other and on top of the public square in Galesburg, the loft apartment superimposed on all previous impositions.

I wasn't sure what was going to happen to me now. I probably wouldn't be going to prison after all, wouldn't be adding my name to the list of those whose lives had been deepened by the experience of incarceration. I had to face the fact that I was a spiritual lightweight.

I'm tempted to say that from where I was standing on the Capitoline Hill I could look down on my life and see things clearly, but I'd fooled myself too many times for that. But one thing I did see clearly. What I'd experienced in the piazza was not homesickness but joy. Even spiritual lightweights can experience joy.

16

The Music of the Spheres
(October–November 2006)

I went through Customs in Chicago and was met by Lois at the
airport in Peoria. Lois had tinted her hair a metallic silvery blue,
and she was getting married. To Jack Banks from the funeral home.
She wanted me to be her bridesmaid. I was stunned.

"Lois," I almost said, "you're sixty-six years old," but I caught
myself in time. Lois had surprised me, and I surprised myself. I was
happy, too. "Of course," I said, embracing my old friend, who had
started to cry.

It took us an hour to get back to Galesburg. I was tired, but before
settling in Camilla, who'd been staying with Lois, I drove around
town, inventing everything anew: the Carl Sandburg house on East
Third Street; the Fourth Street bridge, from which you can see the
second longest railroad hump in the world; the trees in Standish
Park; the orange-and green-striped awnings on Seminary Street;
Old Main, the only remaining site of a Lincoln-Douglas debate. I
pulled over on Cherry Street and looked up into the window of

Paul's old office on the third floor through the windows on the southeast corner; I drove past the house on Prairie Street, not far from the Santa Fe tracks, where we'd spent most of our lives together.

Our old house on Prairie Street had been near the tracks, and the loft apartment is near the tracks, too, the Burlington tracks on the south side of town, and that afternoon I took a nap with the bedroom windows open. The train whistles sounded like the horns of great ocean liners, heading out to sea. And the noise of the musicians setting up for the last street festival of the year made me think, for a moment, that I was still in Piazza Santa Maria in Trastevere. But when I woke up I was home.

That night I took the dog out for a walk. We went down in the elevator. I was singing my little elevator song—"We're going down in the elevator, elevator, elevator, we're going down in the elevator, all the way down"—when the elevator door opened and Dr. Parker from number 5—the doctor who'd done my hernia repair—emerged. We were both slightly embarrassed. "The dog's getting old," I said.

"So am I," he said.

Camilla and I walked down the alley past the barbershop, across Mulberry Street to the little park by the depot. I let Camilla loose for a while and then we walked down Simmons Street to Standish Park. And then on to Hope Cemetery.

You can see Paul's grave from the sidewalk on Academy Street—it's in the first row of graves, the tenth plot from the north side, next to our old friend Luther Carlson, who'd taught history—but we went inside the fence and I unhooked Camilla's leash.

I walked to the back of the cemetery where you get an open view of the western sky. Arcturus had sunk below the Amoco station, below the horizon. I couldn't make out the Swan or Lyra, but Deneb was still in place, and Vega, and I could hear, faintly, the music from Seminary Street.

Camilla had disappeared into the darkness. I called. She came back. I heard her before I saw her. We walked together back to Paul's grave. I stared at my name on the stone, next to Paul's: Frances Dziepak Godwin. No date under my name. Not dead yet. And the inscription: *Pulvis et umbra sumus.* We are dust and shadows. The plot was slightly smaller than most, for some reason, but there was plenty of room for a second box of ashes.

I stayed up late watching one of my favorite *Seinfeld* episodes, "The Pony Remark," where the death of Aunt Mona interferes with Jerry's softball game. After the game Jerry and George and Elaine speculate about the spirit of the dead woman. George doesn't think that Manya's spirit would be hanging out in the back room of Drexler's Funeral Home, not if it could be traveling to distant galaxies and different dimensions discovering the secrets of the universe.

What about Jimmy's spirit? I wondered. What about Paul's? I thought I knew where Paul's was, but where would Jimmy's spirit hang out? Where had he been happy? I thought he'd been happy nailing shingles up on the roof. But not happy enough. Maybe when he thought he was going to be admitted to the Writers' Workshop and was being lionized by Stella and her friends? No, that was a false happiness. I didn't know enough about him, but I could imagine him as a boy, or maybe as a young man on the market. Tommy wanted him to work in the office, but Jimmy wanted to be with the men, pushing a flat truck down the broad sloping sidewalk, unloading eighty-pound crates of cantaloupe and hundred-pound sacks of potatoes. That was the best I could do, and it was pretty good, actually. A physical life. Lifting, pushing, pulling, feeling your strength, the slight ache in your legs, going to work at four o'clock in the morning, looking forward to a beer at the end of the day, or a game of cricket on one of the pitches down by the lake. I could picture Jimmy holding a cricket bat, but I couldn't imagine cricket itself, had no idea what a wicket was or what a bowler did or how Jimmy could have learned this incomprehensible game or why there were cricket pitches in Milwaukee in the first place.

I wasn't sure what I was going to do now. The opera invitation was still on the table. Naples and Reggia Calabria. Stella wanted me to go, kept after me. What could I do?

What did I know for sure? What insights could I count on? I kept coming back to the same ones, kept going around in a circle.

"You're only as happy as your unhappiest child." I'd read that in a Sunday supplement. It's the sort of insight that you can keep drawing on. You don't just say "I get it" and move on. It stays with you. But Stella *was* happy.

"There's more than bed to marriage." If you don't understand this one, you haven't been married for more than six months or so.

"If what you're doing right now isn't meaningful, it won't become meaningful if you keep on doing it forever." Something Father Viglietti used to say.

But there was a fourth thing, too, not exactly an insight, but something that kept demanding to be heard, one that is this: that the *casta diva* experience was now at the center of my life. Beauty, and not just any beauty. The kind of beauty I recognized in Chopin and Brahms, in Vergil's *lacrimae rerum* and in Catullus's farewell to his brother; in the swallows that gather in the sky at the end of "To Autumn" and in the autumnal leaves that strow the brooks in Vallombrosa; in the Caravaggios in the French church in Rome and in still lifes by Chardin, in the glimpse of 3C 273 we had through Professor Moon's telescope back in 1980, right after my father died, and in the tail of Comet Hale-Bopp that had passed our way in 1997, right after Paul's death. It was the kind of beauty I saw in the old house on Prairie Street before we moved in—empty but full of promise—and after we moved out—empty but full of memories. I wanted to be able to command this beauty, to call it forth under my fingers. I was still thinking of it as a kind of window I could open at will, the kind of window through which we can catch a glimpse of our true home. But now I believe I was mistaken about this, as I've been mistaken about so many things.

I tracked down our old Blüthner in a Pentecostal church in the Quad Cities, the Church of the Evangelical Brotherhood. The piano had needed some work when I sold it to a music store in Moline. Frank Johnson, who had tuned the piano for us, said, at the time, that I was lucky to get two thousand dollars for it. The music store had sold it to a church for (I found out later) five thousand. Fair enough. I bought it back for three thousand after lengthy and unpleasant negotiations. The piano looked fine, but it hadn't been tuned in ten years. Middle C didn't play at all. A lot of the notes repeated when you played them. The pastor went to his study to pray on my offer while I negotiated with the chairman of the Stewardship Committee. I never found out what God had told the pastor. I was out of there before he came back. The pastor, that is. The chairman of the Stewardship Committee had already folded up my check and stuck it in his billfold.

The piano was delivered a week later by a big, strong man wearing a Cubs hat, like Ruthy's. It was strapped onto a dolly, a special self-propelled dolly. The elevator was too small, but this dolly could climb stairs, using a special track that the piano man laid down. I went to get my camera and by the time I got back the dolly had negotiated the landing and was almost at the top. I took several photos as the dolly moved, under its own power, down the deck and through the dog gate, and turned into the apartment.

I had spent the previous day moving all the books in the hallway, and the bookcases, into my bedroom and into the living room, to make sure there was room for the piano to negotiate the hallway. The dolly carried the piano into the living room. The moving man went back to his truck to get the legs. And the deck that holds the music. When he came back he gave a command with a little remote, like a TV remote, and the dolly turned the piano to a horizontal position. The mover attached the legs. The dolly set the piano down. The mover went back to his truck to get the lid and the lyre (the pedal assembly). The piano fit beautifully, angled into the bay window. Right where it belonged.

I wrote out a check for three hundred dollars, which seemed pretty reasonable to me, and the mover guided the dolly back down the long hallway and out onto the deck. Without the piano, the dolly fit nicely into the elevator.

That night, when I came out to get a drink of water, the piano startled me. I couldn't see it itself, just a mysterious shadowy space, darker than the dark, like a black hole.

I showed the photos to the piano tech who came to look at the piano while I was in the process of moving the books back into the hallway.

"I hope he was fully insured," he said. "Did he give you a proper bill of lading?"

"He gave me something," I said.

"Humph," he said.

The piano tech's name was Karl Holm. He had retired to Galesburg, his hometown. He'd grown up on Mulberry Street, had apprenticed to a piano tuner, then worked as a piano tech at Lyon &

Healy in Chicago, where Paul's mother had bought the piano in the first place. When Lyon & Healy closed their retail stores, he tuned for the Swedish pianist Magnus Magnusson. Now he lived alone in the house he'd grown up in at the end of Mulberry Street. I drove by his house on the way to the grocery store. His father had known Carl Sandburg, and he himself could remember a time when the seven loft apartments were a sort of dormitory for railroad workers, and the Packing House parking lot had been a coal yard. The little barber shop at the end of the alley had been the coal man's house.

He knew many of the great tuners, including Franz Mohr, Horowitz's tuner. A Bible thumper. He didn't know how Horowitz put up with him, but a lot of pianists did. He was the head tech for Steinway and a great tuner.

I made a pot of espresso as he explained what he could and could not do in the confines of the apartment. He could not refinish the cabinet in the apartment; he could not replace the cast-iron plate; he could not replace the sounding board or pin block. Fortunately, none of these things had to be done, and there were many things that he *could* do.

He jotted down a list as we drank our coffee, which I served on a little tray with sugar and little spoons.

What Mr. Holm proposed to do was this:

- Minor repairs: glue loose joints, remove broken screws, repair loose screw holes.
- Clean.
- Replace strings, hammers, and tuning pins—which would have to be specially ordered. About three weeks.
- Regulate. (I would have some decisions to make about tone and action.)
- Tune. (More decisions.)

All these things could be done in the living room provided I didn't mind letting him use the long harvest table, where I ate, for his work table. Regulating and tuning could be done in two days, but replacing strings, hammers, and tuning pins, which would have to be special ordered, would take much longer.

"Let's do it," I said. "It will be like hearing the music of the spheres."

He didn't laugh. "I'm a Pythagorean," he said. "You have to be, to be a piano tuner. Though it's more complicated than Pythagoras thought. If he'd had a piano instead of a lyre he would have had a better grasp of the problem of fitting fifths and octaves together."

"Do you know that you can still hear the sound from the Big Bang?"

"I didn't know that. What does it sound like?"

"You can't actually *hear* it. It's like the microwave background—outside the visible spectrum. These are sounds outside the audible spectrum. You need a computer simulation."

He spooned the sugar out of the bottom of his cup. "I'll tell you what's really odd," he said. "Do you have any idea what happens when you push down a piano key?"

"No," I said.

"I didn't think so. What happens is, you push the top of the key down. Then the back of the key goes up and pushes on a capstan. The capstan pushes on a wippen. The wippen pushes a jack. The jack pushes on the hammer knuckle. When the hammer is halfway to the string, the back of the key starts to lift the damper lever, and just before the hammer strikes the string, the jack toe hits the regulating screw. The jack slips out from under the knuckle so the hammer can keep going. The hammer strikes the string and rebounds. The knuckle lands on the repetition lever and pushes it down. Then the tail of the hammer catches the back check and stays put till the key is released.

"It's like one of those Rube Goldberg contraptions. You remember Rube Goldberg?"

"You mean like the napkin that opens up when you lift your spoon?"

"Exactly. It's fastened to strings that are tied to the spoon. When you lift the spoon . . . They're called *Was-passiert-dann* machines in German."

"My father used to like them."

"All these things have to be regulated. Everything has to work together, like a Rube Goldberg machine. You have to level the keys, regulate the key dip, travel the hammers, align them to the strings, align the wipes to the hammers, regulate the jacks to the knuckles, adjust the hammer height, the hammer drop, the key stop rail, the damper stop rail, the hammer rail lift, the hammer striking line, the repetition spring tension."

"What's a wippen?" I asked.

He started to explain—"The wippen transmits the motion or the key to the hammer"—but I couldn't follow. I was reminded of God's explanation of baryonic oscillations.

He showed me the wippens in the piano, but they were crowded together so tightly I couldn't really see the mechanism; but I could see that it had a lot of parts. "It's another Rube Goldberg machine," I said, "inside a Rube Goldberg machine!"

"Exactly, and the repetition mechanism is another, and the jack and let-off. Rube Goldberg machines in a Rube Goldberg machine. You'll be able to see what I mean when I replace the hammers."

I fixed another pot of espresso while he poked and prodded the piano, like a doctor auscultating a patient.

After coffee he asked me to play something on the electronic Yamaha. I was suddenly self-conscious. I couldn't think of anything to play, so I played a C-major scale.

"Mrs. Godwin," he said. "You can do better than that."

I rushed through the opening of the Bach Fugue in C Minor from the *The Well-Tempered Clavier.*

"Slow down," he said. "You're not trying to catch a train. Bach said that the piano plays itself. All you have to do is find the right notes and press the keys. But the amazing thing is that a good pianist can transmit his own distinct interpretation by the way he strokes the keys." He had shifted into lecture mode. "Horowitz and Rubenstein were both romantics, they both played Chopin, but totally differently. Horowitz had a clear concept of every piece he played, observing every nuance, every cadence . . . Rubenstein was more impetuous. But in both cases the soul of the pianist entered the body of the piano, if you know what I mean. But you can't do it on this electronic piano. Just listen," he said. "Play the top notes." I played through the top octave. "There's nothing up at the top. You're not really hearing notes. There's no way for the soul to enter the body. You can press the key or strike it, it doesn't matter electronically. You can try to seduce the piano, or you can try to conquer it; it won't make any difference. You need the Rube Goldberg machines."

It was all becoming clear.

"The music of the spheres, though?" I said.

"Oh, yes," he said. "And that's what's so amazing."

Karl—we were now on a first-name basis—took the piano apart while he was waiting for new Swedish steel strings to arrive. He laid everything out on the harvest table. I took pictures. I wanted to document every step of the way. I wanted a record. Wanted to be able to see it. I photographed the pieces of piano—the action, the new hammers, the wippens, the jacks and knuckles, the agraffes (which anchor the strings), and the keys themselves, which were spread out at one end of the table, at the opposite end from the tools. Each one was labeled. They were all different.

I was not allowed near the piano without safety goggles while he was putting on the new strings. "Go read a book," he said. It was difficult to take photos while wearing safety goggles, but I got some good shots. The living room was full of strange sounds, too, as Karl reamed out new bushings, hammered in tuning pins, tightened strings with a coil winder a little at a time. And it was full of strange smells, especially the animal-hide glue that he heated in a thermo-statically controlled electric glue pot, and some piano "dope" that reminded me of the smell of the baby's diaper in Piazza Santa Maria in Trastevere.

Regulating a piano turns out to be like regulating the universe. You have to get the fundamental forces just right (the action, the repetition spring tension, the agraffes, the regulating screws), and you have to tinker with the constants: octaves, fifths, and thirds. These intervals are themselves stable, but they don't fit together as neatly as you'd expect. A series of perfect fifths and perfect thirds will not fit perfectly into a series of perfect octaves. You have to make compromises. That's why the sound of the early universe, the sound that God produced in the back of Saint Clement's, sounded so indeterminate. The early universe needed to be tuned, like a piano, and according to Karl, there were lots of different ways you could do this—Pythagorean, just intonation, mean-tone tempera-ment, equal tuning . . .

"I get the idea," I said.

What Karl proposed was a system of tuning based on a series of loops that Bach had sketched on the title page of the 1722 edition of

The Well-Tempered Clavier. He showed me a photocopy of the title page. The loops looked to me like something someone might doodle during a boring lecture, but they had attracted a lot of attention in recent years.

"I tuned Magnus's piano this way when he was playing Bach and Chopin and Mozart. It was different, of course, when he was playing a concerto, Rachmaninoff or Tchaikovsky. Then you have to tune to the orchestra. You have to make bigger compromises."

The point of using Bach's system, if it was a system, was to minimize the compromises that made "well" tempered sound just a little dull, and also to avoid the "wolf" tones of earlier "mean" tuning systems. Each key would be distinct, would have its own distinct character. I agreed to try it.

I couldn't follow Karl very far. I had no idea what he meant by subtracting one beat per second every time there was an empty loop in Bach's diagram, no idea what he meant by a one-sixth- and one-twelfth-comma layout derived from the loops. But I understood *something*, understood it deep in my whole being, when I sat down to play.

"Good and Bad Times," I started to play in C, just picking out the melody with the right hand and adding a few simple chords with the left. I could hear Paul's voice in the back of my skull, singing along. I forgot how to modulate to G and had to stop for a minute to figure it out. I went to the dominant seventh of G, which is D. Then from D to G. Once I got the idea, I could manage, though I wasn't comfortable with all the keys. I climbed up the circle of fifths to E. The high notes sounded as clear as bells. Then, when I couldn't climb any higher, I started at the bottom F-sharp. The low notes resonated like thunder, like timpani. And then I climbed back up to C, completing the circle. Every key was slightly different. "Different overtones," Karl explained, but that's true in any tuning system.

"The main difference in this system is in the relationships between the fifths and the thirds." I wasn't sure I understood. In fact, I was quite sure I didn't understand. But I could hear the differences, could hear each key telling me the same story over and over again, in slightly different ways.

17

The Recital (November–December 2006)

Overflowing with strong feelings that demanded to be expressed, I decided to give a recital, despite uneasy memories of recitals when I was a girl. I had once played "Flight of the Bumblebee" an octave too high. That was in Mrs. King's living room on her Baldwin baby grand. I became more confident as a student at Knox, but the truth is I was not really a clutch player whose adrenaline flow enables him, or her, to perform miracles under pressure. I was always nervous when I played in front of an audience, and I was nervous now. Just thinking about it. But it was something I wanted to do.

Karl came back once a week to tweak the piano, which had to "settle." Inspired by the sound of the piano, and by dread at the prospect of the recital, I started on a regime of serious practicing. Two hours every morning. An hour every afternoon. I shut down my computer and took the telephone off the hook. It was difficult at first, but after two weeks, practicing became a kind of meditation. Pieces I'd played first in high school and then in college came back to life. Pieces I loved but had never mastered—Bach's Fugue in C Minor and Chopin's Étude in C Minor—started to fall under my fingers, though the Chopin étude was probably too difficult. That's what my music teacher at Knox, Murray Hendricks, had said when I told him I wanted to play it. But then he'd called a couple of days later and told me to go ahead. Why not? I wasn't going to be a concert pianist, after all.

I typed up a program on my MacBook Pro, trying out fancy fonts and settling on one called Harrington.

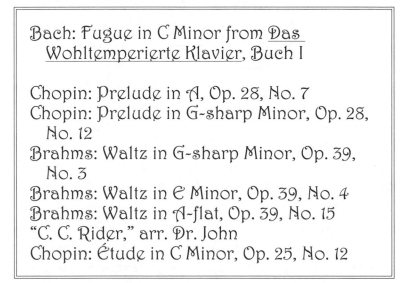

Bach: Fugue in C Minor from Das Wohltemperierte Klavier, Buch I

Chopin: Prelude in A, Op. 28, No. 7
Chopin: Prelude in G-sharp Minor, Op. 28, No. 12
Brahms: Waltz in G-sharp Minor, Op. 39, No. 3
Brahms: Waltz in E Minor, Op. 39, No. 4
Brahms: Waltz in A-flat, Op. 39, No. 15
"C. C. Rider," arr. Dr. John
Chopin: Étude in C Minor, Op. 25, No. 12

I had six weeks to prepare. Three of these pieces—the Chopin Prelude in A and the Brahms waltzes in G-sharp and E minor—are technically simple, within the grasp of a beginning student, though they have to be performed with great care if the soul of the performer, as Karl put it, is to enter the body of the piano. The remaining preludes and waltzes are just the right difficulty for me—not overwhelming, but challenging enough to require total concentration—and after three weeks I could play through them like a person walking confidently on firm ground. The Bach fugue and the Chopin étude were probably too difficult for me. Especially the Chopin.

The only new piece was "C. C. Rider," which Paul used to play in the style of Dr. John, and in fact I learned it from Paul's *Dr. John Songbook*. The notes were challenging, though nothing I couldn't handle, but the rhythm was impossible, the sort of blues rhythm that doesn't lend itself to standard notation. Karl helped me count it out loud and after a while it began to fall into place and I started to hear Paul playing it in my head and singing to me: "If I was a catfish, swimming in the deep blue sea, if I was a catfish, swimming in the deep blue sea, I'd have all you women diving after me."

The common thread, of course, was what I've been calling the *casta diva* experience. But the hard work of concentrated practicing brought me to a new understanding of this experience, and of beauty itself. My inclination had always been to listen *through* the notes, to listen for something beyond, for the music of the spheres. But I was learning to listen to the notes themselves. You've probably heard the Zen riff on mountains and waters. For the novice, mountains are mountains and waters are waters. Then after you gain some real insight, mountains are no longer just mountains, and waters are no longer just waters. And then, when you reach the abode of rest, mountains are just mountains again, and waters are just waters. Well, it was like that. When I was first learning to play, taking lessons from Mrs. King on Academy Street, the notes were just notes, always getting in my way, or jumping out of my way when I needed them. And then when I began to get some insight into the music, the notes were no longer just notes; they were signs, arrows pointing me toward another realm, something beyond this world. I won't claim to have reached the "abode of rest," but after six weeks of concentrated practicing, the notes had become notes again. Not signs pointing toward a more real reality, but reality itself. And the ache I felt was not Augustine's longing for our true home but—and I'm expressing this badly—more like the ache you feel after a good day's work in the garden and you're looking forward to a glass of beer. I wasn't homesick, I wasn't longing for my true home. I was home. I was where I belonged.

Something like this, I realized now, had happened while I was working every night on *Catullus Redivivus*. After translating *"Multas per gentes"*—Catullus's farewell to his brother—a hundred different ways, the magic of the poem seemed to fade into the light of common day, but then a new appreciation, a new *kind* of appreciation, grew up in its place. The poem itself, like the notes, is not a sign pointing at another reality. It is the reality. It is what it is. Just as the stars are what they are, and 3C 273 is what it is. And Rembrandt's *Side of Beef*, and first love, too. Even first love.

I wasn't planning to touch the piano on the day of the recital. Just a few warm-ups before the performance. I was nervous. I watched a *Seinfeld*. I looked at YouTube performances of the Chopin Étude in C Minor. There were a lot of clunky performances, but Horowitz, of course, was astonishing, and so was a skinny little ten-year-old African-American boy. Ten years old. How was it possible?

In the afternoon I went to Saint Clement's. I'd been back since I'd called God a "son of a bitch" and he'd made fun of my Latin. Now I sat in my old spot in the back where I could keep an eye on the confessional line, where I could watch for the little girl who'd always brought up the end of the line, though she would be ten years older now, off in college. I suppose I'd come to say good-bye, and I was glad to hear God's unmistakable voice, glad to hear him mangle my name. Father Viglietti's, too.

"Bene, Frankeska, Pater Wig-li-etti vere iecit nobis curveball." Well, Father Viglietti really threw us a curveball.

"Us?"

"Yes. I allow myself to be surprised from time to time."

"So, you weren't expecting that?"

"Not at all. You could have knocked me over with a feather."

"Really?"

"Not literally."

"Now what?"

"Frankeska, I'm tired."

"Too many things to regulate? Hammers, wippens, jacks . . ."

"I see you've learned something from Mr. Holm." He laughed. "No, Frankeska. I don't have any trouble keeping the universe in tune. It's the people. Did you know that every single individual is more trouble than all the galaxies put together?"

"What are you going to do?"

"I might take a vacation."

"Where would you go?"

"I'm thinking about Ethiopia. That's where the Homeric gods used to go when they needed a vacation—Zeus, Hera, Poseidon—the old-timers."

"What will happen to the rest of us?"

"Nothing. Absolutely nothing. You won't even know that I'm gone."

"Will you come back?"

"Eventually."

"May I ask you something?"

"Of course."

"What's going to happen to the universe? I mean after billions and billions of years? Is gravity finally going to pull everything back together, back to a point, and then there'll be another Big Bang?"

"The 'Big Crunch' theory."

"Or are things just going to keep expanding till everything gives way?"

"The 'Heat-Death' theory. You've been reading about this in the Sunday supplement of the *Register-Mail*, haven't you."

"Yes. The article said that the 'Heat-Death' theory was gaining ground. Everything will burn out. We'll wind up with dead stars and quasars expanding on and on, forever and ever." I gave a shudder.

"You'd rather have a big crunch, then."

"Definitely."

"I haven't decided yet," he said. "I don't know whether it's worth it, starting all over again."

"It's worth it," I said. "Don't just let everything burn out. Just tweak gravity a little. Make it a little stronger, keep everything from pulling apart. You said you could do it."

"It's not that simple, Frankeska, but I'll think about it. Now you need to take the dog out before your recital and then take a little nap. But don't drink anything. No grappa. It might calm your nerves, but it won't help your performance."

"*Ave atque vale*," I said.

At five o'clock I took Camilla out again, singing the elevator song when the elevator door opened. I didn't care if I got caught again. When we came back I started warming up with some scales and arpeggios. I touched the keys lightly, as if they might be hot. The piano cut through the sound of the humidifier.

At five thirty I ate a few crackers and prepared the meal. I opened some red wine—I wanted people to start drinking before I began to play—set out two loaves of bread and several bowls of spiced olives, organized the meat on a serving platter, which I covered and put in the refrigerator. Took the white bean salad out of the refrigerator and set it on the counter.

At six o'clock I turned off the humidifier, adjusted the lights, and arranged the chairs. Three people could sit on the couch, two on Windsor chairs. There were six straight-back chairs at the harvest table. That was eleven. How many people were coming? I always had trouble counting: Stella and Ruthy, and Tommy; Lois and her husband, Jack; Karl, the piano tech. Anna Connolly, who'd moved into Lois's apartment, and Ed Barnes, one of Paul's old colleagues, retired now. That made eight. Maybe someone else would show up. Walk-ins.

I arranged glasses, plates, and cloth napkins on the table.

Karl came early. "This is what I used to say to Magnus," he said," before a performance: 'Remember, no matter what happens tonight, we'll have something good to eat afterward and we'll drink some wine.'" Karl held up the bottle he'd brought. "'It's not like you're a pilot, when if you make a mistake everyone dies!'"

"Open the bottle now," I said. "Make sure everyone has at least one glass of wine before I start playing, maybe two."

I took a shower while he tweaked the piano.

I didn't have a proper evening dress. I was tempted to wear one of the half dozen spaghetti-strap dresses that Paul had given me, but decided against it. I put on the same outfit I'd worn to *Norma*—a light cashmere sweater over a black skirt that hugged my butt, but not too tightly, and then flared out a little. I heard the dog bark. I put on a little makeup, and when I came out, Stella and Ruthy and Tommy were talking to Karl. Or listening to Karl, who was showing off the piano.

"Pour some wine, Karl," I said.

Lois and Jack arrived, and then my new neighbor, Anna.

I arranged the open bottles of wine on the coffee table, in easy reach, but I left the bread on the harvest table because of the dog. Tommy had brought wine too.

While people were drinking wine and eating bread and spiced olives I handed out the programs and then played a few scales to see if my fingers were still working, and then I stood in the curve of the piano till everyone was seated and waited till I had everyone's attention. I said something about the piano, which had originally come from Leipzig, and something about Paul's mother, who'd bought the piano at Lyon & Healy, and about Karl and his theory about the loops that Bach had drawn on the manuscript of *Das Wohltemperierte Klavier*. I passed around a photocopy of the manuscript with the loops, and then I sat down at the piano, stretched out my arms till my wrists stuck out of the sleeves of my sweater, and started to play the Fugue in C Minor.

The alto stated the subject in the tonic key, the soprano answered in the dominant. The bass introduced the counter subject in the tonic again, and the three voices chased each other around the block—Latin *fuga* means "flee"—till the explosion of clashing chords just before the end when beauty breaks through and I could hear the music of the spheres, not coming *through* the notes but *in* the notes themselves, and I knew I'd get through this recital without making a fool of myself.

As I played through the Chopin preludes and the Brahms waltzes and began to go deeper into the music itself, I experienced not longing but completion, not loss but joy, not homesickness but its opposite. I don't think there's a word for it.

"Don't overdo the rubato," Karl had advised, but what's Chopin without rubato? What's "C. C. Rider" without rubato?

"C. C. Rider"' was the next to last number. The blues notes reminded me of Chopin.

The music seemed to be coming out of me, out of the Rube

Goldberg contraption under my fingers as they set in motion series of chain reactions: fingers to keys to capstans to wippens to jacks to hammer knuckles to damper lever to strings to jack toes to regulating screws to repetition levers to back checks. Somewhere along the chain the spirit becomes incarnate. Something welled up inside me and I started to sing. I couldn't stop myself.

"C. C. Rider,
See what you done done,
C. C. Rider,
See what you done done.
You made me love you,
Now your man done come.

And then I started to improvise.

Singing Hey, Hey, Hey Hey,
Singing Hey, Hey, Hey Hey.

I couldn't stop singing "Hey, Hey, Hey, Hey."

Singing Hey, Hey, Hey Hey,
Singing Hey, Hey, Hey Hey.

The last piece on the program was the Chopin étude. It's a simple sequence of ascending and descending arpeggios. The first note in each measure sings the melody, but there is (according to Karl) considerable controversy over where to place the rest of the accents. I'd been practicing slowly—the piano teacher's cure for all ills—till I could move from one arpeggio to the next without clunking.

They're just notes, I told myself, but the simple chord progressions—with a lot of dissonance at the top—are themselves overwhelming.

I took a deep breath, but instead of plunging into the étude, I stood up and bowed from the waist. I didn't apologize. I didn't explain. I just stood up and bowed from the waist. No one seemed to notice that I hadn't played the last number on the program, and I wondered if my guests had heard what I had heard.

The applause was gratifying. Enough to justify an encore, but I'd done what I'd set out to do, so I brushed off compliments and busied myself in the kitchen. It was time to feed people. Everything was ready: the white bean salad on the counter, the prosciutto and thinly sliced *arista* and roasted turkey breast on a tray in the refrigerator; good bread on the table. A bowl of fruit.

One of Stella's poems, one of my favorites—"Setting the Table, Eating What Is Served"—came to mind, not the whole thing, just the ending, and I clinked my glass with a knife and kept clinking till everyone was silent, and then I proposed a toast.

> Earth is our banquet,
> our hall; the feast, richly concocted of desire,
> murder, limitation, serves us all.

*

I'm not dead yet, but I'm going to end my story here.

Do we ever see clearly? Ever see things the way they really are? How many times have I answered yes to these questions—only to realize later that I'd been deceiving myself. How many times have I realized that everything in my life has been leading up to this moment or that moment only to realize, a minute later, that this is always the case, that every moment of your life is leading up to where you are now. That's how you got here, to this moment. And tomorrow you'll see how everything that happened today, which will now be yesterday, was already leading up to tomorrow, which will now be today.

But is this really the case? What about the lightning that bolts out of a clear blue sky? It does happen. We have an expression for it: "a bolt from the blue." What about Paul's cancer? What about the Shelby Cobra in the garage? What about Jimmy? What about June Anderson at the Lyric Opera? What about the young couple in Piazza di Santa Maria in Trastevere? Did everything in my life lead up to these moments? I didn't think so.

Have I got this right? Am I thinking clearly? Am I seeing things the way they really are?

Once again. I think I've come to the end of my story, but of course it can't be the end, can it, unless I drop dead on the spot, right now. Which is not impossible, given the level of anxiety, or is it joy, that I'm experiencing. I made a good confession in Rome. Or at least a confession. I cleaned out my attic. But what about satisfaction? What about absolution?

If absolution is going to come from anywhere it will have to come from Tommy, of course. Or if not from Tommy, then from you, Dear Reader. I can imagine you turning your face away, as God will turn his face away from the damned at the Last Judgment; or smiling, like Father Viglietti, and saying, "Is that all? Frances, what you need is a grappa, and a nap."

Whatever happens, it won't matter to the universe. The universe is indifferent. The stars are indifferent, the quasars, the galaxies, the nebulae, the planets. All indifferent. The molecules and atoms, electrons and quarks, all indifferent. The chemical elements are indifferent. Hydrogen, helium, carbon, silver, gold. They don't care whether I go to Naples and Reggio Calabria with Stella and Ruthy and Tommy or whether I stay at home, whether I step out of the shadows into the light, or whether I remain right where I am. Maybe I'm already standing in the light.

What I need, I think, is the glass of dark red wine that Tommy has poured for me. I'm like Stella looking down from the Fourth Street bridge and watching a man hop a freight train. I am that man, the man in Stella's poem. And I am on the bridge, too, looking down at myself. After all these years I still don't know where I'm going, but I'm going to find out.

Acknowledgments

I would like to thank my first three readers for their encouragement and support: my wife, Virginia; my agent, Henry Dunow; and my editor, Nancy Miller. I would also like to thank other readers at Bloomsbury for their careful work: Lea Beresford, Nathaniel Knaebel, copyeditor Janet McDonald, proofreader Nicole Lanctot, and publicist Theresa Collier.

Special thanks for their expertise to the Latin teachers in my life: my mother (1901–1984); my wife; Tom Sienkewicz, Minnie Billings Capron Professor of Classics at Monmouth College; and Brian Tibbets, Monmouth-Roseville High School; and for their expertise in other areas: to Garry Goddard (Shelby Cobras); Chuck Schulz (astronomy); Jeremy Karlin (legal assistance); Tim Barker (sharp-shooter); Glenn Gore (piano tech); and Rev. Father William Miller I.C. (Corpus Christi Church).

A Note on the Author

Robert Hellenga was educated at the University of Michigan and Princeton University. He is an emeritus professor at Knox College in Galesburg, Illinois, and the author of the novels *Snakewoman of Little Egypt*, *The Sixteen Pleasures*, *The Fall of a Sparrow*, *Blues Lessons*, *Philosophy Made Simple*, and *The Italian Lover*. He lives in Galesburg, Illinois.